On the Edge of After

By: Britt Wolfe

This novel is dedicated to:

Canada — the true north, strong and free, and my incredible home.

I will never stop marvelling at how lucky I am to have this vast, breathtaking, complicated country as the setting of my own story. The mountains, the forests, the quiet strength, the wild beauty — you inspire me every single day.

Sean — my extraordinary partner in every sense of the word.

Thank you for being super hot, for being my safe place, my greatest cheerleader, and my steady hand as I fully disappeared into the universe of Beau and Merritt. You made space for me to chase these characters, sit in their grief, and fall in love with their love. This book wouldn't exist without you. (And thank you for tolerating all the late nights, the rewrites, the obsessive editing — and for letting me shove my phone in your face at 2 AM while whispering, "Just one more chapter — you need to hear this part.")

And — quite frankly — Justin Trudeau.

For being dreamy. For saying things that make feminist romance writers behave... poorly.
Actual words that left me no choice: "I am a feminist. I'm proud to be a feminist."

Sir.

You didn't know it, but you personally funded at least half the scenes where Beau stands in front of a microphone being emotionally available, politically powerful, and devastatingly attractive.

Honestly, I should probably put you in the acknowledgements too. And then go have a cold shower, because *sir*.

Chapter 1
Merritt ~ New Year's Eve

There were moments—more of them lately—when Merritt questioned how she'd ended up here. Not just in this club, but in this unfamiliar, fractured version of her life. It had been eighteen months since Everett passed away, and still, the grief clung to her like fog—insistent, heavy, impossible to outrun. She'd rebuilt the scaffolding of her days with careful precision, but the ache had settled in her bones. Tonight—New Year's Eve—was no exception. She hadn't wanted to come, hadn't wanted to trade the shelter of her townhouse—the soft presence of Sophie curled beside her on the couch, the hum of a life pared down to something survivable—for the chaos of music, strangers, and being seen. But Avery had insisted, and she, too hollow to care, too afraid to lose someone else, had relented.

Her knees throbbed in protest, a sharp reminder of her age in a sea of youthful exuberance. The music pounded relentlessly, each bass drop reverberating in her chest, while the cacophony of voices rose above it, shouting to be heard. She squeezed between two bodies slick with sweat, the acrid tang of alcohol mingling with the unmistakable scent of cigarettes—and something more illicit. She couldn't help but wonder how this had ever been fun.

Each step through the crowd was a battle. Her stiletto-clad feet wobbled beneath her as she navigated the slick, beer-stained floor. The partygoers moved as one, a sticky, steamy mass of glistening skin and plastered hair, drinks clutched tightly in their hands. When she finally reached the bar, she leaned against its wooden edge, ignoring the sticky residue that clung to her forearms. For a fleeting moment, she was grateful to take the weight off her aching feet, silently cursing the over-priced and impractical heels Avery had insisted she wear.

The whole evening—the drinks hastily mixed in her kitchen, the late-night departure into the icy air, the interminable wait to enter this nightclub, even the shiny, slinky dress that barely concealed her—had been entirely Avery's doing. It was just like their early 20s, only now she was painfully aware of how far behind them those days truly were.

"Come on, Mer! We never do anything anymore," Avery had begged, her voice trembling with urgency. It hadn't been simple stubbornness — it was desperation, the kind that comes from watching someone you love slip further into the shadows of their grief. Merritt could still hear it, even now, weeks later.

"I'm just not ready," she had whispered in response, staring into her latte as Avery's piercing green eyes bore into her. Across the table, her friend reached out, resting a perfectly manicured hand atop hers.

"It's been a year and a half," Avery had said softly.

The words had landed like a blow. Merritt flinched, her fingers tightening around her mug. "You don't think I know that?" she'd murmured. "I've counted every single day. And I wish I could move on. But I'm just... not there."

Avery had let out a long sigh. "What happened was terrible..." Her voice blurred as tears filled Merritt's eyes, the pain still as fresh as the day her world had shattered.

It always started with that call. An unfamiliar number flashing on her screen while she soaked in the warmth of the jetted tub in the ensuite she shared with Everett. She could still hear the voice asking for Mrs. Cole.

"My last name is Clarke," she'd corrected absently.

She remembered the shift—the way something as mundane as a phone call darkened in an instant. The words that followed weren't just a message; they were a fracture point. They echoed with a sharpness that refused to fade.

"But, your husband is Everett Cole?" the stranger had asked. The tone was sterile. Clinical. And with the next words out of the caller's mouth, her life split open. "There's been an accident."

No more shared mornings. No more coffee made just the

way she liked it. His accented English would exist only in the permanence of recordings and memory. Loss didn't just visit—it consumed. It pulled her under and left her stranded, forcing her to live with its weight.

"I don't know if I'll ever be ready," she had whispered to Avery, brushing away tears with trembling fingers.

Avery hand't flinched. Her voice sharpened, edged with anger and heartbreak. "Everett wouldn't want this, and you damn well know it. It's like you died, not him. He's more alive in this tomb of a house than you are, standing right in front of me." She'd risen abruptly, dumping the remnants of her latte in the sink.

"Please don't go," Merritt had pleaded. Her voice breaking. How many times had they circled this? How many times had she let down the only friend she still had?

"I'm sorry, Mer," Avery had said, tears threatening her own composure. "I can't just sit here sipping coffee while you live like a ghost."

With Avery's words, *that* day unraveled her all over again. The humid air had clung to her skin. Mist gave way to a downpour. She watched Everett climb into his Audi, jaw set, door slamming. Her heart, caught between fury and despair. When his tires screeched into the storm, she'd turned away from the window, bitterness flickering like a spark.

What a prick. The thought had come unbidden. She'd carried the weight of it ever since.

After he'd left, she resisted the urge to call him. Their fights were rare, but when they came, she always folded first. Always mended them. Not this time. It was his turn.

While she distracted herself—running Sophie, alphabetizing books, texting Avery, diving into the intricacies of a new divorce case that she had taken on—

her husband, always so careful, had neglected to buckle his seatbelt.

He'd taken a corner too fast on the winding roads of Arbourleigh.

She kept moving through her day, oblivious, as doctors fought to save him. She folded laundry while he slipped away.

Ever since, the guilt came in wave after relentless wave. The way she'd let him leave, angry. The silence she'd clung to. She didn't know it would be the last chance to speak to him, but she had chosen not to reach out. That choice—even more than his death—was what haunted her.

So when Avery asked again — New Year's, clubs, dresses, chaos—Merritt reluctantly said yes. Not to celebrate. Not to move on. But to try. To prove to someone—maybe just to herself—that she was still alive. And to make sure no one she loved ever left with resentment lingering.

That's how she found herself here, at forty-one, a widow surrounded by twenty-somethings moving in time to a beat she couldn't feel. She leaned against the bar, invisible to the bartender who was enthralled by the bright, laughing girls with their effortless cleavage and youth. Her own curves were bound by undergarments that felt more like scaffolding than lingerie.

Once, she had been that girl. She remembered being twenty-one like it was yesterday. How had everything changed so fast?

Nearly twenty minutes passed. The bartender never looked her way. She sighed and turned from the bar.

Scanning the dance floor, she spotted Avery easily—a beacon of red hair, swaying with a man who looked barely twenty-five, her body pressed against his. She was luminous. Vibrant. And Merritt... didn't belong here.

Her feet throbbed, too sore to carry her across the crowd to Avery.

Instead, she fished her phone from the tiny clutch dangling from her wrist and sent a text: *I'm leaving. Do you want to come?*

From the dance floor, Avery retrieved her phone from her bra, frowning as she read. With whispered words and a lingering kiss to her dance partner, she made her way over.

"What's going on?" she asked, warmth and alcohol softening her voice.

"I gave it a go," Merritt said, the phrase slipping out—a remnant of Everett's Australian vernacular still rooted in her speech. "But I'm done. I just want to go home."

Avery turned, effortlessly caught the bartender's eye, and ordered a gin and soda. He returned with her drink and a phone number scribbled on a napkin.

"Are you sure you want to go?" she asked, her gaze drifting toward the crowd—then back to the tall, broad-shouldered man still waiting for her at the edge of the dance floor. "It's almost the countdown."

"I'm sure."

"Do you want me to come with you?"

"You stay. You're having fun," Merritt said, nodding toward Avery's waiting companion. A sly smile spreading across her face as she added, "Call me tomorrow," lifting her brows in a conspiratorial arch. "You'll have to tell me everything."

Avery grinned. "Okay." She wrapped her in a tight, warm hug. "Text me when you're home."

"Just one thing," Merritt asked, voice teasing. "How old is he?"

"Old enough," Avery winked, disappearing back into the crowd.

The coat check was a relief. The heavy wool of her coat wrapped around her like armour. She slid on her deerskin mittens—an old pair her mother had given her, hand-stitched and soft with age. A nod to who she was, and where she came from.

The blast of air that greeted her outside stole her breath. But it wasn't the only thing to hit her.

As Merritt pushed open the heavy front door, a sudden gust of frigid air hit her—and so did the door, slamming back with startling force. She stumbled, heels skidding on the icy pavement as the door clipped her shoulder. With a yelp, she went down hard, the cold cracking through her as she landed.

"Stay down," a voice barked—sharp, low, and unmistakably trained in command.

"What the fuck?" Merritt stammered, breath catching as the cold bit into her. Blinking against the wind and a flash of embarrassment, she looked up. A towering woman stood over her—sharp angles, compressed rage, one gloved hand still gripping the door. Her stance was wide and braced, her wool coat pulled tight across broad shoulders. A tension clung to her, volatile and coiled, the kind of hair-trigger energy Merritt couldn't place but instinctively didn't want to provoke.

"Quinn," a second voice said gently, firm but calm. "Let me help her."

From her position on the ground, Merritt turned her attention to the second voice. A hand was extended—leather-gloved, inviting.

The hand belonged to a man in a tailored black wool coat, the collar turned just enough to frame a chiseled jaw dusted with stubble. He looked like he'd stepped off a political campaign poster—clean-cut, confident, and devastatingly handsome in a way that felt both polished and disarming. She took the outstretched hand.

He helped her to her feet, blue eyes kind beneath the brim of a black toque.

"Are you alright?" he asked. He brushed snow from her knees, concern etched into his brow.

She didn't know. Everything hurt. Her knees, her wrists, her lower back—all of it throbbed. Falling at forty-one was not the same as falling at twenty-one; the ground felt harder now, less forgiving. But more than anything, it was her pride that smarted, stung raw by the cold and the humiliating spectacle of it all.

"What happened?" She managed, adjusting her glasses.

He shot a look at the other woman—Quinn, apparently. "She can be... a bit much. I'm truly sorry."

He caught sight of her torn mittens. "Oh no, your hands."

He gently turned them over in his palms. "That looks painful."

She pulled back. "I'm fine."

She stepped to leave—and fell again. Hard. Her traitorous shoes flew in opposite directions, abandoning her completely.

"Fuck's sake," she muttered from the ground. "Could this night get any worse?"

The stranger was already reaching for her again, his bemused smile mercifully free of laughter.

"Let's try this again," he said, voice warm, with the faintest French-Norlandic lilt.

She stared at him, then took his hand, letting him bear her weight as he helped her to her feet.

"My shoes," she muttered. "They're fucking evil."

He released her hand so he could retrieve them. Both heels were broken. "I don't think you'll get very far in these," he handed them back to her. "Let me give you a ride," he offered, gesturing to a sleek black Escalade idling nearby.

"Um, no," she said, brushing his hand away. "I've seen that movie. I'm not ending up in your freezer."

She reached for her phone, preparing to call a Voyagr— but the screen had completely shattered in her falls.

"Fuck," she muttered.

"Please," he said again. "My driver's right here. Just a warm ride. No freezers, I swear."

She let out a slow breath, her feet bare and cold against the frozen pavement. "Okay," she said, voice filled with resignation. "I just want to go home."

He smiled as they approached the SUV and he opened the door for her. She climbed in, flushed and flustered.

He introduced the driver—Sylvie, elegant and poised, with steel-grey hair tied back in a no-nonsense ponytail. Her posture was military-straight, her presence calm and assured. She looked like she'd spent a lifetime keeping people safe and never once asked for thanks.

In contrast, the other woman—Quinn—was hulking, intense, deeply aware. Her wool coat barely contained the breadth of her frame, and her short, dark hair framed sharp, angular features that hinted at strength.

The two chatted softly as Sylvie drove, their voices a muted current beneath the hum of the engine. Merritt sat in silence, the warmth of the car only just beginning to thaw her fingers and her pride. The city blurred past. At her townhouse, the stranger again opened her door for her, helped her across the icy sidewalk, steadying her as she stepped barefoot onto the slick concrete, her broken stilettos dangling from one hand. Her breath came in soft puffs, her exhaustion catching up with her all at once.

She unlocked the door with numb fingers, the ruined gloves buried deep in her purse, and stepped into the dim hush of her townhouse. Familiar shadows stretched across the hardwood, still and undisturbed. She turned to close the door behind her—

—and paused.

Sophie had appeared, silent on her paws. Her long copper fur shimmered in the porch light, and her mismatched eyes—one blue, one brown—were fixed on the man outside.

Merritt froze. She hadn't meant to continue this interaction. She hadn't meant to linger.

As Sophie approach him, he chuckled and crouched, brushing his hand gently over Sophie's head. Then he stood and extended his hand to her.

"I'm Beau," he said, offering a sheepish, boyish smile—just as she realised she hadn't thought to ask his name. Or who he was. Or why he had a driver. Or a bodyguard. Or anything else that might have made her think twice.

"Happy New Year," he said softly, eyes steady on hers.

She stared at the hand, then reached out, her skin meeting

his. Warmth bloomed at the contact—sharp, sudden, and unwelcome. A spark flared through her like a match struck in a dark room.

"I'm Merritt," she said politely. "And this is Sophie."

"Sophie," he repeated, his voice gentle, gaze flicking briefly to the husky before returning to her.

She dropped his hand, heart pounding, and stepped back.

The door clicked shut behind her.

Leaning against it, she slid slowly down until she sat on the hardwood floor, coat still wrapped tightly around her. Sophie padded over and nestled in at her side.

Merritt buried her hand in her husky's thick fur and closed her eyes.

I'm sorry, Everett, she whispered into the hush. *I didn't mean for there to be a spark.*

But there had been.

And in the darkness of her entryway, she couldn't stop feeling it.

Chapter 2
Beau ~ New Year's Eve

The soft chime of the grandfather clock in the foyer mingled with the hum of the movie playing softly. A fire crackled in the hearth, casting flickering shadows across the expansive living room. Beau Laurent sat on the oversized sectional, his youngest child nestled into his side. Juliette's small body was wrapped in her favourite pale-blue cashmere blanket, her golden locks damp with sweat and clinging to her forehead. Her breaths came in shallow waves, each one a struggle.

Her fever was high.

Beau pressed his hand gently to her forehead. Too hot.

He looked down at her, heart aching. She was just seven, still so little despite how fiercely she tried to keep up with her older brothers. She reminded him of her namesake, his younger sister, lost decades ago to a tragedy that had shaped him more than anyone ever knew. Naming Juliette after her had felt like honouring her memory. But tonight, the connection ached like a bruise.

Across the room, Bastien and Émile were sprawled near the fire, lost in a light-hearted card game. Their laughter spilled into the room like warmth. Bastien, sixteen, calm and measured like his father. Émile, thirteen, a spark of curiosity and energy, quick to smile and quicker to challenge. They had no idea how much they grounded Beau just by being themselves.

This wasn't always how New Year's looked for them. There had been joy once—champagne, laughter, Delphine's voice carrying through the halls.

In years past, they'd celebrated here. The house had been full of noise, her laughter lighting up the room as she teased him for playing the same Blue Rodeo record that he so loved. Now she was in Mexico, her brand new, picture-perfect life with Norland's most notorious tech billionaire plastered all over social media and tabloids. And just like that, Sebastian DuPont — once a name Beau barely registered in headlines and at tech summits — had become inescapable.

The divorce had been finalized in September. A formality by that stage. But the wound was still raw. And worse, Beau knew there were truths Delphine hadn't told him. Betrayals she hadn't confessed. The uncertainty gnawed at him.

Still, the kids were here tonight. He had this moment with them. That was everything.

Another cough wracked Juliette's frame. Beau didn't hesitate. "We need something to bring her fever down," he said, standing.

Quinn appeared in the doorway before he finished the sentence. She was hard to miss—tall, broad, and always a little too quick to act. Her movements had a constant tension, like she was on the verge of snapping into action.

Quinn was part of Beau's newly expanded security detail— a personal assignment within the Norland Federal Constabulary, the country's national security and federal police force. His protection detail had grown in recent months, as tensions beneath Norland's polished surface began to shift and murmur in ways that made protection more complicated. But Sylvie remained his constant, and Quinn had quickly become part of the tight circle that moved with him, shadowed him, and stayed within arm's reach.

"It's not safe," she said. "It's New Year's Eve. Sylvie's off. Nothing reliable will be open. And with the threats still circulating—"

"My daughter is sick," Beau said, his voice firm. "Call Sylvie."

Quinn's jaw ticked, but she reached for her phone.

Beau crouched next to his sons. "I need you two to hold down the fort. Keep an eye on Juels."

Bastien gave a steady nod. "Of course."

Émile sat up straighter. "We'll be okay, Dad."

A few minutes later, Sylvie pulled into the underground garage with her usual precision. Her silver-streaked hair was tucked into a sleek twist, and her expression, while composed, carried the faintest trace of irritation.

"There's a pharmacy in The Promenade that agreed to open for us," she said as Beau climbed into the backseat. Quinn huffed as she wedged herself into the passenger seat.

"Of course you already found one," Quinn muttered.

"I don't leave things to chance," Sylvie replied coolly.

The city passed in a blur of frost and holiday lights. Arbourleigh was beautiful at night, dressed in snow and old stone. As they reached The Promenade, it grew more polished—glass storefronts, designer signage, gold and light and curated charm.

The pharmacy was small and understated, tucked beside an exclusive club. A grey-haired pharmacist opened the door as they arrived.

He greeted them with a tired smile and a nod, stepping aside to let them into the softly lit space. The shop was small but well-kept, its shelves orderly, the faint scent of antiseptic mingling with lavender from a nearby diffuser.

"This one's on the house," the older man said kindly, holding out a small white paper bag.

Beau stepped forward, gratitude already forming on his lips—but Quinn reached it first. She took the bag without a word, tore it open with sharp, efficient fingers, and examined the seal on the box inside as if she expected it to be laced with explosives. Satisfied, she slipped the bottle into her oversized coat pocket and, without looking, dropped the paper bag to the floor.

Beau didn't hesitate. He stooped to pick it up, brushing it smooth before glancing up at the pharmacist.

"Thank you," he said, his voice sincere. "Truly. I appreciate you being willing to meet us here tonight."

"No trouble." The pharmacist gave a weary smile and nodded once, clearly surprised to be acknowledged at all.

As Beau and Quinn stepped back out into the crisp night air, the door clicked shut behind them. They had nearly reached the Escalade when the low thrum of music drifted from the upscale nightclub next door to the pharmacy. It was the kind of place frequented by Arbourleigh's wealthiest—the offspring of old money and political dynasties, all designer coats and curated rebellion.

Beau turned his head slightly, the sound catching his attention. The music surged as the door began to open behind them.

Quinn reacted instantly.

She pivoted and slammed into it.

Too fast. Too hard.

And someone was on the other side.

"Jesus, Quinn," Beau muttered, irritation flaring as he turned to her. The woman on the ground was clearly no threat—just startled, dazed, and now humiliated. But Quinn stood rigid, her arm still partially extended, her body braced for a fight that wasn't there. Always too fast. Always too much.

"Stay down!" she barked.

"What the fuck?" the woman snapped, her voice sharp with indignation.

"Let me help her," Beau said, brushing past his bodyguard with a glance that told her—enough.

He leaned forward.

And then everything stopped.

The woman looked up at him, and in the space of a single breath, something shifted. Her glasses were slightly askew, her cheeks flushed from cold, her dark hair tumbling forward in loose waves. Her eyes—deep brown with flecks of gold—locked onto his, wide and wary, but not afraid. Beautiful. Infuriated. Magnetic.

It hit him with a force that almost startled him.

He hadn't felt anything like this in so long—not since Delphine left. And even before that, not like this. Not like being pulled toward someone he didn't know, didn't understand, but *needed* to.

She looked like chaos wrapped in warmth. Like someone who wouldn't let him get away with anything—and he found himself wanting to know what her voice sounded like when it wasn't sharp with frustration.

Still, she took his hand, and Beau was embarrassed by how relieved he felt—like a schoolboy asking for a dance.

He helped her up. She barely got steady on her feet before her heels betrayed her again. She went down hard. Shoes flew in opposite directions, one clattering against the curb.

"Fuck's sake," she muttered, exasperated.

Beau stepped forward again, offering his hand with a soft smile. "Let's try that again."

She stared at him for a moment, clearly weighing her pride against the inevitability of gravity. Then she sighed and took his hand.

"My shoes," she said flatly, brushing snow off her coat. "They're fucking evil."

The words made him grin. Not just the profanity—but the deadpan delivery, the sharpness in her tone. There was something utterly disarming about her. She was flustered, annoyed, and completely unfiltered. And for reasons he couldn't understand, he liked it. Liked her. Instantly.

He bent to retrieve the ruined heels. "You won't get far in these," he said, holding them out. "Let me give you a ride."

She hesitated. "Um, no," she said. "I've seen that movie. I'm not ending up in your freezer."

Beau watched as she fished her phone from a glittering purse. The screen was shattered.

"Fuck."

It made him chuckle again. There was something oddly poetic about the way she cursed—like punctuation, like emphasis. She wasn't trying to impress him. She wasn't performing. She was just... herself.

"Please," Beau said, softer now, bemused by his own pleading tone, and how sincere it felt.

She glanced up at him. For a moment, something shifted in her eyes. Then she sighed. "Fine. I just want to go home."

As they approached the car, Sylvie glanced back over her shoulder, a knowing smile tugging at her lips.

"She could be anyone," Quinn muttered, slipping into the front seat with a scowl.

"She's not," Sylvie replied, her voice dry but gentle. "Relax."

In the backseat, Beau settled beside the woman, unsure where to put his hands. The silence between them crackled —not with awkwardness, but something... charged. Her presence filled the space in a way that unsettled him, made him oddly self-conscious. He, who spoke in front of crowds, who negotiated legislation, couldn't think of a single damn thing to say.

She peeled off her ruined gloves and tucked them into her tiny purse, flexing her fingers in the low light. He looked instinctively to her left hand. No ring. Relief bloomed so fast it embarrassed him. And then—God—her gaze flicked down to his hand. He didn't wear his wedding ring anymore. Hadn't for over a year. Still, something about her noticing made his heart stutter.

She gave Sylvie her address. Beau recognized the street—it was in one of Arbourleigh's oldest neighbourhoods. He knew the area well enough to picture the kind of home waiting at the end of it: classic, understated, and elegantly beautiful. Like her.

Beau stole another glance. She was tall—only a few inches shorter than him, he guessed—maybe 5'10". Something about her posture, even slouched in defeat, made her seem taller. Commanding. Her hair tumbled in loose, slightly chaotic waves around her glasses. Her mouth had a beautiful downturn, like she was perpetually unimpressed, and he couldn't help but wonder what it would take to make her smile.

She didn't need him. That stirred something unexpected in him. Attraction, yes—but also a flicker of admiration.

They pulled up to the townhouse—a three-storey brick beauty tucked into a corner lot, stoic and warm all at once.

Beau found himself scrambling to open the car door for her. She climbed out without a word. He followed, slower, unwilling to let the moment end. If nothing else, he told himself, he was being polite. But the truth was simpler: he just wanted a few more seconds with her.

As she stepped barefoot onto the snowy pavement, he reached for her elbow, steadying her. She didn't pull away. He walked beside her, guiding her carefully up the steps to her front door. Her purse was tucked under one arm, her ruined shoes dangling from her hand. She moved like she was exhausted—but determined to keep her head high. That, somehow, made her even more captivating.

She jiggled the key in the lock, the soft click echoing into the still night. The door creaked open. She stepped inside and turned to close it behind herself.

But before it could close, a copper-coloured husky bounded over to the threshold—long-furred, graceful, curious. She blocked the door with her body, sniffing Beau's hand before giving it a quick, decisive lick.

He smiled. "Happy New Year."

He offered his hand. "I'm Beau, by the way." His eyes met hers, and he held onto her hand for as long as he could without crossing the line from polite to obvious.

She paused, her hand resting in his, and for a split second, he hoped she was holding on for the same reason he was.

"Merritt," she said. "And this is Sophie," she added quickly, her tone bashful as she abruptly pulled her hand away.

Her brief touch was firm but soft, her palm warm against his. It wasn't dramatic. It wasn't earth-shattering. But it was something close—a jolt of recognition that shot straight through him. He hadn't felt anything like it in a long time.

Then she let go and stepped inside, pushing the door closed behind her. The click of the latch echoed.

He stood there, staring at the grain of the wood, as though it might open again. Somehow frozen—caught between the lingering warmth of her hand and the sudden coolness of the closed door.

Slowly, he turned and descended the steps, each one taken reluctantly, as if walking away from something he didn't fully understand but already wanted more of. Merritt. The name echoed in his mind, soft and certain. It was beautiful. Unusual. It suited her.

Back in the car, Sylvie handed him a yellow legal pad.

"What's this for?" he asked.

"For what you'll regret not saying," Sylvie replied knowingly, the corner of her mouth twitching into the faintest smile.

Quinn huffed. "She still uses paper."

Sylvie shot her a sidelong glance that said more than words. "I still believe in gestures."

Beau let out a breath, shaking his head. "You're never going to let this go, are you?"

She smiled, this time fully. "Not when it comes to your love life."

He remembered the time she'd installed Sparkr on his phone without permission—discreetly efficient, entirely unrepentant. She'd even started filling in his profile before he caught her and dissuaded her with a firm but kind *no* .

"You need to at least *try*," she'd said at the time, with that same blend of practicality and tenderness. "You can't rebuild a life if you don't open the door once in a while."

Beau held the pad in his lap, the pen resting idle between his fingers. He hesitated, unsure if a note would be too much—or not enough. But then he thought of Merritt again. The way she'd looked at him. The spark he couldn't quite explain.

This felt different.

And if there was the smallest chance she'd felt it too, he didn't want to let the moment slip away.

He lowered the pen and began to write.

Merritt,

Meeting you tonight has been the best thing to happen to me in a long time. You and your little copper shadow have already made this night unforgettable.

If you ever feel like saying hello, I'd like that.

—Beau

He climbed out and slipped the note into her mailbox, his breath fogging in the cold.

As they pulled away, the lights of her home faded behind them, but the feel of her hand, the sound of her voice, the offbeat rhythm of her presence—none of that faded at all.

He leaned back, letting his head rest against the seat.

The ache of the past year still sat heavy in his chest.

But something about Merritt—her chaos, her stubbornness, her foul mouth and broken heels—had cracked something open.

And for the first time in a long while, it didn't feel like breaking. It felt like beginning.

Chapter 3
Merritt ~ New Year's Day

Sophie nudged Merritt awake early on New Year's morning, her nose damp against Merritt's skin. Merritt, ever the early riser, smoothed a hand over Sophie's soft head as she rose without hesitation. "Happy New Year, baby girl," she murmured, her voice thick with the remnants of sleep, carrying a smile so unexpected it startled her—a smile that felt foreign since Everett's passing.

Sliding her feet into her well-worn moccasins, soft as a whisper and lovingly handmade by her mother, Merritt made her way downstairs. The house sighed around her in its early morning stillness, and Sophie padded faithfully at her heels, the comforting rhythm of paws on hardwood accompanying her to the kitchen.

Merritt slid open the oversized glass door, its weight familiar beneath her touch, revealing the tidy, snow-draped backyard beyond. The freezing winter air rushed in, sharp and bracing, as Sophie darted out into the crisp morning to take care of her business. Merritt shivered, instinctively wrapping her arms around herself, but there was a part of her that welcomed the cold. Winter in Arbourleigh had always been her favourite season—snow glittering like diamonds under streetlights, the air humming with a kind of magic. It had always felt like a season for possibility, for reflection.

But this year, the weight of loss had dulled the enchantment. The world outside sparkled with its familiar winter magic, yet inside, Merritt felt untouched by it, as though the season's beauty had drifted past her without pause. Still, as echoes of the previous night stirred in her mind—along with the memory of the stranger who later introduced himself as Beau, with his steady voice and calm presence—something unexpected flickered within her. For a fleeting moment, she considered the possibility of leaning into the season's joys, of allowing herself to feel even a fragment of its celebration.

And yet, as soon as the thought of his face surfaced— attractive, her mind dared to whisper—she pushed it away with a sharp, internal rebuke. She wasn't ready for that.

Not now, not yet, maybe not ever. The idea of seeing someone who wasn't Everett that way felt wrong. Her heart, still thick with grief, wasn't ready to beat for anyone but the man she had loved and lost.

Merritt cradled a vanilla latte in her hands, the gentle warmth spreading through her palms as she watched Sophie darting playfully through the snow in the backyard. The sight brought a flicker of peace, though her mind refused to stay still. It wandered, unbidden, back to Beau and the startling clarity of his blue eyes. Each time the memory rose, she willed herself to pull away from it, anchoring her thoughts instead to Everett—to the life they had so carefully built together and to the gaping loss his absence had left behind, almost as if punishing herself with thoughts of her late husband.

After making herself a second vanilla latte and calling Sophie inside, Merritt ascended the polished steps to the third floor of her townhouse.

She and Everett had converted the entire top floor to office space, designed with the precision and practicality that had guided much of their life. It was a space that reflected discipline and focus, free from distractions or sentimentality.

For years, she and Everett had poured their energy into their careers with unwavering dedication. They'd made a conscious choice to nurture their work instead of children, crafting a life they both considered perfect—a partnership rooted in mutual ambition and shared purpose. The absence of children hadn't been a gap to fill but a deliberate, shared vision of success on their own terms. It had felt right. It had felt whole. They had been so happy.

As a partner at Haven & Wexler LLP, Merritt had built a reputation as a relentless yet compassionate divorce attorney, guiding clients through the most turbulent moments of their lives. Everett, meanwhile, had risen to prominence as a corporate consultant, crafting strategies that transformed struggling companies into industry leaders. His work was meticulous, demanding, and often unseen, but it left an indelible mark on those he guided.

Together, their careers had provided more than just financial comfort—they had offered a shared sense of purpose and fulfillment, a richness that had been complete. Or at least, it had felt that way. Now, that completeness felt like a distant memory, eclipsed by an ache that had become Merritt's full-time companion.

She settled into the high-backed chair behind her expansive desk, its surface a masterpiece of reclaimed hardwood with a live edge that gave the otherwise orderly room a touch of warmth and imperfection. The desk, like everything else in her office, was deliberate—a reflection of her values and precision. Pulling her laptop closer, she willed herself to dive into her work, determined to drown out the thoughts clamouring for her attention.

The case on her docket was a high-profile divorce involving Sebastian DuPont, a tech billionaire whose notoriety overshadowed even his supposed genius. While lauded by his diehard fans as a visionary, the rest of Norland saw him for what he truly was: a self-obsessed provocateur with a flair for chaos. His public persona was a carefully crafted mix of inflated bravado and calculated cruelty, his social media rants a daily spectacle of arrogance and thinly veiled contempt for anyone who dared question him. Beneath the veneer of innovation lurked a web of shady business practices, whispered allegations, and a string of lawsuits from employees and collaborators who had fallen victim to his relentless ambition. He had the charisma of a cult leader and the ethics of a corporate shark, making him both magnetic and profoundly untrustworthy.

The details of the DuPont divorce were as scandalous as they were heartbreaking. Genevieve DuPont, Sebastian's soon-to-be ex-wife, had filed after discovering her husband's affair with the strikingly beautiful wife of a high-ranking official in Norland's government. The revelation had come after years of Genevieve sacrificing her own career as a journalist to support Sebastian's rise to prominence and to raise their five children.

Merritt couldn't help but feel a pang of sympathy for the woman whose trust and dedication had been so brazenly betrayed.

Merritt found Sebastian DuPont repugnant. His arrogance, paired with a smugness that seeped into every word he spoke, left her ill at ease during their interactions. She had time off over the holidays, and she was using it to dive into the labyrinth of his financial statements—a tangled web of LLCs and shell corporations that seemed deliberately opaque.

Even as his attorney, she struggled to extract meaningful clarity from him, his evasiveness compounding her frustration. The DuPont divorce promised to be a storm of ambition, betrayal, and public scrutiny, and while Merritt didn't relish representing Sebastian, she was bound by her professional duty. Despite her misgivings, she would bring her usual rigour and precision to the case —even if, deep down, she couldn't help but hope that Genevieve's voice, so often overshadowed by her husband's, would still find a way to be heard.

Merritt poured herself into her work, the steady rhythm of her thoughts and keystrokes offering the closest thing to sanctuary she had. At her desk, she could momentarily escape the ache that had taken permanent residence in her chest—an ache now complicated by the unsettling flicker of attraction she was desperately trying to ignore. The flow state her work provided became her refuge, a reprieve from the unrelenting undercurrent of sorrow and loss that shadowed her every step, now underpinned by Beau's eyes.

Even as she poured all of herself into her work, she

opened a tab on her browser and typed the words: Beau Arbourleigh into the search bar. Before she could scroll through the results, she closed it—jaw tight, chest aching—chastising herself not just for the distraction, but for the sharp, guilt-ridden sense that she was betraying Everett.

Her focus shattered around noon when a soft buzz from her computer cut through the stillness, pulling her back to the present. A notification blinked in the corner of her screen, alerting her to someone at the front door. With a sigh, she clicked it.

The camera feed lit up with Avery's radiant, smiling face—a vision of effortless, traditional beauty that could have graced the cover of any magazine. She was still wearing the curve-hugging dress from the posh nightclub they'd visited the night before, the sleek fabric flawlessly accentuating her sculpted figure. Despite clearly not having been home yet, Avery had, as always, gone the extra mile. Her fiery red hair was styled to perfection, each strand falling elegantly into place as though it had been orchestrated by a team of professionals. Her makeup was meticulously reapplied, enhancing her striking emerald-green eyes with the perfect touch of mascara, while her lips wore a soft, flattering shade of lipstick that completed the look. Avery was the kind of woman who turned heads everywhere she went.

Glancing at the clock on her laptop monitor, Merritt realized she'd been working steadily for hours. She stretched her shoulders and allowed herself a moment of gratitude for the welcome distraction of Avery's arrival. She was looking forward to hearing every scandalous detail about Avery and her much, much younger dance partner from the night before. But more than that, she found herself eager to unpack the events of her own evening—the way they lingered in her mind, and in the memory of her hand in Beau's—with the one person who might understand. She hadn't let herself process any of it. Not really. Not yet.

She pressed the button on her laptop to unlock the front

door and watched as Avery pushed it open. Merritt smiled to herself as she hurried down the two flights of stairs to the kitchen.

What she didn't notice as she left her desk was the next document awaiting her attention—a scanned copy of an article detailing the scandal of Sebastian DuPont's affair with Delphine Moreau, the captivating and elegant wife of Norland's Minister of Finance: Beau Laurent. His smiling face was splashed prominently beside the headline announcing Genevieve DuPont's divorce filing, which exposed the sordid details of Sebastian and Delphine's affair.

* * * * *

"Happy New Year!" Avery announced, wrapping Merritt in a warm, lingering hug before crouching to offer the same exuberant greeting to Sophie. Her radiant smile didn't falter, lighting up the room like sunshine after snow.

Merritt turned wordlessly to the espresso machine and began making two vanilla lattes—a ritual between them so ingrained over the past year and a half, no words were needed. "So," she said, her tone teasing as she glanced over her shoulder. Avery had already claimed her usual barstool, elbows resting on the smooth grey marble countertop that tied Merritt's moody kitchen together.

Avery's grin turned impish. "Oh, Merritt," she sighed, her voice positively brimming with mischief.

"What's his name?" Merritt asked, the corners of her mouth twitching knowingly.

"Josh!" Avery declared, eyes bright as she leaned in like they were teenagers again. "Isn't that sexy?"

Merritt chuckled and handed her the latte. They moved to the round, dark-stained hardwood table nestled in front of a large industrial-framed window. Sunlight poured in through the glass, casting long, golden lines across the table's rustic surface as they settled across from one another, Avery already mid-sentence about her whirlwind night with Josh—a 21-year-old architecture student at the University of Arbourleigh. Twenty years her junior.

The age gap gave Avery pause—she admitted as much—but she couldn't ignore the way he'd captivated her. Josh had a maturity that felt rare for someone his age, paired with an enthusiasm that made her feel vibrant again, seen.

Their night hadn't been about sex, she explained with flushed cheeks, but something more intimate. They'd kissed for hours on his worn-out couch, champagne bottle between them, hands roaming respectfully over fabric, the electricity of restraint somehow more thrilling than abandon. When the fire between them began to settle, they just... talked. Until sunrise. About everything and nothing, like they had all the time in the world.

"I haven't even slept yet," Avery confessed with a sheepish laugh, her green eyes sparkling. "But I had to come tell you."

Merritt listened, heart warmed by the sight of her friend so swept up, not by fantasy, but by something real. It was a joy to see Avery like this.

"What about you?" Avery asked, leaning forward. "Did you manage to stay up to ring in the New Year?"

Merritt ran her finger along the rim of her coffee mug, tracing the elegant lettering that spelled out *Paris*. A mug from a trip she and Everett had once taken—a city filled with light and promise. Now, it was just porcelain and memory. A beautiful ghost.

"Mer?" Avery's voice was gentle.

"I think I met someone," Merritt said, the words escaping

before she could stop them.

Avery's eyes lit up. "What?! Who? Tell me everything."

And somehow, she did. Every detail spilled out—the sound of his voice, the snow, Sophie, the stillness. But mostly, his eyes. She kept circling back to those eyes.

"Beau?" Avery repeated, a slow smile forming. "Beau with the beautiful blue eyes," she teased.

"It's nothing," Merritt said quickly, waving it away. The thought of any interest felt too complicated for her life now — and for the routine of grief she'd settled into. "I don't even know him. It was just a moment. It's silly."

But the way she said it—softly, defensively—told Avery it wasn't silly at all.

"Okay, Mer," Avery said gently, letting it go. But she couldn't hide the flicker of hope she felt.

Eventually, Avery yawned and ordered a car through the Voyagr app. As Merritt walked her to the door, Sophie trailing them like a shadow, she noticed something odd —the snow on the mailbox had been disturbed. Curiosity tugged at her. She wasn't expecting any deliveries.

She opened the mailbox and found a single, carefully folded sheet of yellow lined paper. One edge was damp from melted snow.

She unfolded it slowly, eyes skimming the neat, deliberate handwriting. A smile bloomed. Uncontainable. Genuine.

Her breath caught.

Avery noticed instantly. "What is it?"

Merritt clutched the note to her chest, guarding it like a

secret. "Your car's here," she said softly, changing the subject, wanting to keep the note's contents just to herself for now.

Avery studied her, debating whether to press, but finally just gave her a lingering look before stepping away toward the waiting car.

As the street stilled again, Merritt looked down at the note once more, her fingers trembling slightly.

She wasn't ready to share it. Not yet.

She just wanted to feel it.

And for the first time in what felt like forever, Merritt felt something shift inside her grief — a flicker of possibility she couldn't name, but couldn't ignore. Not hope. But something close enough to make her uneasy.

Chapter 4
Beau ~ Five Days Later

The last stretch of Beau's holiday break unfolded gently, with soft morning light spilling across the polished surfaces of his kitchen. It was his final day with the children before they would return to Delphine — and before he escaped to Baie Lueur for the remainder of his holiday.

This morning, Juliette bounded in first, her energy already bubbling over, cheeks flushed with the glow of good health. After four days of fever and sniffling, she was back to her spirited self, and Beau's heart lifted at the sight. She had spent most of the break curled beside him, a shadow. Now she was a whirlwind again, legs swinging beneath the kitchen table.

Bastien and Émile followed, both still yawning, their hair tousled and eyes bleary from too many late nights with holiday movies. Bastien ruffled Juliette's golden hair as he passed, earning a giggle and a half-hearted swat. Émile leaned against the counter, arms crossed, watching her bounce with the resigned air of an older brother who had long since accepted the chaos.

And beneath it all sat the familiar ache — the weight Beau never quite got used to as these stretches of time wound toward their inevitable ending.

"Can we go skating today?" Juliette asked, her eyes bright with hope as she tucked her feet beneath her and looked up at him expectantly.

He smiled and flipped the strawberry pancakes sizzling in the cast iron pan. "Skating, eh?"

The smell of warm berries and sugar filled the kitchen, and with it, a memory crept in. Not of the kids, but of a morning long before them—back in his tiny basement apartment, Delphine curled under his flannel sheets, and him trying to impress her with a romantic breakfast after their first night together. She'd laughed when he served the lumpy, too-sweet pancakes, kissed him with maple syrup on her lips, and said it was the best thing she'd ever tasted.

He didn't think of her often anymore—not unless something pulled her sharply into focus. The past felt like a room he'd shut the door on. Still, its weight lingered, tucked into the corners of his memory, reflected in the curve of his children's smiles, and threaded through the golden strands of Juliette's hair.

"What do you guys think?" he asked, nodding toward his sons. "We could spend the morning skating before you head back to your maman's?"

"Sure," Émile said.

"Yeah," Bastien agreed. "Want me to text Sylvie and Quinn?"

Beau nodded. Their security detail had become an accepted fixture of their lives, and the kids hardly blinked at the coordination anymore.

As the pancakes were devoured and the day got moving, Beau found himself fixated on one specific rink. The one near The Promenade. The one near Merritt's neighbourhood.

It had been five days since he'd helped her across the ice-slicked street, five days since she'd stepped into her townhouse with her copper-furred husky at her side and a quick, bashful "Merritt" on her lips.

Five days since she'd slipped from his orbit—but not from his mind. More and more, his thoughts drifted back to New Year's Eve, to the arresting warmth of her eyes, the way they took hold of him and left behind a smile he couldn't explain.

He told himself the choice of rink was practical. Good ice, less busy than the nearby rinks. Nothing unusual. Nothing deliberate.

Still, when Sylvie pulled the Escalade to the curb and the kids tumbled out with their skates slung over their shoulders, Beau scanned the street—casually, absently, as if expecting something. Or someone.

Sylvie noticed. Of course she did.

"Want me to swing by her place after this?" she asked dryly, eyes on the windshield but clearly enjoying herself. "It's not too far from here," she said with a knowing wink.

Beau didn't answer right away. He tugged his gloves on with exaggerated care, then muttered, "I don't know what you're talking about."

Sylvie let out a huff of laughter. "Sure you don't."

"It's not like that," he said, then paused. "Okay, maybe it's a little like that. I don't know. I forgot to put my number on the note I left her," he confessed.

She turned to look at him, all amusement and affection. "You've been out of the game too long, old man," she joked.

"Tell me about it," he said, half under his breath. "fifty-two doesn't exactly make me a contender in her world." He exhaled, voice quieter. "I keep thinking about her. About that night. I don't even really know why."

"Because it's been a long time since someone caught your attention," Sylvie said simply. "And because you're a human man, and she was beautiful?"

He gave a faint smile. "She was, wasn't she," he agreed. "I can't just show up at her house though."

"No," she agreed. "That'd be pushy. Maybe even a little stalkerish."

"Exactly."

"But," she added, her tone thoughtful now, "if the universe decides to nudge things along again today... well. Wouldn't be the worst thing." They climbed out of the car together, Sylvie walking straight-backed next to Beau, her eyes always scanning.

"No, it wouldn't be." Beau found himself agreeing.

The rink was nestled into a park framed by towering maples. Sylvie joined Quinn and they staked out a spot near the entrance, sipping coffee and watching the perimeter with their usual vigilance. Beau laced up beside Bastien, then followed his kids onto the ice.

He skated with them for an hour, circling wide, catching Juliette's mittened hand when she wobbled, laughing at Émile's show-off spins, high-fiving Bastien after a mock race.

After a while, his knees protested. He coasted to the edge and approached Sylvie and Quinn, tugging off his gloves.

"I'm going to stretch my legs for a minute," he said. "And get a coffee."

Quinn's brows rose. "Alone?"

"I'll stay where you can see me," he promised. "Just the bench by the coffee cart."

Sylvie nodded. "Go ahead. We've got them."

"What about him?" Quinn started to protest before Sylvie silenced her with a sharp look.

The air was sharper near the ice, the cold biting deeper off the rink. Just off the path, a small coffee cart chuffed steam into the morning air, the scent of espresso and sugar curling through the chill. Beau ordered a vanilla latte —his favourite—and nodded his thanks to the barista before making his way to a bench that overlooked the rink and backed onto the sprawl of the park.

He lowered himself onto the frozen wood and took a sip. The latte was sweeter than what he would make for himself at home. He didn't mind.

It had been five days. Five days, and he couldn't stop replaying the sound of her voice, the sharp wit, the startled way she'd looked up at him as if she wasn't sure whether to thank him or hit him.

She'd been magnetic—even in the awkwardness.

He took another sip, surprised by the disappointment that crept in at her absence. What had he expected? That she'd show up here, in the middle of a Friday morning? The odds were infinitesimal.

And then, as if conjured by the thought, a copper blur trotted up to the bench and fixed him with a familiar, mismatched gaze. Her muzzle landed on his knee, tail thumping furiously against the frozen ground.

"Sophie?" he asked, incredulous, his voice catching.

He reached instinctively for her collar, fingers brushing the leather until he found the tag—*Sophie.*

His breath caught.

He looked up.

Merritt.

And there she was—rushing toward him, her expression a mix of panic and determination. She was dressed for a run, effortlessly combining practicality with elegance. Her sleek, black leggings, detailed with subtle reflective patterns, hugged her toned frame, and a fitted, fleece-lined running jacket in a deep burgundy complemented her warm, golden complexion. A soft cream scarf was wrapped loosely around her neck, its ends fluttering slightly as she moved, adding an extra layer of cozy sophistication. Her dark hair was pulled back into a simple braid that peeked out from under a knitted headband in a matching cream hue. The faintest glow from her run highlighted her high cheekbones, a natural beauty that seemed amplified by the winter light.

Even in her haste, leash clutched in one waving hand, she looked composed, graceful—beautiful."It's okay, I've got her," Beau called out, his voice steady as Merritt closed the gap between them.

As she drew closer, Beau took her in, her breath visible in the cold air, and the flicker of surprise in her eyes.

"You," she said, her tone a blend of astonishment and something that might have been playful suspicion. "I mean, of course it's you. You're everywhere, apparently. Should I start worrying you're following me, or is this just fate being... weird?"

The mention of fate caught him off guard, stirring something deep within. It wasn't just the word itself but the way she said it—offhanded yet pointed—that made him wonder if maybe he wasn't the only one who had felt the pull. The thought warmed him in a way the frigid morning couldn't, an unspoken possibility settling between them.

His gaze caught on the yellow piece of paper peeking out of her jacket pocket, barely visible but unmistakable. She'd gotten his note. She'd gotten his note and kept it.

"You," Beau echoed, his smile widening, a playful glint sparking in his eyes. "Following you? If I were, I'd like to think I'd be a bit more subtle about it. But hey, sometimes fate saves me the effort." He gave Sophie a long scratch behind her ears, grinning as the husky leaned into his hand with obvious delight.

Merritt stood for a moment, awkwardly holding Sophie's leash as though unsure of what to do next. Then, seeming to remember herself, she stepped forward and clipped the lead onto Sophie's collar.

"Sorry about that," she said, her voice tinged with embarrassment. "She's usually so good off-lead. That's the first time she's ever taken off like that."

Beau met her apology with a warm smile, privately grateful for Sophie's unexpected detour—and oddly flattered that she'd chosen to run straight to him. "She must like me," he said, his tone more confident than he felt. As soon as the words left his mouth, he cringed inwardly, wishing he could pull them back. Really? That's what you're going with? he chastised himself silently.

But Merritt didn't seem to mind. In fact, she smiled—just enough to make him wonder if, maybe, his awkward charm hadn't gone entirely unnoticed. Maybe that spark he'd felt since New Year's Eve wasn't his alone.

"Would you like to sit down?" Beau asked, patting the spot on the bench beside him.

To his surprise—and, judging by the flicker of hesitation in her eyes, to Merritt's as well—she sat. She left a polite distance between them, a gap Beau had secretly hoped would be smaller, but he wasn't about to complain. She was next to him, and he couldn't believe his luck. His unspoken, not-quite-acknowledged plan had somehow fallen into place.

"What are you doing here?" Merritt asked, her tone casual but tinged with curiosity as she focused on Sophie, who sat at her feet, panting contentedly. "Do you live around here, or is this just some weird coincidence?" She glanced up briefly, a small, awkward smile playing on her lips. "You're not, like, secretly a serial killer and this is part of some long con, are you?" she added, the playful callback to the night they had met making her smile widen despite herself.

"Serial killer?" Beau repeated, a playfully. "If I am, I'm really bad at it. I'm here skating with my kids. My seven-year-old made me pinky swear we'd stop at The Velvet Whisk for a cinnamon roll after skating." He nodded toward the rink with a wry smile. "Not exactly the kind of promise you can break and still keep your super-villain credibility intact."

Beau gestured toward the rink, where Bastien and Émile skated with effortless skill, Juliette darting between them, her laughter occasionally ringing out. Sylvie and Quinn lingered conspicuously near the edge of the rink.

"Juliette, my youngest, wanted to go skating for the morning. Couldn't say no to that," he added with a soft smile.

Merritt followed his gaze, her eyes tracking the movement of Beau's children as they glided across the ice. Beau, watching her more than the rink, noticed the subtle shift in her focus—the way her eyes flicked to his hands, just like they had that night in the Escalade. He knew exactly what she was looking for—a wedding ring.

He decided to put her curiosity to rest. "I'm not married anymore," he said, the words slipping out bluntly, almost too casually.

Merritt's head snapped toward him, her expression caught somewhere between surprise and discomfort. "Oh, I..." she stammered, her cheeks colouring faintly as she dropped her gaze back to Sophie, avoiding his eyes. She didn't finish her thought, and for a moment, silence settled between them, save for the distant laughter of the skaters and the hum of the park.

"So," Beau began, his voice warm, curiosity threading through his words as he carefully tested the waters. He wasn't entirely sure where he wanted the conversation to go—only that he wanted it to continue.

"You seemed... pretty off the other night," he said, his gaze lingering on her a moment longer than intended. His tone was gentle, inviting. "Was everything okay?"

The question hung between them, open but not insistent. Beau held his breath, unsure if he'd overstepped—but unable to let it go. There was something she wasn't saying, and for reasons he couldn't fully explain, he wanted to understand.

"Oh, that. Yeah," Merritt stammered, her voice flustered. "It was my friend Avery's idea. She just wanted me to come out with her. I don't normally go to clubs. Well, at least not in, like, twenty years," she added, punctuating the statement with an expressive wave of her hand—one that unfortunately bumped Beau's cup.

A splash of coffee spilled over the brim, landing squarely on his lap.

"Oh, fuck," Merritt exclaimed, alarmed. "I'm so sorry!" Without thinking, she grabbed the end of her scarf and began awkwardly dabbing at the stain blooming on his pants.

Beau flinched slightly, startled by the sudden nearness of her hands.

"Oh," he said, his voice laced with surprise, a flicker of something stirring beneath the surface. The winter air had cooled the drink, but Merritt's touch—unintentional and close—sent a jolt through him. Not overt, but enough to leave him momentarily unmoored.

"Oh, fuck," Merritt repeated, this time with pure mortification. Her face flooded with regret as she dropped the scarf and scrambled to her feet, clearly ready to make a quick exit.

"I'm going to..." she began, then trailed off as she turned toward the path leading home.

Before she could leave, Beau reached out, his hand gently catching her elbow.

"It's okay," he said, calm but firm. His eyes met hers, and in that instant, he was shocked by how much he didn't want her to go. "Please, stay." He only just managed to keep the pleading from his voice.

Merritt hesitated. Her cheeks still flushed, she slowly lowered herself back onto the bench, her movements tentative. Beau let his hand drop, giving her space, though the moment's warmth lingered.

"Really," he said, a soft smile playing on his lips. "I don't mind. I like talking to you."

She offered a small smile, her hands folded in her lap as Sophie circled back and settled at her feet. For a while, neither spoke. The park filled the silence for them. Finally, Merritt broke it, her voice tinged with awkward humour.

"You know, I really should apologize again for, uh... invading your personal space with my scarf. Not my proudest moment."

Beau turned to her, raising one brow in mock surprise. "Ah yes," he said with faux gravity. "The infamous scarf incident. I wasn't sure we were going to talk about that."

Merritt groaned softly, covering her face with her hands. "Great. It has a name now. Perfect."

Beau chuckled, his laugh warm and gentle, careful not to deepen her embarrassment. "For what it's worth, I've had worse first—or I guess second—impressions," he said, eyes gleaming. "Though this one is definitely... memorable."

She glanced sideways at him, still a little pink, but now with a flicker of humour in her eyes.

"Memorable?" she echoed wryly. "That's one way to put it."

"Absolutely," he replied, his grin softening into something almost tender. "In the best possible way." He couldn't hide the flirtation in his voice.

Her gaze lingered on him. The vulnerability gave way to something lighter. And as Sophie sighed at their feet, Merritt leaned back slightly on the bench, her posture relaxing just a little. It wasn't much—but in the grand scheme of things, it felt like a small victory.

And as the icy world around them softened into the background, Beau found himself secretly hoping there might be more moments like this to come.

Chapter 5
Merritt ~ The Unsettling Quiet

Merritt sat stiffly on the park bench, Sophie sprawled at her feet, her warm body pressed against Merritt's boots. Her cheeks were still flushed—not from the cold, but from everything else. From the surprise of seeing Beau. From the shock of Sophie running to him like he was already hers. From the way he smiled at her, like she was someone worth smiling at.

Oh yeah, and then there was the part where she'd dumped Beau's coffee into his lap and instinctively lunged to clean it up—like they were already on some kind of fast-track to familiarity that absolutely did *not* exist. That was, without question, the most mortifying moment of all. She was pretty sure her face would be permanently flushed until at least spring.

Her heart thudded against her ribs—too fast, too loud. She was mortified, intrigued, unsettled—each emotion layered over the next, all of it threaded through with a low hum of guilt that echoed with Everett's name. The feelings tangled like a mess of loose wires, sparking every time Beau so much as looked at her.

He felt so easy to talk to, disarming in a way that made her feel seen without feeling exposed. But even so, she found herself keeping most things close to her chest. She offered up slivers—details about her work, Sophie, her friend Avery—but never quite peeled back the curtain. Not all the way. Not yet. The grief sat too close to the surface, always just beneath the skin.

But Beau? He was open in ways she hadn't expected. She learned he had three children, that he worked for the federal government, though he downplayed the importance of it with a kind of practiced modesty. He mentioned something vague about a shared custody agreement with his ex-wife who he spoke of but without any negativity. Merritt admired that. There was restraint in it. Integrity.

She could feel herself leaning toward him—

metaphorically, if not physically—drawn by the steadiness he seemed to radiate. And she hated how much she wanted to keep talking. How much she didn't want this moment to end.

A sudden voice broke through the silence.

"Daddy?"

Merritt startled slightly as a small girl ran up the path, curly golden hair peeking out from under a pink toque. Juliette.

Behind her came the two women Merritt now understood where Beau's security detail. One was tall, her posture military-straight, eyes sharp and scanning. The other was older, stylish in a cashmere coat and tortoiseshell sunglasses, her silver hair swept into a low ponytail.

Merritt stood quickly. She suddenly felt like she'd intruded on something, like this entire moment had been a bubble she wasn't meant to enter.

"I should get Sophie home," she mumbled, as Sophie climbed to her feet.

Beau rose with her, something unreadable flickering across his face. "It was nice seeing you again, Merritt."

"You too," she replied, already turning away.

She felt the womens' eyes on her as she walked briskly toward the path out of the park, Sophie trotting beside her.

She was halfway to the park's exit when she heard footsteps catching up.

"Wait," Beau called. She turned. He reached her, his hand resting gently on her forearm—its presence on her body something Merritt suddenly couldn't think past.

"Sorry," he said, slightly breathless. "Didn't mean to make things weird. Sylvie and Quinn just have... presence."

Merritt gave a nervous laugh. "Yeah, I noticed."

He smiled. "Sylvie's my driver—she's been with me forever. Quinn's newer. They added her after some recent... noise around the federal cabinet." He said it casually, but something darker flickered beneath the words. Merritt caught it but didn't ask.

They started walking, their steps falling into a comfortable rhythm.

"I've got time," Beau added, glancing over at her. "Sylvie's taking the kids for cinnamon rolls at The Velvet Whisk and then dropping them off with their mom. Juliette was mostly just excited about the pastry. She didn't mind me skipping the drop-off."

Merritt tilted her head. "You're letting someone else deliver on a pinky swear?"

He laughed, low and warm. "I know. Bold move. But I figured I had an important errand of my own."

She raised a questioning eyebrow.

"I'm walking a beautiful woman home," he said, adopting an exaggeratedly noble tone. "Like a proper gallant escort. Minus the cape. Or the horse."

She rolled her eyes, but she knew the smile tugging at her lips would give her away. Sometimes, the absolute worst lines were perfectly fine — when they came from the right man.

They fell into step together, the sidewalk winding beneath their feet as the city carried on around them. Beau extended his elbow with a gentleman's flourish, and Merritt hesitated only a beat before slipping her arm through his. It was warmer than she expected. Natural. Alarming in how right it felt.

She found herself talking. Not the version of herself that performed in courtrooms or braced against pity, but the one who still existed beneath all of that. She told him about growing up in Norland's Westernmost province, and told him she was a lawyer, vaguely, without offering more. He didn't press. Somehow, she appreciated that more than she could say.

He spoke of his kids, of Bastien's dry humour and Juliette's unrelenting energy, and of the chaos of shared custody. The strain of his job. The scrutiny. But there was joy in his voice too—an ease she wasn't used to. He didn't overshare, but he didn't guard his words, either. He spoke to her like they were already in the middle of something, like he wasn't afraid of where the conversation might go. It felt real. Not small talk. Not flirtation. Just... honest.

Merritt was conscious of how close they were walking, their arms still linked, her side brushing his every few steps. At one point, she laughed at something he said—really laughed—and, without thinking, let her head rest against his shoulder for half a second. Just half a second. Then she caught herself and snapped upright, cheeks burning.

Beau glanced at her, amused but gentle. He didn't comment on it, didn't make it a thing. Just smiled—soft, boyish, utterly disarming. Every time he looked at her, it felt like the world fell away, like his eyes saw only her. It was overwhelming. It was lovely.

And Merritt, against every instinct, found herself wanting to see that smile again. Wanting to know what else might draw it out. Wanting more.

By the time they reached her front steps, Merritt's nerves had all but quieted. Her cheeks were still pink, but not from embarrassment now.

They stood awkwardly for a beat, she let Sophie's lead go and watched her trot happily up the stairs to the front door where she sat like a chaperone at the top of the stairs.

"I don't know, Mer," Beau said softly.

The nickname caught her off guard, but not unpleasantly. It felt unforced, natural on his tongue, like a word he'd always known. Her name—but smaller. Closer.

"This feels like more than coincidence."

His gloved hands came to rest lightly on her shoulders. She looked up. His gaze held hers—steady, sincere, and achingly kind. The world seemed to fall away.

Then he stepped closer.

It wasn't rushed. It wasn't bold. It was permission. A question asked without words.

And when he leaned in, his lips brushed hers in a kiss so careful it nearly undid her. There was reverence in it, like he was afraid to break something precious. The second kiss followed before she could catch her breath—deeper, firmer, threaded with a tenderness that made her chest ache. It told her she was wanted, not just noticed. It told her he'd been thinking about this, too.

When they finally pulled apart, her breath caught somewhere between her heart and her throat. Her lips were still tingling. She parted them to speak, to say something—anything—but no words came.

She just looked at him.

"I better get Sophie inside," she said at last, her voice barely above a whisper.

Beau nodded gently. "Of course."

She turned, stepping toward the door.

"Mer," he called, just as she reached the top step.

She turned back.

He held out a card—simple, clean. His name. His number, Norlands Coat of Arms displayed prominently.

She reached down to take it, their gloved hands brushing for just a moment. "Thank you," she said, the words landing awkwardly between them, too small for the moment. Still, she offered a faint smile before stepping inside with Sophie.

The door clicked softly behind her.

Merritt stood for a beat, staring into the stillness of her home, then exhaled all at once—like she'd been holding her breath since the moment he kissed her. She leaned back against the door, heart pounding, breath uneven, and slowly sank to the floor—just as she had five nights ago.

Only this time, her hands weren't empty.

They held a card.

Beau Laurent, Minister of Finance.

And suddenly, it hit her.

She should've invited him in.

Panic fluttered in her chest as she debated whether to fling open the door and call after him. Surely it was too late.

She rushed to the window, just in time to see Beau ducking into a sleek grey sedan, the *Voyagr* sticker catching the pale winter sunlight before the car turned the corner and disappeared from view.

"Shit," she whispered. "I should've invited him in." And as the words left her lips, she realized just how much she meant them.

She stood alone in her front hall, smiling to herself—caught somewhere between nerves and giddy disbelief.

Then she reached for her new iPhone, the one she'd picked up after shattering her old one the night she and Beau met. She slid open the contacts, entered his name and number, added a crimson heart at the end of his name and without letting herself overthink it, typed out a message:

Hi. It's Merritt (from the park, the bench, the scarf incident, etc). I wasn't sure what the etiquette is after accidentally assaulting someone with a coffee and then kissing them on the sidewalk, but I just wanted to say... thank you.

With the text sent, she tapped Avery's name and brought the phone to her ear, her heart still unsteady in the best way. As the line rang, she let herself hold the thought—just for a second—that maybe this wasn't just a moment. Maybe it was the start of something. Something real. Something that felt like it was finally going somewhere. Something that, even in Everett's wake, she was allowed to want.

Chapter 6
Beau ~ The Thought of Her

Beau couldn't quite believe his nerve—placing his hands on her shoulders, kissing her. Twice. He hadn't planned any of it; he'd simply acted on instinct, on attraction, letting the moment carry him. A first kiss—his first *first* kiss in over thirty years.

And then she'd turned and walked away.

Not exactly the ending he'd envisioned.

Still, she'd taken his card before disappearing inside. That had to mean something.

The whole thing reminded him of dating in high school— when every glance felt charged, every silence filled with potential, and you spent hours analyzing the way someone had looked at you. It was awkward and exhilarating and impossible to stop thinking about. His heart beat a little faster just remembering the press of her lips, the way she'd softened into the kiss before pulling away.

Sylvie would take a while to swing back around with the car, so Beau broke protocol and called a Voyagr. A driver was a minute out, and it saved him the awkwardness of loitering outside the townhouse. He climbed into the backseat just as the sedan rolled up.

Through the passenger window, he caught a glimpse of movement—there she was, standing at the window. For a second, he considered telling the driver he didn't need a ride after all, of knocking, saying something, *doing* something. But then he noticed the driver eyeing the same window in the rearview mirror, his expression unreadable but a little too interested. Something about it set Beau slightly on edge.

He let it go and pulled out his phone, scanning through emails and pretending his chest wasn't still warm from their kiss.

Then a text came in—from a number not in his contacts.

He smiled. Before he could respond, another one landed.

My last name is Clarke. Is that weird to add? I just always need a first and last name before I enter someone into my contacts.

Then: *I mean, if you're going to add me to your contacts. You don't have to.*

And: *Obviously you don't have to. It's Merritt. Thank you for the kiss.*

Beau stared at the screen, bemused and oddly enchanted. One more followed: *Clarke.*

And then, seconds later: *I'm done now. Sorry.*

He laughed, unable to help it. The sound caught even him by surprise, warmth rising in his cheeks. He'd never been thanked for a kiss before—not that he'd had many first kisses in his lifetime.

He started to type a reply, trying to strike the right balance —something that would put her at ease, something that might coax another smile from her the way hers had coaxed one from him.

"You've had a busy week," the driver said suddenly, eyes flicking up to the rearview again.

Beau looked up. "Sorry?"

The driver smirked faintly. "Saw you on the news a few times. Finance Minister's job can't be easy with all those eyes on you, eh?"

Beau forced a polite smile. "I actually get by without being noticed most of the time." He shifted in his seat, trying to focus on his screen, hoping to give the impression he didn't want to be disturbed.

"Not just the news either," the driver continued, his tone

conversational. "Big players probably don't always like what you're doing."

Beau's pulse quickened, though he kept his expression calm. "I'm not sure how to take that."

The driver shrugged; his gaze fixed on the road ahead. "People talk. Especially when you're making moves some folks might not like. You and Hartwell are hitting the big wigs right where it hurts—in their wallet."

Beau studied the man's reflection in the rearview mirror, the casual ease in his tone clashing with the weight of his words. "Accountability is always worth the effort, if that's what you mean," Beau said, keeping his tone steady. "Even when it's uncomfortable."

The driver chuckled softly. "Uncomfortable's one word for it. Dangerous might be another."

Beau's jaw tightened, but he didn't respond. He turned his gaze back to his phone, pretending to read an email while his thoughts churned. This wasn't the first time he'd encountered someone with strong opinions about what he and Prime Minister Hartwell stood for. He'd learned to let these moments pass, even as they left an unease that was hard to shake.

The sedan eased up Beau's long driveway, the engine purring softly as it came to a stop. As Beau stepped out, Quinn appeared at his side, storming toward him with the weight of her frustration written all over her face.

"You took a Voyagr?" she hissed. "What the hell, Beau?"

Beau lifted a hand to calm her. "I didn't think—Sylvie was taking the kids—"

"You didn't think," Quinn repeated flatly. "That's the problem."

Sylvie appeared on the porch, her expression etched with concern. "We've been trying to reach you. There's been an incident."

Beau's entire posture shifted. "What happened?"

Sylvie's voice softened. "Inside. Please."

They moved into the kitchen, the air between them thick with dread.

"There's been an attack," Quinn said abruptly.

"Nice delivery," Sylvie muttered, shooting her a look.

She turned to Beau, her tone gentler. "It's Greyson. He was stabbed at an event."

Beau felt the world narrow. Greyson Hartwell wasn't just the Prime Minister—he was a mentor, a friend, almost family. He gripped the edge of the counter.

"Is he alive?"

"I'm sorry Beau, we don't know yet," Sylvie answered gently.

Quinn jumped in, her tone clipped. "The details are still coming in. It happened right after the Economic Justice Forum. He was doing a walkabout—shaking hands, smiling, the usual." She exhaled. "Someone grabbed his hand and yanked him forward. No one saw what happened exactly. But the next second, he staggered back, holding his neck—bleeding."

Beau sat down heavily.

"We think it's best if you leave for the cottage today," Sylvie said, her voice more measured than Quinn's but just as firm. "You were planning to go anyway—it's remote, secure, and it gets you out of the city."

Beau nodded slowly, the weight of what had happened to Greyson catching up with him. Chalet Écume. He'd intended to spend the rest of his time off there before returning to Arbourleigh. A stretch of coastline, some peace, maybe even a few good books—it had sounded restorative. Now, it sounded like protection.

"I'll get packed," he said softly, already halfway to the stairs.

As he reached his bedroom, his phone buzzed. He glanced at the screen.

Merritt. At the sight of her name, he felt some of his tension ease as a small smile played at his lips.

He answered. "Hello?"

"Hi, is this Beau?" Her voice was warm, hesitant. "It's Merritt. Um. I just wanted to say—I'm sorry for the texts. I got carried away. I'm not usually like that."

Despite the storm still swirling in his chest, Beau found himself laughing.

"I've never been thanked for kissing someone before."

"Oh shit," Merritt groaned. "I've made it worse."

"No," he said gently. "You haven't. Merritt, I want to talk to you too."

There was a pause.

"I know this is fast," he said, the words tumbling out before he could second-guess them. "But I was wondering... would you come away with me?"

"What?"

"I'm heading to my family's cottage in Baie Lueur for a

few days. It's private. Quiet. And I'd really like your company."

She didn't answer immediately. He held his breath.

"Okay," she said finally. "You mean... today?"

"I can send Sylvie to pick you up now."

Another pause. Longer.

"Okay," she said again, softer this time. "Can I bring Sophie?"

Beau grinned. "She's actually who I was inviting. I just assumed you were part of the package."

Chapter 7
André ~ The Watching World

Trailing Beau Laurent was almost laughably easy. It was, without question, one of the simplest assignments André had ever been given. The man practically invited it—constantly slipping away from his security detail, as if he had nothing to fear.

And why would he? Norland wasn't exactly known for danger. Even the Prime Minister, arguably the most powerful man in the country, had operated for years with only a four-person security detail. That number had recently been bumped to six—a correction in light of the swirling threats. André smirked. Six. It hadn't been nearly enough.

He guided his grey Toyota Camry down the residential streets with deliberate ease, keeping a safe distance as Beau strolled beside the woman and her copper-coloured dog. The *Voyagr* decal on his back window gave him cover, a perfect mask. To the world, he was just another rideshare driver—harmless, forgettable. Invisible.

When they arrived at what André assumed was the woman's home, he parked a block away. From here, he had a perfect view. He watched as the two lingered at the bottom of the steps, not one but *two* kisses exchanged. The woman vanished inside without a backward glance.

.
André chuckled darkly. "Ooooh, that's gotta sting, old man," he muttered to no one, his voice curled around a sneer.

He didn't expect what happened next.

A chirp from the Voyagr app on his phone.

A new ride request.

Less than a block away.

Beau Laurent.

André stared at the name for a beat too long, his pulse

tightening.

This wasn't part of the plan. Not yet. The orders were clear: *Observe. Report. Wait.*

But sometimes, plans changed.

He rolled forward, calm as ever, pulling to the curb just as Beau approached. The man climbed into the backseat without hesitation. André gave a courteous nod. Professional. Unremarkable. Just another fare.

As he pulled away, André's eyes flicked to the rearview mirror.

She was standing in her window.

The woman. Watching. Her expression unreadable, her gaze fixed on the departing car.

Their eyes met in the mirror, and something inside André stilled. Not because she frightened him—but because she was *new*. In the months he'd been watching Beau, he hadn't seen her before.

She was unexpected. And André didn't believe in coincidence.

He filed her away.

The ride continued in silence, but the air in the Camry had shifted—dense with something unspoken. André flexed his fingers against the steering wheel, eyes fixed on the road.

He didn't know when the orders would change.

But they would.

And when they did?

He'd be ready.

Chapter 8
Merritt ~ Between Loss and Longing

"Oh, Mer!" Avery's voice burst through the speaker like a firecracker. "You have to call him. This is huge. I so want this for you!"

Merritt couldn't help but smile as she cradled the phone between her cheek and shoulder, the warmth of Avery's excitement filling her tiny kitchen. "I may have texted him," she confessed. "Like, a bunch."

"Mer," Avery said, undeterred by the confession, keys clacking in the background. "I just Googled him."

Merritt groaned softly. "Of course you did."

"He's gorgeous. Like, distractingly, unfairly gorgeous. You definitely have to hit that."

Merritt laughed, the sound bubbling out of her. "I think I want to," she confessed.

"Then I'm hanging up so you can call him. You need to call him. Now."

Merritt stared at the phone after the call ended, Beau's card still clutched in her hand. She took a deep breath, her thumb hovering over his name, freshly added to her contacts with the crimson heart next to it.

She dialed.

It rang twice.

He answered. And her words tumbled out in a rush— apologies, awkward explanations, a thank you that made her cringe even as she said it. But somehow, amid her nervous rambling, she found herself agreeing to go away with him.

Today.

She hung up and called Avery back immediately. "He just invited me to his cottage," she blurted. "Like, now. He's sending his security to pick me up."

"His security," Avery marvelled. "Oh Mer, you're living a dream," she said, utterly serious. "Okay, pack something sexy. Remember that red number I helped you pick out before Bali? That. Pack that."

Merritt couldn't help but notice how Avery carefully dodged any mention of Everett—the one she'd bought the lingerie for, the one she'd spent two romantic weeks with in Bali. The memory tinged her excitement with something more complicated.

Merritt laughed, even as her cheeks flushed. "Okay, I'm getting in the shower."

She moved on autopilot—showering quickly, brushing her damp hair back into a braid, applying just enough makeup to feel polished but not overdone. She packed fast: leggings, sweaters, pyjamas, her softest socks. Her hand hesitated over the red negligee. She touched the fabric, felt the weight of memory in it, and left it behind.

By the time the doorbell rang, she was downstairs with Sophie at her side. When she opened the door, Sylvie stood there—composed, professional, warm-eyed.

"Here," Sylvie said, reaching for Merritt's duffle. "I'll carry this. You've got Sophie."

"Thank you."

They walked to the car together. Merritt paused. "Is it okay if I sit in the back with her? She gets nervous in cars."

"Of course."

The drive wound through the city, the conversation between the two women easy and surprising. Merritt liked Sylvie almost immediately.

"So," Merritt said with a sideways glance, noting just how far they'd driven, "dropping me off the other night wasn't exactly on your way home, was it?"

Sylvie laughed. "Not remotely. I think he might like you."

Merritt blushed. "I think I might like him too."

A silence settled, companionable. Then Sylvie added, "I looked you up."

Merritt glanced at her, surprised.

"Beau didn't ask me to. He doesn't know I did. But I needed to be sure." Her voice softened. "I know you lost your husband. I just wanted to say... it's brave. What you're doing."

Merritt swallowed, but said nothing.

Sylvie's voice dropped further. "My wife didn't come back from Afghanistan. That was a long time ago. I still talk to her like she's listening."

The ache in her voice pierced Merritt's chest. She reached forward, placed a hand on Sylvie's shoulder before leaning back in her seat. Neither of them said anything more.

Eventually, Sylvie turned onto a long, winding drive. Merritt blinked as the house came into view—grand and secluded, set deep within a stretch of forested land, its modern architecture softened by the surrounding trees and winter stillness.

"This is Beau's?" she asked.

Sylvie nodded.

Before she could say more, the rear door opened. Beau climbed in just as Quinn slid into the front passenger seat, clearly annoyed. "This is not a good idea," she grumbled.

Merritt stiffened, but Beau reached across Sophie and took her hand.

"I'm really glad you said yes," he said softly.

Merritt smiled. "How could I not?"

She meant it, even if Beau's presence—this trip, this whole whirlwind—felt less like a plan and more like a tornado. A welcome one, but a tornado all the same.

They drove in companionable silence and comfort. The city faded. Trees closed in. Sophie dozed on the leather seat between them. Eventually, Merritt drifted off too, her head resting against the cool window, her hand still in Beau's, both nestled in Sophie's thick fur.

When she woke, the world outside was cloaked in darkness. The car was pulling up to a modest yet striking cottage, carved into the landscape and set against the vast backdrop of the Atlantic Ocean.

Inside, Sylvie moved with ease, kneeling to coax a fire to life in the hearth. Flames licked the kindling, casting flickering light across the room. The space filled quickly with a kind of warmth that settled deep and made the room feel lived in, real.

Sophie trotted from room to room behind Beau's security team, tail wagging, her nails tapping lightly against the hardwood as she explored her new surroundings with unbothered confidence.

With the cottage secured, Quinn disappeared out the front door with the ominous pronouncement, "all cameras are active."

Sylvie lingered a moment longer, pausing by the threshold. "We'll be up at the guest cabin," she said, her tone reassuring. "It's not far—just past the bend in the road you came in on."

She gave Merritt a small, knowing smile before stepping out into the night, the heavy door easing shut behind her with a soft click.

Merritt watched the oak door close. The mention of cameras lingered. "Cameras?" she asked, her tone edged with unease.

"Not in here," Beau assured her quickly. "Just the perimeter. It's a precaution—nothing invasive, I promise."

Sophie, having completed her own search, drifted back into the main room with the unhurried grace of a husky. She claimed her place in an overstuffed armchair, where a light grey faux fur blanket was draped deliberately over one side. The textures blended seamlessly, casting an effortless warmth across the space.

Merritt watched her for a moment longer, grateful for the distraction—a beat to collect herself before facing Beau again. She perched nervously on the edge of the expansive white linen couch that dominated the room, her fingers brushing over the hem of her sweater in a small, absent motion that steadied her.

When her eyes finally met his again, there was softness in his expression, combined with an intensity that felt like an unspoken challenge. It unsettled her, as though he could see past every wall she had so carefully built—and yet, she didn't look away.

"Thank you for coming," Beau said. His smooth voice mingled with the fire's low crackle, adding a kind of rich ease to the room. "This all must seem so... I don't know, fast?"

"To be honest," Merritt said with a wry smile, "my main concern is how everything here is so white and beautiful. It's like this room is daring me to spill something—or trip over something—just ruin something, really. It feels personal."

He laughed, and the sound loosened something in her.

Slowly, he stepped closer and reached for her, his hand finding the curve of her neck with a tenderness that made her breath hitch. His thumb brushed lightly against her skin.

"I think this room's been waiting for someone like you to shake it up," he murmured. The words weren't flirtation —they were something closer to a truth.

And then he kissed her. Warm, searching, unhurried. It unravelled her. The fire crackled. The world faded. It was just his mouth on hers, and her hands finding his chest, his shoulders, anchoring herself to him like he was something steady.

When he pulled back, he rested his forehead to hers. Their breath mingled. His hands stayed steady on her.

And Merritt knew. She was going to let herself fall.

He kissed her again, slower, deeper.

Then he slid his hands lower, lifting her to him, and she wrapped her long legs around him without thinking.

And in Beau's arms, Merritt felt like the kind of woman who could be carried. The kind who didn't have to carry everything alone.

And for the first time in a long time, she let herself go as he carried her to one of the cottage's bedrooms.

Beau set Merritt's feet back on the ground and pulled away just enough to look at her, close enough that his breath still mingling with hers as his hands lingered on her waist. His eyes, dark blue pools in the low light, held hers with an intensity that made her feel utterly exposed and entirely seen. Slowly, he straightened, his fingers trailing reluctantly from her sides as he moved to the corner of the room.

The soft click of a lamp broke the silence, followed by another, until the bedroom was bathed in a warm, golden glow. Shadows played gently along the walls, softening the space and wrapping them in a cocoon of intimacy.

When he turned back to Merritt, his gaze caught hers and didn't let go. He stood still for a moment, letting the weight of his stare speak louder than words. Finally, in a voice as steady and unshaken as the way he looked at her, he said, "I want to see you."

Merritt's heart stuttered, her pulse quickening as his words settled over her, their meaning reverberating deep within. Beau stepped closer, reclaiming the space between them as his hands returned to her hips. He bent slightly, bringing their faces level, his eyes searching hers with tenderness.

"You're beautiful," he whispered, his tone unhurried, as though each word had been carefully chosen. The sincerity in his voice and the way his eyes never left hers made the moment feel like a confession.

She couldn't bring herself to look away, drawn into the power of his gaze. There, in the warm light and the steady presence of his hands on her, Merritt felt as though she was standing on the precipice of something she didn't know, but desperately wanted to embrace.

Her breath hitched, but before she could respond, his lips found hers again. This time, the kiss was deeper, pulling her into a slow unraveling. His hands moved with deliberate care, slipping beneath the hem of her sweater to skim the bare skin of her waist, the warmth of his touch igniting something that had been smoldering between them almost since they met.

She matched his movements, her own hands exploring the breadth of his shoulders, the curve of his back, committing every detail of him to memory. The world outside ceased to exist; there was only Beau, only this moment.

As they sank into the bed, the soft layers of blankets and pillows cradling them. Each touch, each kiss, felt like an affirmation of the connection they shared. Merritt surrendered to it completely, feeling not just wanted but cherished. In Beau's arms, she didn't feel like the strong, self-reliant woman she was used to being. She felt safe. She felt desired. She felt whole.

The soft glow of the lamps continued casting long shadows over the room as their breathing slowed and Merritt lay nestled against Beau, her head resting on his chest. The steady rhythm of his heartbeat was a soothing metronome, grounding her in the aftermath of a night that felt both surreal and magical. Their bodies were entwined beneath the layers of blankets, the warmth between them an echo of the connection they had just shared.

For a long moment, neither of them spoke, content to exist in the silence. Beau's hand moved lazily over her back, his fingers tracing small, absent patterns against her skin, as though he couldn't bear to let her go even in rest. She sighed softly, a sound of contentment, and he shifted beneath her, his voice a low murmur as he broke the hush.

"Stay here," he said, his words more a gentle plea than a command.

Merritt lifted her head to meet his gaze, her hair falling messily around her face. His expression was open, unguarded in a way she hadn't seen before, and it sent a pang of tenderness through her.

"I wasn't planning on going anywhere," she replied, a hint of a smile playing at the corners of her lips.

Beau chuckled, the sound a low rumble that seemed to fill the room. He rose from the bed with an easy grace, crossing to the small dresser tucked against the wall. Pulling open a drawer, he retrieved one of his t-shirts—a loose, faded thing softened by time and wear. "Thought this might be more comfortable," he said, turning back to her as he held it out.

Merritt sat up, letting the blankets pool around her waist, enjoying the way his eyes made her feel as he watch her, and took the shirt from his outstretched hand. She slipped it over her head, the fabric brushing against her skin and carrying the faint scent of the cottage—wood smoke, pine, and something else that was purely and unmistakably Beau.

By the time she looked up again, he had returned to the bed, sliding beneath the covers. Propping himself up with one arm behind his head, he watched her with a satisfaction that made her pulse race. The way his gaze lingered on her made her feel as though she belonged—not just in this moment, but in the space they were creating together.

Sliding back down beside him, Merritt fit herself into the curve of his body, her legs tangling with his beneath the blankets. The room felt cocooned in warmth, their voices drifting softly in the stillness.

Beau continued to trace lazy circles along her back with his fingertips as he spoke, his tone low and steady. "This cottage has been in my family for a long time," he told her. "My grandparents built it. I used to come here as a kid—every summer, without fail. It felt like the one place where time slowed down, where I didn't have to think about anything except the ocean, the woods, and how many marshmallows I could roast before someone caught me sneaking extras."

Merritt laughed softly, her head resting against his chest as she listened.

"Now, I bring my kids here as often as I can," he continued, his voice taking on a reverence. "It's different as an adult, but there's something comforting about watching them fall in love with the same trees and water I did. I wanted it to stay a place that feels...safe. Like it belongs to them, too."

Merritt tilted her head to look up at him, his fingers tracing the edge of the t-shirt she now wore. "It must be incredible," she said softly, "to share something like this with them."

He smiled, his gaze meeting hers with an openness that felt rare and precious. "It is," he admitted.

When the silence stretched between them, Merritt took her turn, her voice soft but steady as she began to share memories of her childhood. She spoke of growing up on the misty, forested coast of Cascadia—where towering cedars and rocky shorelines met the wild blue expanse of the Pacific Ocean. Her mother had been a member of the Tsa'huk Nation, whose traditions were deeply tied to the land and sea.

"I spent hours climbing trees when I was little," she said, a hint of a smile in her voice. "There's something about sitting in the branches of an old cedar, high above the ground, that makes the world feel... safe. Like it's just you and the wind and nothing else matters. My mother used to say the trees carried our stories, that when we climbed them, we were connecting with the generations who came before us."

She paused, her fingers tracing circles over Beau's exposed chest. "But my dad is British, so I always had one foot in two different worlds. On the reserve, I'd be teased for not knowing enough of the language or traditions. And with my dad, people would always ask where I was *really* from, as if being mixed made me an outsider. It's strange, carrying pieces of both worlds but never feeling like you fully belong in either."

Her voice softened as she continued, sharing how her mother had taught her to gather cedar bark and weave it into rope or baskets, and how she and her cousins would spend hours fishing or harvesting berries. She told Beau about the Pacific Ocean, how its tides and endless horizon had always felt like home.

As she spoke, her words flowed easily, as though she'd known Beau far longer than she had. And as his steady gaze held hers, Merritt felt the warming sense of being understood.

Together, they wove their stories into the fabric of the night, their voices blending into the soft glow of the lamps and the hum of the cottage around them.

As the conversation continued, their voices grew quieter, their pauses longer, and eventually, Beau's breathing slowed, deep and even, as he drifted into sleep. Merritt stayed awake a little longer, her eyes tracing the shadows on the ceiling, before she finally drifted off to sleep.

Chapter 9
Beau ~ The Weight of Want

Beau stirred awake in the early hours of the morning, his senses sharpening slowly in the hush of the room. Outside, the sky remained dark, the first light of this winter day still hours away. His gaze settled on Merritt, curled beside him, her body warm against his own. There was a rightness to the way she fit against him—an almost startling sense of comfort, like coming home to a place he hadn't known he'd been searching for.

It caught him off guard, how natural it felt. How easy. Especially after everything he'd lost. After Delphine.

Her name didn't come to him often anymore, not like it used to. But in the stillness of early morning, when the world held its breath and the past pressed softly at the edges of his thoughts, she sometimes returned. Not as the woman he had once adored—but as the breaking point that had redrawn the shape of his life.

They had met during their freshman year at Norland's prestigious Montrose University. Beau was already deeply entrenched in his political science degree, laser-focused on law school and the public service career that would follow. Even then, his resolve had been unwavering—fuelled by determination to create change in a country he loved, a country whose corruption had left personal scars.

Delphine, by contrast, had begun in general studies, her path uncertain. There was a lightness to her—curious, creative, free-spirited in a way that both captivated and confounded him. Where he was order and discipline, she was movement and spontaneity. It shouldn't have worked. But it did, for a really long time.

They met at a freshman mixer, one of those awkward university events meant to forge connections. Beau and Delphine barely noticed anyone else. They found a corner and talked for hours, and by the end of the night, something between them had already taken root.

He proposed the following year. Their wedding came

quickly, despite their families' gentle protests for patience. But they had been sure. And for thirty long years, Beau had believed their certainty had been well placed. Their marriage had become a solid, steady thing—tested, shaped, and refined over decades. They built careers, a home, and raised three extraordinary children together. It had felt like a life.

Until it didn't.

The first whisper of Delphine's betrayal came as an anonymous email, subject line: *About Delphine*. Against his better judgment, Beau opened it. Inside was a grainy photo —Delphine's hand entwined with Sebastian DuPont's. Beneath the image, speculative text hinted at secret meetings and a potential engagement. It read like tabloid fiction.

Beau deleted the email. Told himself it was nonsense. But something sharp lodged in his chest and refused to dislodge.

Sebastian DuPont.

Of all people. A tech billionaire with a hand in almost every sector of Norland's economy. A political adversary. An opportunist. A man whose interests ran counter to everything Beau and Prime Minister Hartwell stood for. There were always whispers about DuPont—the way he operated, the shadows behind his empire. To see Delphine's name tied to his was almost laughably implausible.

Almost.

But that image haunted him.

Over the following week, Beau watched his wife through new eyes. Her lateness. Her distance. The subtle unraveling of her once-impeccable composure. Dinner as a family, once sacred, became optional to her. Her apologies were hurried, her excuses thin. And still, he waited. Hoping he was wrong.

Then came the night he couldn't ignore it anymore. The kids were in Viremont with Delphine's parents, and the house was silent. Beau sat in the formal sitting room, nursing a glass of whiskey he didn't particularly like. He must've dozed off because he startled awake to the sound of the front door opening.

Delphine crept in like a ghost, her hand smoothing her hair, her coat slung carelessly over her arm. She caught his reflection in the mirror and froze.

"Beau," she said, a smile flickering across her face. It didn't reach her eyes.

"Delphine," he replied evenly, using her full name. A rarity.

"I'm just going up to bed. Long night—Winslow wedding prep."

He gestured to the armchair she'd chosen for the room. "Why don't you sit for a minute."

She hesitated, then crossed the room slowly, placing herself as far from him as she could. Her posture stiff, her smile brittle.

He watched her for a long moment before the words came.

"How long?"

Her reaction was immediate. Tears. Big, dramatic ones. Her whole body folding as she sobbed. Once, Beau might have gone to her. But not now.

"Oh, Beau," she cried, voice trembling. "I've just felt so alone."

His tone stayed level. "How long?"

Delphine sat up sharply, her grief morphing into anger.

"Don't pretend this isn't your fault," she snapped. "Everything has revolved around *you*. Your work. Your name. I disappeared."

She stood, pacing now. Her fury building. "He saw me. Not as your wife, but *me*."

Her confession struck like a slap. His whiskey slipped from his hand and hit the rug with a muffled thud.

"I've been nothing for 30 years," she spat.

He sat frozen.

And then, without warning, she crossed the room and climbed into his lap, kissing him with a fierce, almost punishing desperation. Her hands gripped his shoulders like she was trying to anchor herself, or maybe shake something loose from him. Beau let it happen. His body responded out of habit, out of sorrow, out of some raw, misguided need for closure. His hands moved to the buttons of her blouse, fumbling with a mix of muscle memory and disbelief, the fabric parting beneath his fingers like a memory he couldn't quite hold onto.

And then he saw it.

A ring.

Not the modest engagement ring he'd once placed on her finger, but a large, emerald-cut diamond threaded onto the same chain that held the birthstone charms he had given her after each of their children were born.

He froze.

Delphine stilled. Her eyes followed his, and her hands dropped. She stood quickly, buttoning her blouse with shaking fingers.

"I need to go," she said.

And she did. Just like that. No apology. No answers. No goodbye.

Beau never asked for the details. He wasn't sure he could survive knowing them. But he knew the truth. Their marriage was over. And in the process, so was the life they had built together.

The memory of that night flickered and receded like a shadow.

Now, in the warmth of the cottage, with Merritt curled against him, Beau felt something he hadn't dared to hope for. Not a replacement. Not a remedy. Just peace. The kind that didn't erase what had come before, but softened it.

He rolled onto his side, slid his arm around Merritt's waist, and tucked himself into the space she made for him. Her scent—soft, clean, faintly sweet—settled over him. He pressed a kiss to the back of her neck.

She stirred, then turned to face him, her smile slow and sleepy. Her hand found his cheek.

And then she kissed him, warm and unhurried.

For the first time in years, Beau didn't brace himself for what came next. He let it be.

This moment. This woman. This peace.

Chapter 10
Merritt ~ The Gravity Between Them

Merritt woke to the sensation of a strong arm sliding beneath her, pulling her close with a gentle insistence. A soft kiss landed at the nape of her neck, warm and lingering, sending a shiver through her that felt equal parts romantic, familiar, and utterly disarming. She stilled, breath catching as her mind registered the intimacy of what was happening.

When she turned to face him, Beau's eyes were already on her. That sleepy, boyish grin—so at odds with his commanding presence—made her heart flip. Before she could overthink it, she reached for him, her fingers trailing along the light scruff of his jaw.

Their lips met, unhurried but charged. Every kiss built on the last, deepening, drawing them closer until the only thing between them was heat and want. His hand slid down her back, gripping her hip, then trailing lower, fingertips brushing her thigh and setting every nerve alight. She gasped into his mouth as he pressed her back into the mattress, her body already arching to meet his.

Her fingers tangled in his hair, her touch urgent now, her breath quickening as he kissed his way down her neck, his mouth mapping her skin like a prayer. When he finally moved over her, she welcomed him with a soft cry, wrapping herself around him, pulling him into her. Their bodies moved together with a rhythm that was slow and aching, every thrust deep and deliberate.

It wasn't rushed or frantic—it was fiercer than that. Focused. Intimate. Consuming.

Her hands roamed his back, memorizing every line, every muscle, her breath hitching as his whispered words washed over her skin. The pleasure built, sharp and steady, until it crashed over her in waves, leaving her shivering beneath him. His release followed moments later, his forehead pressed to hers, breath ragged as they clung to each other.

No words. Just warmth. Breath. Skin.

And then came the knock.

They both froze as the sharp rap of knuckles hit the front door. Merritt blinked, disoriented.

Then the unmistakable sound of a key turning in the lock.

The bedroom door was ajar offering an unobstructed view from the cottage's front door.

"Beau?" Quinn's voice rang out, brisk and to the point. Footsteps followed. Then she stepped into view.

Her eyes locked on them. She paused. Merritt froze. The shirt Beau had peeled off her moments before lay in a heap on the floor.

Beau sat up slightly, Merritt scrambled to pull the blankets around herself. "Quinn, could you give us a minute?" he said, calm but firm. "Close the door, please."

Quinn didn't so much as blink. "Sure." She turned without another word and shut the door.

Merritt burst into laughter. "You're cursed," she said, still breathless.

She stood, letting the sheet slip from her body as she reached for the discarded shirt. When she caught him looking—really looking—it gave her pause. There was no judgment in his gaze. Only admiration. Reverence. The warmth in his eyes stirred something in her chest—an understated confidence, a rare willingness to be seen, fully and without apology. In that moment, under his gaze, she didn't feel scrutinized. She felt beautiful. Wanted. Enough.

She tugged the shirt over her head, the hem brushing the tops of her thighs, and began gathering her jeans from the night before.

"Okay," she said, hopping slightly as she pulled them on. "It's me who's cursed. Think about it—I meet a gorgeous man while having the worst night, fall on my face, twice, spill hot coffee on him, and basically grope him in apology." She buttoned her jeans, gesturing wildly as she continued. "And now? Security barges in mid-afterglow and sees me naked! How am I supposed to look that woman in the eye again?"

Beau chuckled, climbing out of bed and slipped on navy sweatpants and a white t-shirt. "All I heard," he said, moving toward her, "is that you think I'm gorgeous."

He paused in front of her, his eyes sparkling, smile softening—shifting from joy to something deeper. Then, slowly, his hand rose, fingertips grazing the curve of her neck and trailing upward with a kind of awe, until he gently tucked a loose strand of hair behind her ear.

The gesture was so tender, so precise, it caught her off guard. For a second, the air shifted.

She was somewhere else.

Another room. Another bed. Everett propped up against pillows, his laptop long since pushed aside to make room for her. She'd crawled over his legs, straddling his lap with an easy kind of confidence, grinning as she settled into their rhythm. He'd looked up at her with that soft, half-laugh she knew so well, his hands finding her thighs as though drawn there instinctively. Then one hand drifted upward—tracing along her hip, brushing her ribs, before gliding up the slope of her neck to tuck her hair gently behind her ear. A touch so familiar it lived in her skin.

It had been one of those small, wordless moments that stayed.

The memory pierced her, sharp and sudden. Her heart stuttered.

She blinked, forcing herself back into the now. Back to Beau. His touch still lingering. His eyes on hers, steady and open.

"Where did you just go?" he asked softly, leaning back to search her face.

Merritt met his gaze. "I'm right here," she reassured him, pulling him toward her for a long, warm kiss. But even as their lips met, her mind spun with the sharp flash of Everett—of what they once shared, of how fully she was giving herself to Beau now—and the guilt tangled tight in her chest.

Beau accepted the kiss gratefully.

"You don't know Quinn," Beau said, settling briefly on the edge of the bed. He leaned back, gazing up at Merritt. "I'm not sure that woman would notice awkward if it walked up and smacked her in the face." He laughed, then stood and reached for her hand.

"We'll just have to face her together."

"Okay, but you first," Merritt said, nudging him playfully toward the door.

Hand in hand, they stepped into the great room. The smell of fresh coffee greeted them. Sylvie stood at the counter, calm and efficiently manning the espresso machine that looked even more complicated than Merritt's own, while Quinn sat casually on the couch, playing with Sophie.

"We have more information," Sylvie said, pouring expertly steamed milk into two mugs and handing them over. "Vanilla lattes," she explained of the mugs.

Merritt took hers, grateful for the caffeine and hoping there was much more where that came from.

"Maybe we should take her somewhere before we talk?"

Quinn asked, motioning toward Merritt.

"It's already on the news," Sylvie replied smoothly. "Nothing classified."

Quinn frowned but didn't argue.

"News about what?" Merritt asked, sipping at the foam on her coffee.

They all migrated to the large couch. Merritt sat beside Beau, coffee in hand, his arm draped around her. When he leaned in and whispered, "Don't spill," she gave him a bashful smile before turning her attention back to Sylvie and Quinn.

Sylvie set her own mug down and sighed. "We don't want to alarm you," she began.

Quinn stood abruptly and began to pace. "Someone stabbed Hartwell in the neck," she said flatly. She turned to Merritt, clearly directing the news at her—everyone else in the room already knew. "He's in hospital. He'll recover."

Merritt blinked. "What?" The word came out too fast. "Wait—stabbed? Like... actually stabbed?" She looked around the room, trying to catch up. "I didn't turn on the news this morning. Or yesterday. Or—God, it has been a while?" Her eyes landed on Beau. "You knew? Is that why we are here?"

She didn't mean for her voice to sound so exasperated. It wasn't anger—it was shock.

"I was coming here anyway," Beau said gently, his hand sliding from her shoulder to her thigh. "Selfishly," he added with a wry smile, "the last twenty-four hours have been a little... distracting." He gave her leg a light squeeze. "Or I would have found time to tell you."

"No, no—I'm not mad," Merritt said quickly. "I just... wow." She took a sip of her coffee, trying to reset her brain.

"Okay, so. You're in the government. Like, really *in the government*. You probably have the Prime Minister in your phone. As a contact."

Beau smiled softly, but Merritt wasn't finished.

"Wait—does he text you? Do you have group chats? Is there a Minister of Finance emoji I don't know about?" Her voice pitched higher, somewhere between horrified and amused. "I cannot believe it's just hitting me now that you run the economy."

"You make it sound so dramatic," Beau murmured. "I've known Greyson since before I joined the government."

"You call him *Greyson*? It *is* dramatic!" she said, eyes wide. "I just slept with a man who could crash the economy if he sneezed on the wrong spreadsheet—and he's on a first-name basis with the guy who runs the whole fucking country!"

Beau's gentle laughter filled the space between them, and despite herself, Merritt laughed too. Heat crept into her cheeks, but it wasn't embarrassment—not exactly. It was awe. It was disbelief. It was the surreal realization that she was tangled up with someone who was... actually important.

Really, *really* important.

Quinn turned away, annoyed as Sylvie cut in, her tone more careful. "Last night, the NFC recovered the attacker's phone."

"That's... good?" Merritt said, glancing at Beau, calming a little at Sylvie's serious tone.

"We think so," Sylvie said. "But it held more than we expected."

Beau's hand tightened on her thigh. "What was on it?"

Quinn stopped pacing. "There was a photo of the two of you," she said, eyes narrowing. "Kissing. Outside her house." She jabbed a finger in Merrit's direction.

Merritt's stomach dropped.

"And a list," Sylvie added, her voice lower now. "Names of people connected to Beau—collateral. Merritt's name was on it."

Beau's expression changed instantly, his jaw tightening. "My kids?"

"They weren't listed," Sylvie said. "And there's no indication they're in immediate danger."

"They're targeting Merritt because she's more accessible," Quinn explained, arms folded, tone clinical. "It's about pressure, not destruction. Leverage, not carnage."

Beau's grip on Merritt didn't loosen. Merritt, still reeling, placed her free hand over his, grounding herself with the feel of his skin beneath her palm.

"We're adding extra security for the kids and Delphine," Sylvie said. "But for now—for both of you—staying here is safest."

"They think they're being smart," Quinn muttered. "Let's keep it that way."

Merritt's gaze flicked between the two women, briefly catching the way their stances had shifted into unspoken alignment. It struck her as oddly intimate—how crisis had closed the distance between them—but even that thread of thought dissolved under the weight of what she'd just heard.

Her name. On a list. A list of threats.

The room felt like it had tilted slightly, reality slanting on a sharp, unfamiliar axis. She wasn't just a woman on a spontaneous weekend away anymore. She wasn't just slipping into something warm and intoxicating. She was... part of something bigger. And potentially dangerous.

"I'm sorry," Sylvie said gently, her tone softening. "But wherever you go now, we go too."

"No more slipping away," Quinn added, her eyes flicking toward Beau for just a beat longer than necessary.

Beau exhaled, his voice low. "How far can we go?"

"To the front door," Quinn said dryly.

Sylvie offered a small smile. "We'll talk options."

Then Beau turned to Merritt, the strain in his expression giving way to something softer. "I'm sorry," he said, taking her hand and lifting it to his lips, pressing a gentle kiss to her knuckles. "I hate that I've dragged you into this." The sincerity in his voice made her chest tighten. "Maybe you and Sophie would like to explore the property a bit—with me." He glanced toward Sylvie and Quinn, a resigned smile playing at the corners of his mouth. "Well... with us."

"I think Sophie would love that," Merritt said softly. "And I know that's who you're really trying to win over." The joke, light as it was, made her chest loosen slightly. She could still find laughter in this.

"Is it okay if I shower first?" she asked.

"Take your time," he said, brushing his lips to her cheek.

Inside the bathroom, she shut the door and leaned against it, exhaling hard. Her pulse was still fast, her nerves frayed.

The shower took its time warming up, but eventually the steam rose around her like a gentle cloak. She stepped under the water, letting the warmth seep into her skin.

But her thoughts didn't follow. They flickered and tangled, refusing to settle. Images collided in her mind—Beau's steady eyes, Sophie curled up contentedly, the word collateral ringing like a bell, shrill and echoing. And beneath it all, the dull, familiar ache of Everett.

What was she even doing here?

She tried to make sense of it. It was just a few days. Just a holiday escape. And okay, yes—there had been sex. Really good sex. And kisses that felt like they meant something. And maybe she liked him. Maybe more than liked. But that didn't mean she was ready. It didn't mean it made sense.

She scrubbed shampoo through her hair a little too hard.

What if this was reckless? What if this was selfish?

What if she was betraying Everett? Her mind clung to that thought, circling back to it with every excuse it could find —and there were plenty. It was unfair. Untrue. He was gone. She hadn't betrayed him. And yet, the guilt lingered, low and constant, whispering through the corners of her heart like something she didn't know how to silence.

She stayed under the water until it began to cool, hoping it might rinse the noise from her mind. But it didn't. Her thoughts were still tangled—grief woven into wonder, guilt twisting around the edges of something that felt dangerously close to joy.

Beau had kids. A demanding, high-profile job. That job had put him in danger. That danger meant he had a security detail. A detail that had followed him everywhere. Someone had been following him, had seen their first kiss —not just seen it, but captured it. Saved it. Her name was now on some list. A list. And yet...

As she stepped out of the shower and wrapped herself in a

towel, she caught her reflection in the mirror. Damp hair. Flushed cheeks. A stupid smile tugging at her mouth.

She looked like a teenager. Like a girl with a crush. Like someone who'd just been kissed behind the gym and couldn't wait to tell her best friend all about it.

It didn't make sense.

Chapter 11
Beau ~ The Edge of Want

Beau stood in the small kitchen, hands wrapped around his second cup of coffee—a rare indulgence for a man who prided himself on discipline. But this morning, with its stillness and the low thrum of unease under his skin, he allowed it.

Sylvie and Quinn had gone to the guest cabin to gather their things. Outside, Baie Lueur was still. The whisper of wind through the trees mixed with the lapping of waves against the rocky shore and the sound of Merritt's shower. This place had always been his reset button. His compass. A return to simplicity and breath. And now, somehow, it held her.

Beau glanced down at his mug, the heat warming his hands. She was here, and it didn't feel temporary. It felt... right. Like he'd brought her to the one place where his life made sense so she could see the truest version of him.

And the truth was, he was already in deep. He worried for her—her safety, her peace, what it meant to draw her into his world. But he couldn't deny the clarity that had settled in his chest like something unshakable: he wanted this. Her. However fast it was happening, however messy the circumstances.

She had brought something vivid and alive into the stillness of this place. And for the first time in a long time, Beau felt like something was beginning instead of ending.

The shower shut off. Silence returned.

A moment later, Merritt stepped out of the bathroom, wrapped in nothing but a thick, sky-blue towel. Her skin was still flushed from the heat, damp hair clinging to her shoulders, and she padded barefoot across the cottage with a startled, awkward smile when she caught him watching her.

She disappeared into the bedroom, the door swinging half-closed behind her.

Beau exhaled, grounding himself in the mundane act of making their lattes—foamed just right, sprinkled lightly with cinnamon the way he'd noticed she seemed to like. He was still smiling to himself when he brought hers into the bedroom, only to find her already dressed in leggings and a fitted long-sleeve shirt, her back to him as she brushed her hair in the mirror.

"Tragic timing," he said, leaning against the doorframe. "Missed the whole show."

Merritt caught his eyes in the reflection, smirking. "Next time, move faster."

He stepped behind her, their eyes meeting again in the mirror as he handed her the coffee. His fingertips brushed hers. She sighed, long and dramatic, after her first sip.

"Coffee is my world," she murmured, her shoulders relaxing visibly.

Beau grinned. "Noted."

She twisted her hair into a loose ponytail, securing it with a tie from around her wrist. Then she turned to face him, her expression softening.

"Are you okay?" she asked.

He hesitated, then gave a slight nod. "I should be asking you that."

Her brow furrowed, then lifted with a flicker of humour. "Well, no one's ever snapped a secret picture of me kissing someone before. Our first kiss, no less." She shook her head, then added, "Maybe when they catch the person, we can ask for a copy. Frame it. Hang it on the wall next to the thermostat."

Beau laughed, but there was something deeper behind it—something warm. He liked how she spoke as if they would have a shared wall. A shared future.

But Merritt's playfulness dimmed a touch. "I also... I'm sorry for earlier. For how I reacted when Quinn told us about the Prime Minister. I didn't mean to be insensitive. I don't really keep up with politics or the news. I work all the time, and I didn't connect the dots. I didn't even think about how close you might be to him."

Beau's smile softened. "You have nothing to apologize for." He reached for her hand. "Honestly, I haven't thought much about Greyson at all today. I haven't had time. I've been a little distracted."

His hand came to her waist, then slid higher, his lips finding hers. She melted into him, her fingers curling around the front of his shirt, and for a moment, it was only them again—everything else fading.

And then the front door creaked open.

Boots on wood. Voices.

Beau groaned against her lips. "They really don't want me to have any fun," he lamented.

Merritt pulled back with a grin, lifting her mug. "It's fine. I wasn't finished my coffee anyway. You wouldn't like me with less than two coffees in my system."

Beau chuckled. "Noted," he said again, brushing his thumb across her hip before he stepped back. "Come on."

They walked together into the main room of the cottage, where Sylvie and Quinn were peeling off jackets and setting down bags—none the wiser, or at least polite enough to pretend they hadn't caught anything intimate.

"Ready to go?" Quinn asked, her tone brisk as she glanced between them.

"You really know how to kill a moment," Sylvie teased, her usual professionalism cracking just enough to allow a rare laugh. She nudged Quinn's arm lightly, her expression uncharacteristically warm.

Beau turned back to Merritt, his focus narrowing to her alone. "Do you like hiking?" he asked, a hopeful note in his voice. "I probably should've checked before planning the day."

A flicker of amusement crossed his mind—he'd already envisioned showing her the trails, the hidden lookout points, the beauty surrounding the cottage—without ever thinking to ask if she'd even enjoy it. But the thought of Merritt beside him in this wild place stirred something deeper than just optimism.

Merritt's lips curved. "Do I like hiking?" she echoed. "Beau, I grew up climbing cedar trees tall enough to brush the clouds, wading through streams to catch salmon with my cousins, and foraging berries with my mom. A good weekend meant disappearing into the woods until sunset with nothing but a fishing line and a knife."

She paused, eyes softening. "The outdoors isn't just something I like—it's part of who I am. My mom used to say the land carries our stories. That when we walk it, we're never alone."

Beau held her gaze, moved by the obvious pride in her voice.

Then she tilted her head, a spark in her eyes. "I just hope you can keep up."

He laughed, delighted by her fire. "I'll do my best."

His gaze dropped to the outfit she'd put on. "But I think you might need something more... weatherproof."

He nodded toward the storage closet near the back porch.

"That closet's basically a museum of outerwear fashion disasters. Three generations of Laurents left their mark. You'll find everything from my grandfather's wool hunting jacket—permanently scented like campfire—to my dad's neon windbreaker. Loud enough to scare off wildlife."

When he opened the door, the closet practically groaned —bulky jackets, garish parkas, and an objectively criminal pair of plaid snow pants spilled forward. "Take your pick," he said with a grin, then ducked away to shower.

By the time he returned in his own modern thermal gear, Merritt was standing in the middle of the room, fully suited up in blinding neon emblazoned with the '88 Rider's Rest Olympic crest.

Beau stopped in his tracks.

The gear was unmistakable. He'd been fifteen that winter. His dad had worn that exact jacket to the Olympic opening ceremonies. Beau could still hear his booming voice echoing through the crowd, cheering for every flag, every moment. One of the rare joyful memories.

Now, Merritt wore it with casual confidence, unbothered by its age or absurdity.

"It's the only thing long enough," she said, shrugging with mock resignation.

Beau smiled, the nostalgia catching him by surprise. "It's perfect."

As the group ventured out into the crisp morning air, Beau and Merritt walked hand in hand, Sophie bounding ahead, revelling in her leashless freedom. Sylvie and Quinn followed at a measured pace, their presence unobtrusive but unmistakably watchful. The cold bit at Beau's face, sharp and invigorating.

The cottage's rear opened onto a private stretch of snowy shoreline, the Atlantic Ocean lapping softly at the rocks. Beau led Merritt to the edge of the water, pausing as he glanced at her, a faint smile spreading across his face.

"I know you grew up near the Pacific," he said. "But the Atlantic has its own kind of beauty."

He gestured toward the silvery expanse before them— endless ocean meeting a snow-dusted beach, tall trees circling the landscape like sentinels. The only break in the forest was the winding drive that led to Chalet Écume.

Merritt slipped off one neon glove, knelt at the water's edge, and dipped her fingers into the frigid waves. She lingered there, her hand skimming the surface in a delicate, reverent motion.

Then she rose and, with a mischievous gleam in her eye, flicked cold droplets toward Beau.

He gasped at the chill, laughing. "Oh, sorry, did I get you?" she asked, her voice pure mock innocence. "I thought you might want a little connection with your Atlantic Ocean."

"I feel so connected," Beau said, catching her cold hand in his. He pulled her close, pressing a soft kiss to each of her frigid fingertips.

Then, without warning, his free hand slipped behind her and dusted a light shower of snow down the back of her neon snowsuit.

"You started it," he teased, grinning as she arched away with a gasp, wriggling in protest as the icy crystals slid down her spine.

Merritt launched herself at him, laughing. Beau caught her easily and brought them both down into the snow, twisting so he straddled her hips. He hovered, lips just above hers—until she shoved a handful of snow down the back of his jacket. He yelped, flinching. "Okay, okay! You win."

Still grinning, he pulled her up, then kissed her, warm and lingering. Sophie barked her approval, darting around them in excited loops.

"Is there any chance you two could keep your hands to yourselves before this gets too hot and heavy?" Quinn called, approaching with Sylvie in tow. Her tone was dry, but her smile gave her away. "We're stuck with you—let's keep it G-rated."

They continued their hike, falling into an easy rhythm. Sophie raced ahead, her copper coat flashing between the trees. Beau pointed out the weathered rocks where he used to fish, the driftwood forts, and the inlet where his grandfather's rowboat had once rested.

As they moved inland along a snow-dusted trail, Beau's stories shifted to his children. "That hill there—Bastien built a ramp one summer with scrap wood. Émile nearly broke his arm going down it on a skateboard." He chuckled. "And Juliette... she would follow them everywhere, dragging her stuffed rabbit behind. Her adventure bunny."

Merritt smiled softly at the image.

He grew quiet for a moment. When he spoke again, his voice was laced with grief.

"My little sister was named Juliette too," he said. "She died on the first day of school when she was 8 and I was 10. She was running ahead of me and Mom, rushing into a crosswalk. A sportscar came speeding around the corner and hit her." His jaw tightened. "Mom ran to her, but the car didn't stop. Juliette died right there on the pavement."

Merritt's breath caught, but she stayed silent, sensing he

wasn't finished.

"The driver was drunk. It was eight-thirty in the morning. But he was also a federal politician—someone well-connected. The justice system protected him. He gave a statement, issued a hollow apology, and went on with his life. Meanwhile, ours shattered."

Beau's gaze drifted out across the water, the waves crashing like a steady heartbeat against the shore. "My mom never recovered," he said, the weight of the words thick in the air. "She tried, but she spent the rest of her life hollowed out by loss. She died a few years later—still aching, still mourning. My dad stayed. Held on. He poured everything into me after that. I think being a dad to me was how he kept going." Beau's voice softened. "He was a good man. He passed two years ago. I'm grateful he got to meet all three of my kids."

His throat tightened, but he didn't look away. "Losing my sister... it changed everything. It pushed me—first into law, then to the Crown Prosecutor's Office. Greyson found me there and brought me into politics. Every decision I've made since has been about making things right. About justice. So no one else has to live through what we did."

After a while, Beau glanced back at Sylvie and Quinn, who had been keeping their distance—a token gesture of privacy. "Everyone ready to head back?"

Merritt nodded. Sylvie and Quinn did too, already turning toward the trail.

But even as she answered, Merritt's mind drifted elsewhere.

To someone else.

She remembered Everett. And his sister.

Rachel had always struggled, even before Merritt met Everett—but during their second year together, everything unraveled. The relapses. The late-night phone calls. The frantic drives to pick her up from places she never should have been.

Everett had carried so much of it, and when the overdose finally came, it had nearly broken him. Merritt could still feel the weight of him sobbing in her lap that night, the way his hands gripped her as though she was the only thing keeping him from falling apart.

It was a different kind of loss than Beau's, but the grief sat in the same part of her chest now. An old ache waking under the weight of Beau's story.

She tugged her collar a little tighter, and they began walking again.

Chapter 12
Merritt ~ The Undoing

For the rest of their time at the cottage, Merritt and Beau lived in something that felt like a dream—not the kind that disappears upon waking, but the kind that lingers in the bloodstream. What began with tentative glances and soft kisses when they'd first arrived had grown into something bigger. They shared everything—mornings wrapped in wool blankets, long walks through snow-blanketed trails, touches that felt like answers to questions she hadn't known she was asking.

But even in the warmth of it, doubt began to hum at her temples. Soft at first. Distant. Like the faintest crack in a frozen lake, miles from shore.

Prime Minister Greyson Hartwell was recovering and had already requested a meeting with Beau—proof that reality was waiting just beyond the tree line. And Merritt, who had grown used to the calm of the cottage, couldn't ignore the tightening in her chest as her phone lit up with unread emails and missed calls.

She had built a life that depended on her being present— on always showing up. Her firm allowed her flexibility, yes, but that didn't change who she was. She was the partner who pulled the all-nighters. Who never turned down a case, even the unsavoury ones. Who carried her clients' burdens like her own. It was more than identity—it was certainty.

Still, for her, leaving didn't feel like freedom. It felt like leaving something delicate mid-sentence.

Beau remained close—steady and disarming in a way she hadn't expected. He made her laugh. He made her feel wanted. Not just desired, but truly seen. And yet, the very ease of it began to unnerve her. When had anything in her life ever felt this easy? This good?

Was that what scared her?

She wasn't sure. Not yet.

Earlier that afternoon, after returning from a hike up the ridge, Merritt had begun silently packing her duffle. Each item folded felt heavier than the last. She hadn't thought about work since Avery's visit on New Year's Day, but now the responsibilities began to push in.

An extra day off the following day had been a gift—a pause she desperately needed—but the DuPont case loomed large, with its endless spreadsheets and ethical knots. Merritt reminded herself she cared about her clients. Even the difficult ones. Her work had always been her constant. Even now, as she zipped the bag shut, she clung to that truth.

Still, something tugged at her. The cottage had been more than a retreat from the city. It had peeled back layers of grief she hadn't realized she was still wearing. And with Beau—what they had built here—it felt like the beginning of something, but she wasn't sure she could let herself be honest about what it was.

She didn't want to go. But she wasn't sure if she could stay, either.

As the sun dipped behind the trees, she curled beside Beau by the fire. A worn copy of *The Shipping News* rested in her lap. The fire crackled softly, casting shadows across the walls. The novel transported her back to her teens—back to the girl who believed in second chances and finding solace in remote places.

Now, that place was real. But for how long?

Sylvie emerged from the guest room, all business. "I'm going to start loading up the car," she said. "Quinn and I will get everything packed so we can head out."

Beau stood to help, brushing off Quinn's predictable protests. Merritt stayed behind, watching the fire burn low. She reached for the poker, nudging the coals apart before closing the flue. The glow dimmed to embers, and with it, something inside her dimmed too.

Beau returned and wrapped his arm around her waist, pressing a kiss to the crown of her head.

"Ready?"

She nodded, though her chest said otherwise.

Outside, the air was sharp and bright. Sylvie was already behind the wheel, Quinn on alert by the passenger side. Beau opened Merritt's door, his hand brushing hers as she climbed in. Sophie jumped up behind her, tail thumping.

The drive passed mostly in silence. Merritt reached across the seat and found Beau's hand over Sophie's fur. They didn't speak. They didn't need to. But the closer they came to the city, the more the silence felt heavy.

When they pulled up outside her townhouse, Quinn hopped out first, retrieving Merritt's duffle. Beau took it from her without a word and carried it up the steps.

Sylvie followed, her voice level. "We'd love to give you two a proper goodbye," she said, "but protocol doesn't allow us to leave you unattended—not yet."

"Too easy for someone to slip in unnoticed," Quinn added. "Especially here."

Merritt placed her hands on Beau's chest. His kiss was slow, lingering. When they pulled apart, her voice was soft. "I don't suppose you can come in?" she asked, feeling —somehow—as if this was an ending, not just a brief return to their separate lives. She wanted to hold on a little longer. To linger in the togetherness.

Quinn shook her head. "Absolutely not."

Sylvie's tone was gentler, but resolute. "Not with what we know. Not right now. I'm sorry."

Merritt sighed, the disappointment more than she wanted to admit. Beau's thumb brushed her cheek.

"I'd love nothing more than to spend time in your world," he murmured. "But one of us has to work tomorrow. Not all of us get the golden employee treatment," he teased lightly, his hands lingering on her shoulders.

She groaned. "Fine." Her voice was affectionate but resigned.

She kissed him once more before stepping back. From the doorway, she watched him retreat, Sylvie and Quinn falling in behind him.

Just as she was about to step inside, her gaze caught on a grey sedan idling across the street. A *Voyagr* sticker glinted in the rear window. Just a rideshare.

Inside, she locked the door and leaned against it, the hum of the furnace replacing the hush of the cottage. The warmth felt unfamiliar. So did the silence.

Sophie padded over and flopped beside her with a sigh.

Merritt slid down to the floor, her back to the door, knees drawn in. The tears came softly. Not just grief, not just longing—something else too. A weight pressed down on her.

Eventually, she rose. Fished her phone out of her jacket pocked. Dialed Avery as Sophie padded after her.

On the third ring, the line connected, and Merritt's sobs filled the silence.

"Mer," Avery said softly, voice laced with concern. "What happened?"

In the background, Merritt caught a man's voice—groggy, curious. "Who's that?"

"Oh no," Merritt stammered. "I'm interrupting. I'm so sorry. I'll let you go—"

"Mer, it's okay," Avery cut in, calm and steady. "Josh, I'll just be a minute." The faint rustle of linens, a door creaking closed. Then just Avery, always creating space when Merritt needed it most.

Words tumbled out, heavy and cracked. Merritt wept as she poured guilt into the phone. She spoke of the way everything came crashing down as soon as she returned home. She spoke of Beau. Of how she had let herself fall—too easily, too soon—and how shame had clawed its way in as soon as she crossed the threshold.

And then, finally, she said it.

She told Avery what had happened the day Everett died.

How they'd fought. Not about anything important. Dinner plans. She had scheduled a work dinner with a partner and his wife. She'd told Everett about it days in advance. But that afternoon, he'd made other plans. When she reminded him, he accused her of never consulting him. Said she always did what she wanted.

It escalated.

Sharp words. Rolled eyes. Her temper matching his. He grabbed his keys, said something awful—something neither of them meant—and slammed the door. Merritt had watched his car pull away, anger still simmering.

"And then," she whispered, "he never came home."

Avery was quiet for a beat, her breath catching. "Fuck, Mer. Why didn't you ever tell me?"

Merritt couldn't answer. Couldn't speak over the sobs as they broke again.

"I just..." she gasped. "I slept with Beau. Like, a bunch of times," she confessed, "And now I feel—God—I feel like a filthy adulteress."

"You're not," Avery said gently. "You're grieving. And you found someone who makes you feel alive again. That's not betrayal, Merritt. That's surviving. And okay—maybe thriving a little. I mean, cottage sex with a hot politician? That's some next-level healing." Her words made them both giggle.

A pause. Then Avery announced, "I'm coming over."

"What about Josh?"

"You've earned me more than he has," Avery replied, no hesitation. "I'll be there in fifteen."

True to her word, Avery was at Merritt's door just over fifteen minutes later. Merritt opened it, red-eyed and hollow. They didn't say much. Avery toed off her boots, and they curled up on the couch—Merritt's head in her lap, Avery's fingers combing gently through her hair.

"I don't know what to do," Merritt said, voice a whisper. "Being with Beau felt good. But it also felt like cheating," tears still dripped from her eyes.

"You're not cheating," Avery said. "You're healing. Those aren't the same."

But Merritt didn't respond. She just stared at the ceiling, trying to believe it.

Eventually, Avery coaxed her to bed. She took the guest room—the one she'd half-lived in for months after Everett's death—and Merritt retreated to her own.

The next morning, Merritt made coffee while Avery leaned against the counter, still in pyjamas, watching her with sleepy eyes.

They didn't mention Beau at first.

Instead, Avery broke the silence with a sigh. "So... I think I'm ghosting Josh."

Merritt gave her a sarcasticly withering look. "You spent half the night in his bed."

"Exactly," Avery said. "It was fine. But I don't know. He's sweet. Young. And—God—I can't date someone who thinks TikTok is a valid news source."

Merritt let out a weak laugh, grateful for the shift in energy. "You know," Avery continued, stirring sugar into her coffee, "I'm probably doing the kid a favour. He can go find someone who can unironically say 'no cap.'"

Merritt snorted.

"But there's someone else," Avery added, a spark lighting her eyes. "Luca Montgomery."

"That name sounds expensive."

"Oh, he is," Avery said. "Smart, my age, ridiculously well-read. We went for drinks. Ended the night at his place. Merritt—he has a fireplace that could swallow you whole. And the bookshelves. My God. I don't know if I'm more into Luca or his first editions."

Merritt smiled genuinely for the first time in hours. "I'm happy for you."

"You could be happy too," Avery said softly. "I'm not saying Beau's the answer. But you felt something. That matters."

Merritt nodded, though she didn't speak. As she walked Avery to the door a little while later, her phone buzzed with new notifications—emails, texts, work reminders.

None from Beau.

She stared at the screen, trying to decipher what she felt.

She didn't know.

With a breath, she headed upstairs with her fourth latte of the morning, Sophie at her heels.

Work was waiting.

Dropping into her chair, Merritt traced her fingers absently across her laptop's trackpad. The screen blinked to life, stirring from days of sleep mode. As she waited for it to fully wake, her gaze landed on the stack of papers and notes on the corner of her desk—an untouched mountain of responsibility. She'd been reading through them just before Avery had arrived on New Year's Day.

And there it was.

Beau's face stared back at her—smiling, unmistakable— even in the grainy reprint of a news article. Her chest tightened as disbelief swept through her.

"What the fuck?" she muttered into the stillness, voice sharp and unsteady. She reached for the paper and accidentally sloshed coffee onto the corner. Her eyes scanned the headline, each word a punch to the gut:

Elite Scandal Shockwaves: Billionaire Sebastian DuPont Affair Exposed!

The air thickened as she skimmed the article, her stomach clenching with every line:

The glittering world of Norland's elite has been rocked to its core by a bombshell revelation: tech billionaire and notorious social media conspiracy theorist Sebastian DuPont has been having a steamy affair with none other than Delphine Moreau, the stunning wife of Norland's Dreamy-eyed, but little-known Minister of Finance, Beau Laurent.

Both Laurent and the jilted Genevieve DuPont have filed for divorce, though their filings tell very different stories. While Laurent diplomatically cites "irreconcilable differences," Genevieve's filing doesn't hold back, detailing "an affair with the wife of one of the country's top political figures." She doesn't drop names, but come on—who else could it be?

Multiple outlets have already published photos of Delphine and Sebastian looking more than cozy together, their body language screaming "couple goals"—if you ignore the part where they're blowing up their families. Meanwhile, Genevieve, a former journalist turned full-time mom, claims this wasn't some one-time slip-up. Oh no. According to her, Sebastian's philandering has been going on for a long time, dragging their family into this messy love triangle with Delphine Moreau.

Sources close to the DuPont family say Genevieve's finally had enough. "She gave up everything for him—her career, her independence—to raise their five kids and support his empire," an insider spilled. "This affair? It's the ultimate betrayal."

And then there's Delphine. Once seen as the epitome of grace and sophistication—the perfect political wife—her reputation is in shambles. This scandal doesn't just drag her down; it casts a shadow over Beau Laurent's career and potentially even Prime Minister Hartwell's administration. Talk about collateral damage.

Beau Laurent, for his part, has been radio silent. No statements, no comments—just a picture of him accompanying this very article, where he looks as composed (and dashing) as ever. But don't let that poker face fool you. Sources close to the Laurents say Beau was completely blindsided by the affair. Still, whispers about the state of their marriage have been circulating in political circles for months. Guess the rumours weren't far off.

As the dust settles, one thing's for sure: this scandal will be the talk of Norland, and its ripple effects are just getting started. The carefully curated images of Norland's power players are cracking, and we're all here for the drama. Stay tuned—this one's only going to get juicier.

The second page was worse. There were photos. A family portrait stared back at her—Beau, Delphine, their three children. Delphine was radiant, one hand resting easily on Beau's arm. The picture twisted something in Merritt's chest.

She tore her gaze away, catching her own reflection in the laptop's dark screen. The heaviness of doubt pressed down. She glanced back at the paper, rereading the byline and first paragraph as if the words might change. They didn't.

Her stomach churned. This wasn't just personal anymore. It was professional. She was representing Sebastian DuPont in what promised to be one of the messiest divorces Norland had seen in years—and now she was sleeping with the ex-husband of her client's new fiancé.

Her hand trembled as she set down her mug, splashing coffee across the article again.

"You fucking idiot," she muttered to herself, her anger turning inward.

This was a disaster. Not just emotionally—ethically. A conflict of interest so glaring. How had she let this happen?

She shoved the article aside and reached for her case files, forcing herself to focus.

"This is better," she said aloud, voice flat and unconvincing. It didn't matter. She was committed now. Committed to fixing her mistake the only way she knew how—by burying it under work.

Her phone buzzed.

A message lit up her screen: *Missing you. And imagining you chain-drinking coffee while taking over the world. God, I adore you.*

Her breath hitched.

She stared at the screen, her chest tightening with something that felt dangerously close to longing. Then, slowly, she turned the phone face down.

And got back to work.

Chapter 13
André ~ The Undercurrent

André tapped his fingers against the steering wheel, eyes tracking the rhythm of the street. Fourth night in a row. Same block. Same view. The assignment was simple—watch Merritt Clarke—but the repetition was beginning to grate. Every evening had followed the same script: houses dimmed, streets emptied, and her townhouse stayed still.

Until tonight.

Just after 9 p.m., a sleek SUV pulled up and Merritt stepped out. André leaned forward slightly. She was not alone. Laurent exited next, followed by two women—his security detail, one of them towering, even taller than Laurent himself. They flanked Laurent as he approached the woman's door, a picture of careful coordination.

André didn't move. That was the new directive—stay.

It wasn't a hard job. Boring, sure. But boring meant quiet, and quiet meant clean. The *Voyagr* sticker in his back window gave him cover, made his presence easy to dismiss in a city where rideshares were constant. No one questioned a parked driver with his phone in hand.

The next morning, just after sunrise, the striking redhead reappeared—same one who'd arrived the night before. Sexy as hell. He snapped a few discreet photos as she descended Merritt's front steps, coffee in hand, and climbed into her Range Rover parked out front. Merritt didn't follow. Just watched her go from the doorway, then stepped back inside. Nothing remarkable on the surface, but André logged it all. These things didn't matter—until they did.

That night, the light on her top floor burned late. According to the building records, that room was her office. Around 3 a.m., it finally blinked off. Seconds later, another one flicked on on the second story.

That's the bedroom, he noted.

He adjusted the recline of his seat, pulled his coat tighter against the cold, and let his body settle. The street was hushed, broken only by the occasional bark of a dog or the hum of a passing car.

The house was still.

André closed his eyes. Whatever came next, he'd be here to see it.

Chapter 14
Beau ~ The Call to Lead

The estate was silent.

With the kids at Delphine's, Beau moved through the sprawling house alone. Outside, the early January morning pressed against the floor-to-ceiling windows—black and impenetrable, broken only by the glow of distant security lights across snow-covered grounds.

He'd texted Merritt the night before. Something flirty. Tender. Honest. He couldn't help himself.

She hadn't responded.

At 5:30 a.m., he'd stirred. After five uninterrupted days together, he knew Merritt was always up by 4:30. At the cottage, he'd wake to the scent of coffee and the sound of her moving through the kitchen.

This morning, he'd reached for his phone before his feet touched the floor.

Still no response.

But then—three dots.

He froze.

They vanished just as quickly.

Sitting on the edge of the bed, he'd watched. The dots blinked back. Disappeared again.

The pattern had repeated—uncertain, halting. Then: nothing.

His jaw tightened. He's set the phone on the nightstand and rose in silence.

Downstairs, in the home gym—a sleek, temperature-controlled space lined with free weights, a climbing wall, and cardio equipment—he fell into routine. Incline sprints. Weighted push-ups. Rows. Split squats. Core circuits. The kind of training that kept him lean, focused—strong enough to carry everything that came with the job.

But today, the clarity he usually found in motion never came.

Afterward, he climbed the stairs slowly, towel slung around his neck. The house remained still. Waiting. Like him.

In the ensuite—remodelled after Delphine left, all slate tile and burnished gold—he stripped off his gear and set his phone on the counter.

Just before he stepped into the shower, he glanced at it once more.

The dots.

He reached for it—

Gone.

"You're reading too much into this," he said aloud. But his voice sounded too taut. Too unsure.

He stepped into the spray, letting the water thunder down.

There wasn't time for distraction. Not today. Not with Greyson waiting. Not with the administration in recovery. Briefings. Strategy. Damage control. Reform.

He needed to get out of his head.

* * * * *

Greyson Hartwell, Norland's long-standing Prime Minister and leader of the Progressive Alliance, had governed through three consecutive five-year terms. His leadership was marked by bold social reforms, fiscal pragmatism, and a magnetic presence that dominated the country's political landscape. But lately, the rumblings of change had grown louder. Just before the attack, Greyson had formally requested the dissolution of Parliament. The Governor General approved it the following morning, triggering a federal election with just eight weeks' notice.

Beau had barely absorbed the news before everything shifted. A campaign was coming, and his calendar was already full—now with a dangerous undercurrent that had been previously theoretical.

Greyson's stabbing rewrote the stakes.

The security briefings, once tedious and overly cautious, were now loaded with hindsight. Beau had always operated within the paradox of political service: visible but vulnerable. There were always risks, but he had never let them change how he moved through the world. Until now.

Because this wasn't just political anymore. This was personal.

Greyson wasn't a colleague. He was a mentor. The man who had pulled Beau from the courtroom and into public life. Who had taught him how to wield power without losing his integrity. Who had stood by him during his divorce, even as the tabloids attempted to feed on his pain. Greyson was the closest thing Beau had to an older brother.

And now he was injured—stabbed in public by someone who'd gotten too close.

It changed everything. Not just for the country. For Beau.

He thought of Merritt again, of how close she had already come to danger. His first instinct was to call, to offer private security, to beg her to stay out of sight. But he didn't. Merritt didn't take well to being handled, and he knew better than to undermine her independence. Still, the impulse was a low roar in the back of his mind.

As Sylvie steered the Escalade through Arbourleigh's

downtown, Beau sat forward slightly in the back seat, hands braced on his knees.

"Do we know how he's doing?" he asked.

Sylvie exchanged a glance with Quinn, then nodded. "He's upright. Walking. Stubborn as hell." Her voice softened. "But he's okay."

Beau's chest eased slightly. "Thanks," he murmured.

Sylvie gave a small smile but didn't look away from the road. Quinn, in the passenger seat, kept her gaze scanning the sidewalks, always watching. Since the attack, they both carried themselves with an extra layer of alertness.

The SUV glided off the main road, cutting along the scenic Seaview Highway, a route that hugged Arbourleigh's Atlantic cliffs. The sea crashed far below, hidden now by a dense winter mist.

Up ahead, Dominion House emerged through the haze— Norland's official residence of the Prime Minister. Its stone façade was severe in the low light, tall wrought iron fences casting long shadows across the drive. The historic building had become a fortress in recent days. NFC agents patrolled the perimeter in high-visibility gear, sidearms holstered, tactical vests secured.

Sylvie pulled into the first of three gated checkpoints. IDs were checked. Faces scanned. Even the Escalade's undercarriage was inspected by mirror and canine. At the final gate, all passengers were required to disembark.

Beau climbed out first, coat buttoned against the wind, eyes scanning the compound. Sylvie and Quinn flanked him automatically.

A senior NFC officer greeted them. "Minister Laurent," he said briskly. "The Prime Minister's staff is expecting you. Just you."

Sylvie gave a short nod, and Quinn's jaw flexed—but both stayed behind.

Inside, a staffer escorted Beau through the inner corridors of Dominion House, bypassing the ceremonial salons and heading straight for Greyson's private domain. Eleanor Hartwell met him at the door.

Her composure, always impeccable, was slightly frayed around the edges today. Her white hair was swept back, her makeup minimal. Her hands, however, remained clasped at her waist with white-knuckle tension.

"Beau," she greeted.

"Eleanor," he returned, nodding gently and embraced her.

She led him into a private office—a far cry from the grandeur of the main house. Wood-paneled, lined with photos, old campaign posters, and books stacked neatly in curated disarray. A worn leather armchair faced a gas fireplace. Greyson sat in it, collar unbuttoned, a white bandage visible beneath the starched edge of his shirt.

"Beau," he said, his voice thinner than usual but intact.

"Good to see you vertical," Beau said softly.

Greyson managed a dry smile.

Eleanor crossed to stand beside him, tension still radiating off her in waves. Beau noticed how she hovered, never more than a hand's breadth away. Her entire frame was alert—not afraid, just exhausted. Ready to fight if she had to.

Then Greyson spoke.

"I'm stepping down."

Beau blinked. "What?"

"The party's already moving to announce it," Eleanor added. "We've drafted the language. Framed it as a proactive transition, not a response to the attack."

Beau looked between them, stunned.

Greyson leaned forward slightly. "I want you to run."

The words landed like a body blow.

"I—Greyson, with all due respect..." Beau shook his head. "This election is eight weeks away. You're the face of the party. We're polling strong. This doesn't make sense."

Eleanor's voice rose, sharp and sudden. "He was stabbed."

Silence.

She stepped forward, her posture tight, hands clasped so tightly her knuckles paled. Her voice was still composed, but trembling beneath the surface.

"You all keep talking about the party. The election. The optics." She paused, her gaze flicking toward the tall window behind Beau. The drapes were drawn, but they all knew what was out there—reporters, cameras, speculation piling at the gates. "Out there, he's the Prime Minister. To them, he's a symbol. A leader."

She turned back to Beau, her composure starting to crack. "But to me, he's my husband. The man I eat dinner with every night. The man who makes me laugh when no one's watching. The man I sat beside in an ambulance, covered in his blood."

Her voice broke. "And I will not watch him die to win a fourth term."

Beau didn't speak. Couldn't.

Greyson reached for her hand. Eleanor let herself sink into

the moment, the rest of her words caught behind an uncharacteristic swell of grief.

The room was still.

Beau swallowed hard.

He understood.

Of course he did.

"I don't know if I can win," he said quietly.

Greyson straightened. "You're the only one who can."

Eleanor nodded. "You'll need ten endorsements from sitting MPs or executive members. You'll get them. Then you launch your platform. Two weeks of voting—ranked ballot. It's already in motion."

Beau hesitated. "And the scandal?" His voice dropped lower. "Delphine. Sebastian. The whole circus. You don't think voters will connect me to that mess? DuPont's divorce is still in the press."

Eleanor's eyes sharpened, her tone clipped but measured. "Some might. But they won't see a man dragged through scandal—they'll see a man who didn't retaliate. Who protected his kids. Who kept his dignity. That's what we've shown them. You kept your head down. I handled the noise."

She leaned forward slightly. "It's not about pretending it didn't happen. It's about showing who you were through it. That matters."

Beau exhaled slowly and leaned back in the chair, tension still settling at the base of his neck—but her words lodged somewhere deeper.

He wanted to talk to Merritt.

He wanted to talk to his kids.

He needed time.

"How long do I have?" he asked.

"End of the week, maybe," Greyson said simply. "We'll start background support now. The rest is up to you."

Beau stood slowly and extended a hand. Greyson clasped it.

Then Eleanor stepped in and hugged him.

He didn't hesitate.

Outside the office, the NFC agent escorted Beau back through the security wing. In a small waiting room near the exit, Sylvie and Quinn stood when he entered.

Sylvie's hand found his shoulder again—light but comforting. Quinn said nothing.

"How is he?" Sylvie asked.

"He's Greyson," Beau said. "He's recovering. Stubborn as ever."

Sylvie gave a soft laugh, her eyes shining with obvious relief.

As they stepped outside, the cold bit through Beau's coat. He climbed into the Escalade and pulled out his phone.

Still no response from Merritt.

He stared at the screen.

Then tapped it off.

And let the silence settle in.

Chapter 15
Beau ~ Almost

Beau woke later than usual on Friday morning, the soft light of a winter dawn creeping past the heavy drapes and brushing the edges of the room. The estate was still and silent, the children had been at Delphine's for the week, but were set to return to home today. The stillness should have brought a measure of peace, but it only deepened the ache that had settled in his chest.

He reached instinctively for his phone on the bedside table, his thumb unlocking the screen before he could think better of it. Maybe, just maybe, Merritt had texted.

She hadn't.

There were no missed calls. No unread messages. Nothing but the usual flood of work notifications and—oddly—a string of texts from Delphine.

He opened them with caution, expecting her usual clipped coordination about the kids' schedules. But her tone caught him off guard.

Morning, Beau. I'm heading out with the kids. They've been looking forward to seeing you, and I thought we could have some time to catch up too. It's been a while since we talked properly. I'll bring croissants from that café you like—still remember how you like your lattes. See you soon.

The warmth was unexpected. So was the familiarity. For the first time in over a year, her words sounded almost like the Delphine he'd once known—the one he'd built a life with. But rather than comfort, it left him disoriented. Especially against the cold silence from Merritt.

He let the phone fall beside him onto the bed, rolling onto his back as he stared up at the ceiling. His thoughts tangled together, the familiar pull of responsibility battling the ache of confusion. Merritt's absence throbbed louder than he wanted to admit. He didn't know what her silence meant, but, even as days past, he wasn't ready to believe it meant an ending.

After a few minutes, he forced himself out of bed and padded to the ensuite, tugging off his flannel pajama pants and stepping into the steam of his rain shower. The bathroom was a study in slate and glass, a masculine retreat carved from the ruins of his marriage. It was a space that had once given him comfort.

This morning, it barely registered.

He let the hot water pound against his back, trying to rinse away the static in his mind. But it clung to him—Merritt's silence, Delphine's text, and the career decisions that would reshape not just his life, but the future of the entire country.

And then, through the curtain of steam, movement.

Beau blinked, wiped a clear streak across the fogged glass —and froze.

Delphine.

She was moving through the ensuite with practiced ease, bending to collect the pajama bottoms he'd left behind like she'd done it a thousand times. Her long hair was twisted back, her dress immaculate, her posture entirely too comfortable in a space that no longer belonged to her.

"What the hell?" Beau barked, shoving the glass shower door open, water trailing down his skin as he grabbed a towel and wrapped it around his waist. "What are you doing here?"

Delphine turned, a soft smile on her lips. "Oh, Beau," she said with a teasing lilt, her fingers flicking at the towel around his waist like they were still married. "It's nothing I haven't seen before."

"Get out," he said flatly, his voice a controlled growl.

She laughed, light and maddeningly unbothered. "Fine,"

she shrugged, dropping the pajama bottoms in the hamper and strolling from the room as if it were hers.

Beau stood motionless for a moment, the towel clinging to his skin, his jaw clenched. Whatever game she was playing, he didn't have the energy—or patience—for it.

He dressed with methodical care, pulling on a navy suit, a crisp white shirt, and a deep red tie. His shoes gleamed as he descended the stairs, bracing himself for the chaos he expected to find in the kitchen with the kids.

Instead, he found only Delphine.

She moved through the space like she had never left. A pink pastry box from his favourite café sat open on the counter, steam still curling from the fresh croissants inside. She pulled out their old china—the set she'd insisted on when they got married—her movements elegant and deliberate.

"What are you doing?" he asked, his voice sharp.

Delphine turned with a smile that didn't reach her eyes. "Trying to be civil," she said lightly. "I thought we could talk. I'm so sorry about Greyson."

Beau stiffened. She hadn't answered a single one of his calls from the cottage — calls made to reassure their children that he was safe, and that Greyson, who had always been like family to them, was recovering. And now she wanted to catch up?

"Where are the kids?" he asked instead, ignoring her attempt at warmth.

Her smile faltered. "You can't even stand to be near me," she said bitterly. She closed the distance between them, reaching for his tie. Beau caught her hands and pushed them gently but firmly away.

"Where are they, Delphine?"

Delphine's smile vanished, replaced by a flash of anger.

"They're upstairs. Getting ready for school," she said sharply.

She spun toward the counter, snatched her leather clutch, the morning light catching the large emerald-cut diamond glinting on her ring finger. With a swift motion, she knocked the croissants into the sink, flipped the faucet on, and turned back to Beau with a cold, satisfied smile. "I'll see myself out."

Once the front door clicked shut, Beau exhaled slowly and leaned against the counter. The silence left in Delphine's wake was sharp and disorienting.

Everything felt to be spiralling into confusing territory, and he suddenly couldn't take the silence anymore.

He took a breath, pulled out his phone, and tapped out a message to Merritt: *I know you've probably been buried in work, and I want to respect your space. I saw a clip of you on the news the other night—just a flash of you outside the courthouse. I didn't catch what it was about, but it reminded me how much I miss you.*

No pressure. Just thinking about you.

He read it over once, then hit send.

A short while later, as he helped his children gather their things and load into the Volvo, his private vehicle. As he climbed behind the wheel, his phone buzzed.

Beau's heart sped up and the chatter of his children faded when he saw Merritt's name on the screen. He eagerly tapped the message to read it, even though he was stopped at a red light, and was fiercely against driving and texting.

I think we need to talk. Came Merritt's message.

Beau's chest lifted. His fingers moved quickly: *Of course. Name the time and place.*

A second message from her appeared: *Near your office?*

Beau suggested an unassuming café and added a crimson heart emoji. As he slipped the phone back into his pocket, a flicker of hope steadied his steps. This might not be easy. But it wasn't over. It couldn't be over. Not yet.

He dropped off each of his children at their respective schools. Bastien's thoughtful wave, Émile's animated goodbye, Juliette's tight hug—each moment stitched a bit of calm into his frayed nerves.

Beau drove toward Parliament Hill, pulling into his secured parking spot. Sylvie and Quinn were already waiting near the staff entrance. Quinn was all business, scanning the perimeter as she greeted him with a nod.

"The Prime Minister is expecting you this afternoon," she said.

Sylvie offered him a knowing smile as they fell into step beside him. "You seem lighter this morning. Something happen?"

Beau tried to downplay it, but his expression betrayed him. "Merritt texted. We're meeting for lunch."

Sylvie grinned. "It's about time."

"We'll see," he said nonchalantly, not wanting to give away how much Merritt's text had left him worried and relieved at the same time. "I'll need a ride," he added, giving her a glance.

"Of course," she said. "We'll drop you. Quinn will behave."

"I make no promises," Quinn muttered.

The morning unfolded in its usual blur of back-to-back meetings and high-stakes decisions. As Norland's Minister of Finance, Beau's hours were tightly choreographed—briefings with senior economists, consultations with cabinet ministers, calls with provincial finance officials. His staff cycled through with data sheets and fiscal reports, prepping him for his upcoming presentation to the Standing Committee on Budget and Economic Affairs.

He reviewed updates to the upcoming infrastructure stimulus package, debated carbon pricing targets for the next quarter, and signed off on a short-term funding extension for the National Transit Recovery Program.

There were early murmurs about interest rate adjustments, and he had to weigh the political consequences of his position against the soundness of fiscal policy. Somewhere between the trade numbers and a half-eaten protein bar, he also signed off on payroll adjustments for civil servants affected by a longstanding arbitration process.

But even with the flurry of numbers and policy talk, his mind kept drifting. Lunch wasn't far off now. And with it, Merritt.

Beau checked the time again, barely registering the words of an aide presenting the latest financial forecast. The morning's demands, once the centre of his focus, felt distant now, eclipsed by the promise of a moment outside the noise—a moment with Merritt.

"Ready to head out?" Sylvie asked, knocking gently on his office door. Quinn loomed beside her, as always, alert and stone-faced.

Beau stood, smoothing his tie. His pulse kicked up a notch.

The drive to the café passed quickly, the city blurring past the Escalade's tinted windows. When they pulled to the curb, Sylvie turned in her seat. "We'll be just around the corner," she said.

"We'll give you space, Minister," Quinn added, her tone clipped but respectful.

Beau nodded his thanks and stepped out.

As he rounded the corner into the small café, he scanned the tables and found her. Merritt. Sitting near the window, her posture straight, her plum blazer elegant and crisp.

She looked composed, professional—like someone preparing for a deposition, not a date.

He crossed the café and greeted her with a warm embrace, pressing a soft kiss to her temple. "I'm so glad you could meet," he murmured.

But she didn't return the hug. Her arms stayed at her sides.

They sat.

"I've been wanting to talk to you," Beau said.

Merritt didn't answer. She glanced down at her menu. "Are you getting anything to eat?"

Beau blinked. "I don't know. Are you?"

She didn't reply.

Beau's hands curled slightly in his lap. "What's going on?" he asked, leaning forward. "Please. Just tell me."

Merritt slid her phone across the table. On the screen was a photo of Sebastian DuPont.

"Do you recognize him?"

Beau's stomach dropped. "Of course," he said — everyone did. DuPont was a regular fixture in the media. Between his affair with Delphine, his attention-seeking antics, and constant social media rants, DuPont rarely stayed out of the headlines for long. "Why?"

Her eyes didn't waver. "At the risk of breaking attorney-client privilege—he's my client," she explained. "That is why you saw me on the news."

The words hit like a gut punch.

He understood immediately. The ethics. The implications. The conflict of interest, and the decision Merritt would have to make between her personal and professional lives.

"I'm sorry," she said, reaching to squeeze his hand briefly. She stood. Her decision clear.

"Wait," Beau's voice was small, pleading.

Her expression softened, but her resolve didn't falter. "I'm sorry," she said again. Then she turned and left.

Beau remained in place, staring at the empty seat across from him. The hum of the café faded beneath the weight of the moment. His phone buzzed, but he ignored it.

Eventually, Sylvie and Quinn approached.

"We were worried something had happened," Sylvie said gently, sensing what had just happened. "Ready to head back?"

Beau nodded. Outside, the air was cold and clear. Each step to the car felt heavier than the last.

* * * * *

Back at the Hill, Beau moved through the lobby on muscle memory alone. Inside his office, Sylvie handed him a coffee without a word.

Fifteen minutes later, she returned. "He's ready for you."

Beau rose.

Greyson Hartwell stood by the window of his private office, hands clasped behind his back. The bandage was gone, revealing a brutal scar along his neck. He looked paler, leaner—but sharp.

Beau stepped inside. "Prime Minister."

Greyson turned. "Close the door."

Beau obeyed.

Greyson didn't waste time. "Are you ready to do this?"

Beau hesitated. Then he exhaled. "Yes."

Greyson studied him. "You sure?"

"No." Beau's voice was dry. "But I will be."

Greyson nodded once. "The party's behind you. The executive council will finalize the nomination timeline this afternoon. We've secured your ten MPs."

Beau felt the ground shift beneath him. Not in panic—just gravity.

"I'll need to announce before Monday," Greyson added. "Let the country see this wasn't chaos. It was transition."

"Right."

Greyson took a step forward, his eyes steady. "We built something worth preserving. You're the best shot we have at keeping it alive."

Beau nodded. "Then I won't let it fail."

They shook hands.

Beau stepped back into the corridor, the door shutting behind him with a soft click.

He had said *yes*. The future was already underway.

Chapter 16
Merritt ~ The Work of Forgetting

Merritt moved briskly across the café, willing herself not to look back. The soft chime of the door sounded behind her as she stepped into the biting cold. Tears blurred her vision, but she kept her head high, her stride purposeful even as her chest tightened. The icy air stung her cheeks, mingling with the warmth of the tears that escaped despite her efforts. She tugged her blazer tighter around her, as though the fabric could shield her from the storm inside.

Beau's voice echoed in her ears—warm, hopeful, impossible to bear. She'd seen the hurt in his eyes, the confusion.

Turning onto an emptier street, Merritt stopped and pressed her hand against a cold brick wall, the other clutched tightly around her phone. She muted the short text thread that now marked the outline of their relationship, then blocked his calls.

"Pull it the fuck together," she whispered, voice cracking as she pushed forward. She swiped at her cheeks with a trembling hand. There were clients to meet, a life to uphold. But the image of Beau, and the devastation in his eyes, refused to let her go.

Hadn't she wanted an out? Wasn't this cleaner? Easier? Now she could stay rooted in the grief she knew. But the deep ache in her chest told her it wasn't that simple.

Her phone buzzed. A text from Avery: *Did you do it?*

They'd had coffee that morning. Merritt had laid out her reasons. "There's a conflict of interest," she'd said.

Avery had pressed gently. "Mer, if this is about your career, okay. But if it's about Everett... you keep mentioning him. You have to stop living like you owe it to his ghost. He loved you. But he's gone."

"It's not about that," Merritt had tried to deflect. "I can't give up a client for a fling."

Avery hadn't flinched. "You know it's not a fling."

Still, Merritt had said it: "I'm going to tell him it can't happen."

Now, she typed back: *It's over.* The words brought fresh tears.

Another vibration: *Was it awful?*

I'm okay, Merritt replied — not exactly answering, because she most definitely wasn't anything close to "okay". But she would be. She had to be.

I know you're not. Popcorn and a movie tonight. Came Avery's response.

That was Avery. Twenty-five years of unwavering support, beginning when Merritt moved to Arbourleigh at sixteen, trading the fractured closeness of her mother's new life in Cascadia for her father's modest apartment.

Arbourleigh hadn't been easy. Her mixed heritage and darker skin marked her as different in a city ruled by polished privilege. The curiosity of classmates carried an edge—"Did you grow up on a reserve?" or "Is that how you tan so easily?"

She found solace working at the local movie theatre. It was there she met Avery—charismatic, self-assured, and unrelentingly kind. Over the years, their friendship became the most solid thing in her life.

That sounds perfect, Merritt typed back, guilt blooming.

Since Everett's death, Avery had carried Merritt more than the other way around. As she slipped her phone into her blazer pocket, she welcomed the discomfort of the cold. It felt earned.

Her office loomed ahead, all glass and steel under a slate-grey sky. Inside, the familiar rhythm of work waited, but it brought little comfort.

By the time she reached her desk, Sebastian DuPont had arrived. Her assistant Malcolm knocked gently. "They're ready for you in the conference room."

Merritt straightened her skirt, adjusted her blazer. Normally her outfit made her feel powerful. Today it felt like armour she couldn't quite bear the weight of.

Inside the conference room, Sebastian and Genevieve sat side by side, their energy markedly different from past meetings—less charged, less brittle. Tentative. Merritt noted the subtle shift, the way their bodies angled slightly toward one another, as though something between them had softened.

At the head of the table sat Richard Voss, attorney for Genevieve DuPont, sharp-eyed and effortlessly composed. Merritt had faced him in court more than once—he was a tactician, polished and cold-blooded, known for leveraging optics as deftly as legal precedent. He leaned back in his chair now with an ease that belied the ruthlessness beneath.

"We need to finalize the property transfers," Voss began crisply, his voice slicing through the room. "Starting with the Cascadia estate."

Merritt nodded slowly, maintaining her poise, but the insistence on that particular property lit up something instinctual in her. There was no reason for it to be prioritized—at least not one that had been disclosed. "My client has already agreed to equitable terms," she replied, evenly but pointedly.

Sebastian interjected, his tone smooth but evasive. "It's a strategic decision. For stability."

Merritt didn't respond. Her gaze flicked briefly to

Genevieve, who shifted in her chair before speaking.

"We have to put the children first," Genevieve said, her voice low but clear. "Even when you and Delphine..."

She paused, offering a slight, knowing smile. "Let's just say we handle this with more grace than that."

Sebastian looked down at his hands. "I know I haven't..." He cleared his throat. "I could've done better. For you. For the kids."

Genevieve nodded slowly. "We both could have."

There it was—that warmth again, soft and flickering, like a candle catching flame in a drafty room. Merritt watched it carefully, wary of what it might mean.

The meeting adjourned soon after, the usual legal language wrapping up loose ends. Merritt left quickly, eager to escape the fog of strange new feelings and unspoken reconciliations. But halfway down the hallway, she stopped short.

Her notes.

Turning back, she retraced her steps. Just outside the conference room, she spotted Genevieve lingering near the elevators, arms crossed, expression unreadable. Inside, through the narrow glass pane, Merritt could see Voss and Sebastian still seated, mid-conversation.

She pushed open the door. The conversation stopped. A folder lay open between them on the glass table. Sebastian leaned forward, signing with a flourish. Voss snapped the folder closed almost the moment Merritt entered.

Her eyes narrowed. "Did I interrupt something?"

"Unrelated matters," Voss said briskly, tucking the folder under his arm as he stood. He didn't meet her eyes as he swept past her, his expression unreadable. Merritt watched as he joined Genevieve at the elevators.

Sebastian rose more slowly, adjusting his tie with deliberate ease. His smugness had returned in full.

"Something wrong?" he asked, his voice light, almost amused.

Merritt stared after him but didn't answer. Whatever was in that folder, she knew better than to press without evidence —but there was no way it was good. Both Voss and DuPont would know that any document DuPont had just signed could be challenged later, which made it all the more troubling that Sebastian seemed complicit in whatever they were orchestrating.

And yet, for the first time in her career, she didn't care— not with her meeting with Beau still weighing so heavily on her. She didn't want to dig.

She hated DuPont. And that hatred dulled something she usually guarded with precision: her vigilance.

Back at her desk, she picked up the phone and dialed her assistant's desk. "Malcolm," she said, her voice steady, "please forward my calls. I'll be working from home the rest of the day."

She pulled on her long coat, wrapped the cream scarf she couldn't bring herself to wash around herself, and headed out.

Outside, the air was metallic and sharp with the promise of snow. Arbourleigh pulsed around her. The world continued.

As she descended the steps into the underground train station, warmth enveloped her—an immediate, welcome contrast to the winter chill she'd left behind. Merritt swiped her transit card at the turnstile, the familiar beep sounding like a small affirmation. She followed the platform signs on instinct, her steps purposeful even as her mind drifted.

The platform was comfortably busy, commuters gathered in loosely formed clusters, the air tinged with damp wool and faint perfume. Merritt tucked herself beside a column and closed her eyes, letting the low rumble of an approaching train vibrate through the soles of her boots.

She had once loved to drive. Her Fiat 500 had been her little pocket of peace—a capsule of independence where she could blast Taylor Swift and sing like nobody was listening. After long days of managing other people's unraveling lives, the solitude behind the wheel had been sacred.

Now, the car sat untouched in her garage, dust softening its mint-green paint. Since Everett's accident, she hadn't been able to get behind the wheel. Even the thought made her hands sweat. She'd told herself it was about convenience, about reducing her carbon footprint. But she knew the truth. The trauma had anchored itself in her body in ways she hadn't yet learned to undo.

The train pulled into the station with a gust of air and a screech of metal. Merritt boarded quickly and slipped into a window seat. The reflection of her fellow passengers shimmered faintly on the glass as the train slid into motion, a blur of shadows and light racing past.

She tried to focus on her phone, scrolling through emails from smaller clients—clean, simple cases she could compartmentalize. A shared vacation home to divide. A separation between two people who still liked each other. These were the kinds of cases that kept her grounded.

But her mind wouldn't settle. The DuPont divorce clung to her like smoke—its confusion, its contradictions, that folder. And beneath it all, Beau. His expression when she left the café. The warmth of his voice. The devastation in his eyes. She blinked it all away and turned back to her phone.

The train slowed. Merritt rose, smoothing her scarf and coat. The sky outside the station had darkened prematurely, dusk settling over the city like a veil. Snow dusted the sidewalks in thin, untouched layers, and her breath fogged as she made her way through the streets.

The townhouse came into view, lights glowing softly in the front window. But her pace slowed as she noticed the grey sedan across the street—idling again, its engine a low hum in the silence. She narrowed her eyes. The same Voyagr car. It had been there the night before. And the night before that.

Coincidence? She wasn't sure. But tonight, she was too tired to investigate. She climbed the steps to her door, pushed the thought aside, and forced herself to focus on something lighter.

Avery.

Their movie night would been an anchor in an otherwise unmoored day. She smiled despite herself, already picturing the blanket they'd share, the takeout they'd argue over, the inevitable bottle of wine. As she stepped inside, warmth enveloped her once again—and this time, it didn't feel hollow.

Sophie bounded toward her, tail wagging in eager, wolfish arcs. Merritt crouched down and buried her hands in the husky's thick fur. "Hey, sweet girl," she whispered, her voice catching just slightly.

For the first time that day, she didn't feel like she had to hold everything together.

Chapter 17
André ~ The Quiet Advance

André sat in the driver's seat of the grey sedan, fingers drumming lightly on the steering wheel as he watched Merritt ascend the steps to her townhouse. Her movements were brisk, purposeful—almost routine. But as she neared the door, she paused. Her eyes flicked toward his car.

Instinctively, André shifted deeper into the shadows of the driver's seat, as if the darkness alone might render him invisible. He knew better than to linger in plain sight, but he'd taken a chance tonight, circling back after losing her when she left the office. He'd gambled that she'd return home eventually—and she had.

Merritt Clarke wasn't careless. She noticed details. André could see it in the way her eyes lingered for just a beat too long on the curb. It wasn't enough to confirm anything, not yet. But it was enough to make him uneasy.

He reached for his phone and opened the surveillance app provided by his employer, tapping quickly to log the time of her arrival. Her habits were largely predictable—early departures, punctual returns, morning coffees with her redheaded friend. That level of consistency made his job easier. But this afternoon's hesitation? That was a variable. One that might complicate things.

He made a mental note to adjust his routine. A new parking spot, a different vehicle rotation. Subtle changes, nothing drastic—just enough to stay invisible a little while longer.

His gaze returned to the townhouse, its windows glowing warmly against the fading light. He couldn't see Merritt anymore, but the faint shadow of movement behind the curtains told him she was home, settling in.

André exhaled slowly. His role, at least for now, was simple: observe, record, report. Nothing more.

But still, he watched the windows a moment longer.

Just in case.

Chapter 18
Beau ~ Snowfall and Silence

Beau's afternoon unfolded in muted shades of grey. He found himself digging deeper than usual, grasping for the purpose and momentum that his career had always provided. Yet his mind kept drifting back to Merritt—the stiffness in her body under his embrace, the way she'd felt so distant despite his warmth. Hurt and frustration simmered beneath his professional demeanour.

He knew he should be focusing on his decision to run for Prime Minister, but instead, his mind was focused on her.

After his time away with Merritt, Beau had been so sure. Sure of her, of them, of the possibility that their connection was the start of something real. The brokenness left in the wake of that sureness cut deeper than he'd expected, leaving him embarrassed by the weight of his own feelings. The ache clouded his thoughts, even as he tried to immerse himself in the afternoon's endless stream of paperwork.

His children's afterschool extracurriculars offered a practical rhythm to his evenings—Bastien had debate club, Émile hockey, and Juliette was busy with ringette. Their schedules meant Beau could work uninterrupted at his desk in the evenings, his black-framed reading glasses perched on his nose, his head resting in one hand as he willed himself to focus. Though Beau was ever-present for morning school drop-offs, afternoons often ended with carpooling arrangements, other parents driving his children home.

Just after six, the buzz of his phone cut through the quiet of his office. Beau blinked, pulled from his reverie, and glanced at the screen. Despite himself, a flicker of hope rose, unbidden—a hope that it might be Merritt. But it wasn't. Instead, Delphine's name flashed across the screen, tugging the corner of his mouth into a frown. With a resigned sigh, he tapped the notification and read her message.

I'm sorry about this morning. I miss you.

Beau exhaled sharply and clicked the screen into darkness. Frustration and confusion prickled at his composure as he stood and reached for his coat. Shrugging it over his tailored suit, he slipped his phone into his pocket, determined to leave the office and the day's lingering emotions behind.

Sylvie and Quinn struggled to keep up with his determined strides as he made his way through the halls.

Making his way to the secure parkade, Beau's Volvo waited where he'd left it that morning. He climbed in, the soft click of the door echoing in the stillness of the garage. Sylvie and Quinn followed close behind in the very conspicuous Escalade.

As he pulled out of the parkade and onto the quiet streets of Arbourleigh, Beau tried to shake the weight of the day. Yet, even with the city's muted evening lights flickering around him, the tension lingered—a mix of unresolved feelings for Merritt, and the frustration of Delphine's message. He tightened his grip on the wheel.

The drive home did little to calm his nerves. Still, he paused at the driveway to his home, taking a steadying breath. He needed to compose himself for his children. No matter what weighed on him, he was determined to be present for them as he always had been.

As he climbed the steps from his private underground garage, Sylvie and Quinn staying with the car, his hand lingered on the door handle that entered into the expansive living room just off his home's foyer. Through the door, he could hear the faint hum of the television and the soft murmur of his children's voices. A small smile tugged at his lips, the familiar sounds easing some of the tension in his chest.

Pulling the door open, he stepped inside, his voice warm as he greeted each child in turn. Bastien was seated at the coffee table, legs crossed, his head bent in focused concentration over his homework. Beside him, Émile worked on a colourful drawing for a school project, occasionally tilting his head as he considered his next stroke. Juliette was curled up on the couch, her attention glued to the television.

Beau breathed in the scene, gratitude washing over him. Moments like this reminded him of what truly mattered. His children's presence was his constant—a steady anchor in a life that so often felt chaotic, especially lately.

After exchanging warm, brief conversations with each of them about their day, Beau headed upstairs to change. He traded his crisp, tailored suit for something far more comfortable: a pair of soft, warm flannel pajama pants and a black V-neck t-shirt. Running a hand through his hair, he made his way back downstairs, his steps lighter now.

He paused in the doorway of the living room, taking in the sight of his children again. Their energy, their focus—it always amazed him. Clapping his hands together, he broke the quiet. "What if we ordered something in for dinner tonight?" he suggested, his voice carrying an easy warmth.

The room lit up with excitement, his idea met with enthusiastic responses from all three of them. Beau moved to sit beside Juliette, pulling up Voyagr's app on his phone and navigating to the food delivery section. Together, they debated their options, the occasional laugh breaking through as they narrowed it down to a healthy but delicious choice everyone could agree on.

The food arrived, and they ate dinner in front of the television—a rare bending of the rules on a school night that felt as much for Beau, whose heart ached beneath the layers of joy his children brought, as it was a treat for them.

As, one by one, his children headed off to bed, Juliette was the only one who still received a tender tuck-in, complete with a warm hug and a kiss on her forehead from Beau.

The boys, growing older and more independent, accepted only a quick goodnight and a heartfelt "I love you" before retreating to their rooms. Once the house fell silent, Beau turned his attention to his phone, which had buzzed periodically throughout the evening, its notifications syncing with his watch. Each glance at his wrist revealed the same name: Delphine.

Now, with the children asleep and the house quiet except for his own movements, Beau moved through the kitchen with practiced ease, loading plates into the dishwasher, and tucking takeout containers neatly into the fridge. After wiping the marble countertop clean, he sat down on a stool at the sleek kitchen island, his forearms resting on the cool marble surface as he finally picked up his phone. The screen unlocked automatically with Beau's face, and he began scrolling through the texts, all from Delphine:

Can we talk? read her first unanswered text.

I miss the way we used to laugh together! followed the next, Delphine's words dripping with nostalgia.

I haven't stopped thinking about this morning, she continued, undeterred by his silence. Beau scoffed at the memory of her unwelcome intrusion into his bathroom, the invasion of his privacy still fresh in his mind.

Do you ever think about what we had?

I know I made mistakes, but doesn't it feel like we could fix this? Her words pressed on, insistent despite the absence of a response from Beau.

I don't want to give up on us.

I miss you. ALL of you. Her final message had arrived just moments ago, its implications lingering like a heavy fog in the stillness of the room.

"Jesus," Beau muttered into the emptiness, shaking his head in frustration as his hand moved to scratch at his brow. He exhaled sharply, pressing both hands over his face, his elbows resting heavily on the marble countertop. He stayed like that for a long moment, his mind reeling, thoughts spiraling in every direction. A sardonic laugh escaped him, hollow and sharp, an attempt to stave off the sting of tears. The laughter broke off into a low groan, a mix of frustration, hurt, and uncertainty knotting in his chest.

Finally, he rose to his feet, resigning himself to an early bedtime—a stark departure from his usual night owl tendencies. He climbed the sweeping staircase, his steps echoing faintly in the spacious, high-ceilinged expanse of his grand estate, and headed down the softly carpeted hallway that stretched toward the expansive primary suite. Once shared with Delphine in what now felt like a different lifetime, the suite remained a sanctuary of understated luxury, its oversized windows offering a moonlit view of the sprawling grounds beyond.

Peeling off his T-shirt, Beau sank onto the edge of the bed, the cool linen brushing against the skin of his palms. He paused for a moment, and as he reached to place his phone on its charger on the bedside table, he hesitated, his gaze lingering on the brief text thread between him and Merritt.

Surely, we can work something out? he quickly texted and sent before he could think better of it, the words a plea for connection, his heart refusing to accept what his mind already knew. Merritt was unwavering in her dedication to her career—a quality he admired deeply. Yet, the sour luck of their timing, of their lives colliding in this moment, left him searching, hoping, for some way to make it work anyway.

* * * * *

Beau woke early on Saturday morning to the winter sun bleeding through the edges of his curtains. He hadn't bothered to close them the night before—too tired, too wrung out to care—and now the light cut across the room in a wash of pale gold.

Instinctively, he reached for his phone, the motion so habitual he didn't register it until the screen lit up in his hand.

No new messages.

Nothing from Merritt.

Her silence was beginning to take up space.

With a soft sigh, he set the phone back on the nightstand and sat on the edge of the bed, dragging both hands down his face. The house was still hushed, though he could hear the muffled stir of movement downstairs— his children easing into the morning.

He padded across the floor into the ensuite, took a quick shower, and dressed in a pair of worn jeans and a dark blue hoodie. Something easy. Something familiar.

The scent of toast met him as he stepped into the kitchen.

Juliette stood on a chair by the counter, reaching for the jam with determined little fingers, while Émile and Bastien sat at the island, each halfway through a bowl of cereal. The scene was blissfully ordinary, the kind of morning Beau never took for granted.

He smiled as he moved to the espresso machine and began making himself a latte.

"The Winter Carnivale is today," Bastien said casually between spoonfuls of cereal.

Juliette lit up. "Can we go, Daddy?"

"Of course," he said, planting a kiss on the top of her head. Then, glancing at his sons, he added, "But before that... I have something to tell you."

The boys looked up. Juliette paused mid-spread.

Beau set down his mug. "Yesterday, I agreed to run for Prime Minister. The party made the request official. And I said yes."

A heavy beat of silence followed.

"What?" Émile's brows drew together. "You didn't even talk to us first."

"I know," Beau said quietly. "I should have. I wanted to talk to you about it, I just—everything happened so fast. You all had been at your mother's..." He trailed off, knowing how flimsy the excuse sounded.

Émile pushed his bowl away, frustration sharp in his features. "You always say we're a team. But then you go and make this massive decision without us."

Beau flinched. Émile had taken Delphine's affair harder than either of his siblings. The public scrutiny that came with Beau's role had only deepened the wound. More than once, Émile had urged him to step away—to choose a quieter life, one free from headlines and the constant shadow of security. What Émile wanted, more than anything, was privacy. Peace. A life untouched by the spotlight.

"You're right," Beau said, his voice thick with regret. "I wasn't thinking about how it would feel for you. I got caught up in timing and logistics. But I should have thought about you. About all of you."

There was a pause, taut with tension. Then Bastien spoke.

"He's not wrong to be upset," Bastien said, glancing at Émile. "But maybe... Dad's doing this to help people. All kinds of people. And I think we need to trust that he's still our dad first. That part's not going to change."

Émile didn't answer. He stood abruptly, chair scraping back, and walked out of the kitchen.

Juliette's eyes followed him, wide and worried. "Is he mad?"

"He's just... feeling a lot," Beau said gently. "Give him some time."

Then he crouched to Juliette's level. "But yes, we're still going to the carnival."

Her face brightened. "Yay!"

The tension in the room eased slightly, though Beau's chest still ached as he rose. Upstairs, a door clicked shut. He hoped Émile would be ready to talk later. Or at least ready to listen.

Juliette climbed down from her stool and padded over to Beau, wrapping her arms around his waist. "Does this mean you'll be, like... famous?"

Beau chuckled, resting a hand on her back. "Maybe a little. But more than that, it means there's going to be a lot more attention on our family—journalists, cameras, questions. And I need to know you're okay with that."

Bastien looked thoughtful. "Will we still have family dinners? Hockey games? Can you still come to my debate finals?"

Beau nodded. "I'll do everything I can to keep things

normal. But there will be changes—I won't lie about that."

"You better not miss Émile's playoff games," Bastien added.

Beau smiled gently. "I wouldn't dream of it."

Juliette tugged on his hand. "So... we're still going to the carnival?"

"Absolutely," Beau said. "Let's bundle up."

* * * * *

The carnival was already in full swing by the time they arrived. Tents lined the snowy main street of Beau's exclusive community, Wintermere Heights, a private, sprawling enclave nestled in Arbourleigh's northernmost ridge—where the estates looked more like boutique lodges than homes, and the driveways were longer than some suburban blocks.

Each year, the Wintermere Heights Winter Carnival transformed the normally hushed wealth of the neighbourhood into something luminous and alive. Locals bundled in wool coats and designer snow gear meandered between booths as children raced from stand to stand, cheeks pink with cold and fingers clutching sticks of maple taffy. Vendors sold everything from hot pretzels to hand-knit mittens, and soft music from a local quartet drifted from a small stage near the centre square.

Proceeds from the day's events would go to *The Juniper Fund*, a beloved local charity that provided safe housing and trauma therapy for women and children fleeing domestic violence. It was an elegant kind of revelry— purposeful, curated, but joyful.

Beau walked alongside his kids, breathing in the crisp winter air, the sound of their laughter weaving through the hum of the carnival. For the first time in days, something inside him eased. Even Émile, who had been distant that morning, seemed to let the magic of the Carnival soften his mood.

They were just approaching the skating rink when a familiar voice cut through the cold.

"Beau!"

He turned, a reflexive smile already forming, only to feel it falter as he spotted Delphine striding toward them. She looked radiant, draped in a tailored ivory coat with a soft cable-knit scarf looped elegantly around her neck. Beside her stood Bastien, his cheeks flushed from the cold.

"Thought I'd crash the family outing," Delphine said, smiling broadly.

Beau's posture tightened. "You didn't think to text first?" His tone was sharper than intended, irritation bleeding through in front of the kids.

Delphine tilted her head, unbothered. "I did. Émile said you were here. He sounded a little upset," she added, lowering her voice just enough to keep the comment between them.

Juliette ran over, throwing her arms around her mother. "Maman! We're going to skate!"

"Are you coming with us?" Bastien asked, looking to Beau.

He sighed internally but nodded. "Alright then. Let's skate."

Despite himself, Beau found his shoulders loosening as the afternoon wore on. Delphine was in rare form— playful with the kids, engaging with other parents, laughing easily. He caught himself smiling more than once.

At one point, as he helped Juliette tie her skates, he glanced up and saw Delphine helping Émile with his scarf, their heads bent close together. It looked, impossibly, like a family.

And something about that felt good.

Later, they all walked together to the nearby café, hands tucked into mittens, breath clouding the air.

Inside, the kids crowded around a small corner table while Beau ordered drinks. "Four hot chocolates and a vanilla latte, please."

The barista nodded.

Delphine raised an eyebrow. "Vanilla latte?"

Beau didn't answer right away. As he ordered his vanilla latte, a familiar ache stirred beneath the surface— Merritt's favourite, too. The simple act of choosing it made him feel tethered to her, even in her absence. She was uninvited in the moment, but there all the same, pressing gently at the edges of the unexpected warmth of the day.

"You know me," he said lightly. "Creature of habit."

When the drinks arrived, Juliette announced proudly, "Daddy's going to be Prime Minister!"

Delphine blinked. "What?"

Beau met her gaze evenly. "It's in the works. The party asked. I said yes."

Delphine's expression shifted, surprise softening into something unreadable. "Well. Congratulations. That's... quite something."

She sipped her hot chocolate, then added, "Let me know if you want help with your campaign. I have connections, you know."

Beau gave a non-committal nod. "I'll keep that in mind."

When they left the café, Delphine hugged each of the kids and then turned to Beau. She wrapped her arms around him. He allowed it, standing still as her body pressed to his.

"I'm proud of you," she murmured, her lips brushing his ear before she pressed a light kiss to his cheek without letting him go.

"Thanks," he said, his voice low.

The hug lingered. His return embrace was brief, half-hearted. But he didn't pull away as Delphine held on.

That night, after the kids had gone to bed, Beau sat at the marble counter with his reading glasses perched on his nose, laptop open, poring over early policy memos and scheduling requests from his new communications team. There were constituent notes to review and early drafts of speech messaging to approve. All of it felt both thrilling and utterly overwhelming.

Eventually, he gave up. His eyes burned. His focus fractured.

He climbed the stairs slowly, the house quiet around him.

In his bedroom, he changed into pyjamas and reached for his phone again, opening the thread with Merritt.

Merritt, I miss you. He sent, quickly giving into his desperation to talk to her.

Please, talk to me. He sent the message seconds later, then shook his head, cringing at how unappealing his desperation must look.

The messages sat there, blue and silent.

He hesitated, then typed: *I'm sorry. I get it. I'll leave you alone.*

He clicked the screen dark and set it on the charger. Then, with a sigh that reached all the way down to his bones, Beau lay back against the pillows and stared at the ceiling, the weight of the day pressing in.

Sleep came slowly. And when it finally did, it was dreamless.

Chapter 19
Merrit ~ March

More than a month had passed since Merritt met Beau at the café.

Now she sat curled on the living room sofa, Sophie sprawled contentedly at her feet, her copper fur rising and falling with each slow breath. The early-March wind rattled the back door, carrying with it the faintest whisper of spring—just a trace of softness beneath the chill, like a promise the season wasn't quite ready to keep. Merritt held a glass of white wine, its muted warmth a small comfort against the cold that had settled into her bones lately, a cold that felt less like winter and more like absence.

The television cast shifting shadows across the room, and for once, Merritt's attention lingered on the evening news. She had developed a habit of watching political coverage—something she never would have done in her pre-Beau life. That was how she thought of time now: pre-Beau and, achingly, post-Beau.

Before him, she had avoided the news entirely—especially anything to do with politics. But now, the federal election coverage in Norland had become a nightly ritual, her eyes drawn to the screen with a growing urgency she was beginning to recognize for what it was: not just curiosity, but the pull of longing—an attraction she had tried, and failed, to keep at bay.

Lissa Tremblay, Norland's most trusted political anchor, filled the room with her clear voice, recapping the second leadership debate with brisk efficiency. The election loomed just over two weeks away, and the stakes, Tremblay reminded viewers, couldn't be higher. The footage cut to a clip of Beau standing before a jubilant crowd, his expression open and steady, that understated charisma she remembered radiating through the screen.

Merritt's lips curved into a small, involuntary smile. Despite everything she was feeling, she was proud of him.

She'd followed the Progressive Alliance leadership race more closely than she cared to admit—cheering silently when it was announced that Beau would be stepping into the role of Prime Minister, taking over for Greyson Hartwell ahead of the federal election. The press had dissected every nuance of the transition, from Beau and Greyson's easy camaraderie to the symbolic hand-off of power, and Merritt had consumed it all—each article, each headline—like a woman looking for signs in tea leaves.

Prime Minister Laurent, she corrected herself silently, the title still strange to her. Her mind wandered back to the stillness of the cottage, to the quiet morning light spilling across Beau's features, to the feel of his hands on her body. It didn't feel that long ago.

He'd made headlines again just days after his appointment, declining the official residence at Dominion House in favour of keeping his children in their home and routines. Victor Hargrave, the leader of the Norlandic Conservative Union, had leapt at the opportunity to criticize the move, accusing Beau of being "un-Norlandic." Merritt, already a supporter of the Progressive Alliance, even before Beau, found herself liking that smug, rat-eyed bastard even less with every passing day.

The television continued to chatter, but Merritt's gaze drifted to her phone on the coffee table. Her wine glass hovered near her lips for a moment before she set it down. Her fingers reached for the device almost unconsciously, scrolling to the message thread with Beau.

She hovered over his name, her thumb pausing above the screen.

Earlier that day, Sebastian and Genevieve DuPont had walked into her office—smiling, poised, completely at ease—and announced their reconciliation. The storm of their divorce had passed, and they were withdrawing all filings. The conflict of interest that Merritt had once clung to as a reason to walk away from Beau had evaporated with a single sentence, and with it, the last convenient excuse she had been clinging to.

She had regretted her decision to push him away almost immediately.

Now, that realization pulsed in her chest. There was nothing stopping her—not ethically, not professionally. But she still didn't know whether what had bloomed between them could survive the silence she'd enforced. She didn't even know if he wanted it to.

But she wanted to find out.

Bolstered by the wine she'd already had, Merritt opened the thread she had silenced weeks ago, her heart thudding a little faster with every second.

A series of unread messages stared back at her—each one a time capsule from the aftermath of their final meeting.

Surely, we can work something out? Sent not long after she'd walked out of the café.

Merritt, I miss you. Three days later.

Please, talk to me. The ache in those words hit her square in the chest.

And finally: I'm sorry. I get it. I'll leave you alone.

That last one had arrived all those weeks ago.

She hadn't read any of them at the time, knowing full well that if she did, her resolve might crack. Instead, she'd buried herself in work—telling herself she was being professional, principled. But as she sat here now, watching him take on a role of national significance with the same sincerity that had captivated her from the start, she couldn't help but smile.

Maybe there was still something there—not a rewind to what might have been, but a step forward into whatever was still possible.

Her fingers moved before she could talk herself out of it.

I hope you know you have my vote, she typed.

But before sending it, she hesitated. She tapped Avery's number, hoping for a familiar voice. The call went straight to voicemail, as it had for weeks now. Merritt left a quick message, more out of habit than hope. It had been three weeks since she'd heard anything from her friend. She had called Avery's office and been told by her assistant that Avery was there. So Merritt knew nothing terrible had happened—but the silence was unshakable.

With no advice to anchor her, Merritt glanced at Sophie.

"What do you think?" she asked softly.

The husky shifted and crossed her paws, lifting her mismatched eyes to meet Merritt's.

"Okay then," Merritt whispered, nodding to herself.

She hit send.

The familiar whoosh of the message being delivered broke the stillness. Merritt set the phone back on the table, her heart thudding, alive with nerves.

Three dots appeared.

Then disappeared.

Reappeared.

Vanished again.

This pattern played out for ten agonizing minutes as Merritt poured another glass of wine—bringing the bottle back to the couch with her this time. By the time a reply finally came, her heart had settled into something equal parts hope and dread.

Thank you, Merritt. It's good to hear from you.

She read it once. Then again.

The words were simple. Polite. Ambiguous. Neither the warmth she'd hoped for, nor the coldness she'd feared.

Her fingers hovered over the screen, brushing lightly against the glass. She told herself to be grateful—grateful he'd responded at all, grateful she hadn't lost the thread completely.

But as the quiet settled around her again, that message lingered, cool and careful.

It was a reply.

But not yet a connection she was certain of—though now, more than ever, she wanted it with her whole heart.

Chapter 20
Beau ~ The Opening

The hum of downtown Rider's Rest traffic drifted faintly through the windows of Beau's high-rise suite in the city's bustling core. He sat on the stiff, modern couch, its sharp edges and cold design mirroring the unfamiliarity of his surroundings. Beside him, Delphine leaned in, her thigh brushing his, their faces so close they could have been sharing a secret. Together, they peered at the laptop balanced on his knees, the smiling faces of their children filling the screen with a warmth that softened the sterile room.

As Beau embarked on the campaign trail, Delphine's parents, Philippe and Charlotte, had flown to Arbourleigh from Viremont to stay with the children in Arbourleigh. Their presence ensured that the kids' routines remained undisturbed, allowing Delphine to join Beau on the road. It had been her idea—something she had insisted upon— and now, three weeks in, the toll was beginning to show. The grueling schedule pressed heavily on Beau, the fatigue settling into his shoulders and creeping into his voice. With the election only two weeks away, there were more long days and sleepless nights ahead.

They had one more stop and then they would be wrapping things up in Port Reinier, on Norland's western coast, before a weekend off. Then it was back to Arbourleigh for the final leadership debate and soon after, the election.

This evening, Beau and Delphine sat side by side on the small couch in his suite, their faces, nearly touching, lit by the soft glow of his laptop screen as they chatted with their children.

Philippe and Charlotte's voices carried in the background, speaking to the children in perfect French, urging them to begin their nighttime routines. The two-hour time difference meant it was already late in Arbourleigh, and the children responded cheerfully in French before turning back to the screen to wave their goodbyes to their parents.

Beau smiled as he blew three kisses toward the monitor,

his expression softening with warmth. Delphine leaned in, her own smile mirrored by their children's as they signed off and Beau closed the laptop.

"I miss them," she said softly, her voice threaded with wistfulness as she placed a hand on Beau's thigh. Her touch lingered, deliberate and familiar. When her gaze met his—bright with unspoken emotion—it held for a beat too long. "We did good when we made those babies," she added, her lips curling into a gentle smile as she shifted closer, daring to rest her head on his shoulder.

Beau rose abruptly, brushing her hand away with a smooth, practiced motion that left no room for lingering. "They are incredible," he said, his voice measured, though his body carried a tension that spoke of boundaries he didn't want to have to reiterate. He adjusted the hem of his snap button shirt as he moved, the worn denim of his Wrangler jeans—a deliberate nod to Rider's Rest cowboy heritage—creasing slightly as he stepped away from the Delphine, creating deliberate space between them.

He watched as Delphine crossed the suite, her movements a study in elegant seduction. She came to him, pressing her body into his with a forcefulness that felt more determined than inviting. Beau shifted away, his body tensing as he gently nudged her back. "It might be time to go to your own suite," he said, his tone firm, the words leaving no room for argument.

"How long are you going to punish me?" she asked, her voice lilting with a pout that softened her striking features. She looked up at him, undeniably beautiful, but the sight no longer stirred the desire she seemed to expect. Beau's resolve remained unshaken, even in the wake of her sudden and dramatic break with Sebastian DuPont. Delphine had reappeared in his life, seductive and eager, as if ready to pick up where they had left off.

It had started subtly enough—her unexplained early

morning presence in his bathroom while he showered, as though the intimacy of shared space still existed between them. But it quickly escalated: overtly flirtatious texts, unannounced visits to the home they had once shared, lingering touches, and advances laced with unmistakable intent.

Beau, distracted by the grueling demands of the campaign trail, had let his guard down just enough to allow her presence to creep back into his life. Her charm, practiced and persistent, worked its way past his defenses to a point, but only so far. When Delphine pressed him to use her event-planning expertise for his campaign, her argument well-crafted and persuasive, he had agreed almost reflexively, too consumed by his focus on the road ahead to fully consider the implications.

Now, as she stood before him with that familiar mix of seduction and determination, Beau felt the weight of her intentions pressing against his already burdened resolve. He knew what she wanted, but the wounds of her betrayal still lingered. The question loomed unanswered, leaving him uncertain whether the space for reconciliation existed —or if it ever could.

Beau was acutely aware of how easy it would be to surrender to her, to accept her warmth, to lose himself in the comfort of their shared history. Her body was familiar, her touch achingly recognizable, and the memories of their ecstasy lingered just beneath the surface, ready to pull him under. Without fully thinking through his actions, Beau reached for her, his arm encircling her waist and drawing her closer. He held her against him, his chin resting on the crown of her head as the cloying, familiar scent of her enveloped him.

For a fleeting moment, he allowed himself to linger there, his mind warring with his heart. He wanted so badly to let go, to give himself over to the familiarity of her body and the illusion of their marriage as it once was.

A soft knock at the door interrupted the moment. Sylvie

used her keycard to open the door, with Quinn following behind.

"Oh shit," Sylvie gasped. "Sorry, we'll be out here," she stepped backward, her body bumping into Quinn's as they backed out of the room.

Beau dropped his arms from Delphine's body. "I can't," he murmured, his grip loosening but not fully releasing her.

Delphine tilted her face upward, rising onto her tiptoes, and pressed her lips to his. Beau kissed her back for an instant, a reflex born of muscle memory and emotion, before pulling away sharply. He forced his body from hers, breaking the connection that had felt both magnetic and unbearable. "I can't," he said again, his voice firmer now, carrying the weight of his resolve. "Please go."

For a moment, Delphine lingered, her eyes searching his face as though trying to find a crack in his resolve. When she found none, she stepped back, the space between them growing vast and unbridgeable. She turned toward the door, pausing briefly to look over her shoulder one last time before slipping out and closing it behind her.

As Delphine exited, Sylvie and Quinn re-entered the room. "What was that about?" Quinn asked brazenly. She and Sylvie settled onto Beau's couch, their bodies close, legs touching. Sylvie rested her hand on Quinn's thigh, quieting her.

"We just wanted to go over security for tomorrow," Sylvie began. With weeks having passed since Greyson's attack, the NFC were no closer to uncovering who was behind the attack, nor the continued threats. With nothing resolved, it seemed the added security, now multiplied thanks to Beau's new position, was here to stay.

Beau sat on the edge of his bed, staring absently at the ornate pattern in the carpet beneath his feet. The room was quiet now—Delphine had gone, but a trace of her remained. Her perfume, soft and floral, lingered in the air like a whisper that refused to fade. He exhaled heavily, dragging a hand down his face. In her absence, the weight of her presence still clung to the room, as if her attempts to weave herself back into his life hadn't left with her.

Beau turned his attention back to Sylvie and Quinn, listening as they outlined his schedule for the following day. He nodded along, surrendering to whatever they had planned, before they wrapped up and headed toward the hallway. Quinn's hand rested lightly on the small of Sylvie's back as she led the way, a gesture that did not escape beau's attention and left him smiling in spite of his own inner romantic turmoil.

Beau didn't linger on the thought of whether his primary security detail had fallen into a more intimate relationship. In fact, he welcomed it. Someone deserved to have a healthy, happy connection—and if it wasn't going to be him, he was glad it could be them.

Now alone in his room, Beau's thoughts drifted back to Delphine. Was he really considering forgiving the unforgivable? The idea lingered—heavy and far too tempting. Some part of him was. A part that longed for the ease of familiarity, even if it came at the cost of his heart—a heart he knew could never truly love Delphine again.

His phone buzzed against the nightstand. Without thinking, he reached for it, his thumb swiping across the screen to reveal the message. The sight of her name stopped him cold. Merritt Clarke, the crimson heart still part of her name in his phone. His children's smiling faces beamed at him from the wallpaper behind her notification, their joy a sharp contrast to the sudden chaos in his chest.

Beau's breath hitched, his fingers hovering over the notification as though touching it might shatter the moment. Finally, he tapped it, the message opening to reveal her words.

I hope you know you have my vote.

The room seemed to tilt slightly as Beau staggered to his feet, his back hitting the closed door to the suite's bathroom. He slid down to the ground, his heart pounding. A surge of adrenaline coursed through him, leaving his thoughts racing. His thumb began moving over the keyboard almost instinctively, his mind grasping at words to match the storm in his chest.

I've been thinking about you ever since that day at the café. He typed it quickly, then froze. Too much. He deleted it.

Would you like to get dinner with me when I'm back in town? The thought felt too forward, too open. Deleted.

Every time I get a text, I hope it's you. His chest tightened as he read the vulnerable truth in the words. Deleted.

I'd give anything to hear your voice right now. The realness of it burned, but it wasn't what he could, or should say—not now. Deleted.

He stared at the empty text box, his hands trembling slightly as his emotions churned. Merritt's message had cracked something open inside him, a flood of feelings he had tried to suppress. He didn't know what her words meant or why she had chosen this moment to reach out, but he didn't want to push her away. Not again.

Finally, he settled on something safe, something neutral. *Thank you, Merritt. It's good to hear from you.* He pressed send before he could overthink it, watching the message appear on the screen, the word 'read' appearing underneath it almost instantly.

Leaning his head back against the door, Beau closed his eyes. He read Merritt's message again, the stark simplicity of it leaving him hollow. He felt foolish for hoping. It was just a friendly text, he told himself. Nothing more. He tried to shake it off, but Merritt's name still glowed faintly on his screen, a reminder of the connection he had tried so hard to bury.

Beau exhaled sharply, pressing the heels of his palms into his eyes as his thoughts spiralled. The weight of his past pressed down on him, while the uncertain pull of Merritt loomed like a shadow he couldn't outrun, and didn't want to. The quiet of his suite wrapped around him, the deepening night casting the room in a dim, reflective stillness.

He remained on the floor a few moments longer, willing a reply to appear. None came.

With a shake of his head, Beau gave up and climbed to his feet. In the suite's bathroom, he stripped off the cowboy-themed clothing piece by piece and stepped into the cold shower, letting the icy stream crash over him. The shock tore through him, clearing the fog in his mind, if only for a moment. Afterward, he dried off and prepared for bed, his body heavy with exhaustion and his thoughts no quieter than before.

Climbing into the hotel bed, he wrapped the bleach white blankets tightly around himself, pulling them all the way up to his chin. His body, still adjusting to the unfamiliar time zone, felt heavy with exhaustion. Sleep came quickly, pulling him into its peaceful embrace.

* * * * *

The low hum of his phone vibrating on the bedside table jolted him back to consciousness. Night had fully descended, and the muffled sounds of the city—sirens, distant voices, and the occasional honk of a horn— filtered through the window. The large red numbers on the suite's dated digital clock glowed in the darkness, announcing it was just after 11.

Beau was instantly alert, his heart racing as he reached for the phone. A call at this hour could only mean an emergency. His mind immediately went to his children, panic tightening his chest as he grabbed for his phone.

Turning the device over, he was met with a different kind of emergency. Merritt's name glowed on the screen, couple with the photo he had snapped of her after their first night together. She had been lying beside him, her hair tousled, a soft, shy smile on her lips as the early morning light framed her face. The image stirred a rush of emotions—desire, longing, and more.

It would have been after 1 a.m. in Arbourleigh. Beau quickly accepted the phone call, eager to find out what had kept her awake so late into the evening.

As the call connected, a soft, girlish giggle carried down the line, light and unexpected.

"Merritt?" Beau said, his tone communicating his surprise.

"I'm sorry," Merritt replied, more composed but her voice still tinged with laughter before another wave of giggles overtook her. "I'm... a bit drunk," she confessed, her voice warm and slurred with alcohol. "I drank wine," she said by way of explanation.

Beau chuckled softly, his worry easing slightly. "Is everything okay?" he asked, his voice steady but gently probing.

The line went silent, and Beau frowned, pulling the phone away from his ear to check if the call had dropped. Seeing the connection still active, he shifted, pulling his feet toward him and creating small tents with his legs beneath the bleach-scented hotel bedding. He set the phone atop one knee, switching to speaker, and waited patiently.

The silence stretched far too long, the weight of it building until Merritt finally spoke again. Her voice was barely above a whisper. "It's... it's not okay," she said.

Then, after a hesitant pause, she added, "I miss you." The words were so quiet, they might have gone unnoticed if Beau hadn't been straining to hear. "Is that okay?" she questioned, her voice tiny, as if bracing for rejection.

Beau leaned back against the headboard, a broad smile spreading across his face. The simple confession sent a warmth rushing through him, a feeling so immediate and overwhelming that it left him momentarily breathless. He felt like a teenager again, the giddiness of something new and precious overtaking him. The word love drifted through his mind, startling him with its sudden presence. He bolted upright, the realization sending a jolt through his chest. Was that what this was?

"I..." Beau began, his voice catching. He stammered, searching for words, desperate to say the perfect thing. His mind, sluggish with exhaustion, failed him. "Yes," he said finally, the single word sounding both inadequate and exactly what he needed to say. "Yes," he repeated, his voice soft but steady. "That's okay."

There was a silence that again dragged out, and then...

"Good," Merritt blurted, her voice unfiltered and bold. "Because I keep thinking about your eyes, and your shoulders, and your arms. It makes me want to do...things."

Beau froze, her words hitting somewhere between a playful tease and a raw confession. "Things?" he asked, his voice low, a slow smile curving on his lips.

"Yes, things," Merritt slurred, her tone dipping husky and sultry before descending into a giggle. "You remember the things we did at your cottage? I'd like to do that again...and more." Her breathy words hung in the air, bold and unrestrained from the alcohol coursing through her. Then, as though realizing what she had just said, she groaned, half-laughing. "Oh fuck, I cannot believe I just said that out loud."

Beau laughed softly, his breath catching in his throat, the sound rumbling deep in his chest. "I'm not sure I should encourage this... but I'm definitely intrigued," he said, his tone warm and teasing, even as her words sent a jolt of heat through him.

"Of course you are," Merritt mumbled, embarrassment flickering in her voice, though she couldn't stop the giggle that escaped. "I'm sure you're used to getting whatever you want with those eyes."

Beau shook his head, though a grin lingered on his lips. "You give me a lot of credit," he said, his voice rich with amusement. "But I don't think my eyes are *that* persuasive."

Merritt let out a soft laugh. "Oh, they are," she countered, her tone dipping into something quieter, more intimate. "It's unfair, really. Those eyes could probably convince me to do just about anything."

Beau felt his pulse quicken at her words, his usual steady composure slipping slightly. "I'll keep that in mind," he he almost a whispered. He leaned back against the headboard again, the phone warm on his knee as he stared at the dark ceiling of his hotel suite. For a moment, the air between them was charged, the silence heavy with possibilities.

Merritt sighed softly, her voice breaking the quiet. "I didn't mean to call and make things... weird," she said, a flicker of self-consciousness creeping into her tone. "I just... couldn't stop thinking about you."

Beau closed his eyes, her words sinking into him like a balm and a burn all at once. "Merritt," he said, her name rolling off his tongue with a tenderness he didn't try to hide. "You didn't make things weird. You made my night."

She laughed again, softer this time, and he could hear the relief in her voice. "Well, I guess I should go before I make it weirder," she said, though there was hesitation in her voice.

"You don't have to," Beau said quickly, his own voice surprising him with its intensity. "Stay on the line. I don't mind... I like hearing your voice."

Merritt paused, the quiet stretching between them like a thread pulled taut. "Okay," she said finally. "Then talk to me, Beau. Tell me something real."

He smiled, the vulnerability in her words cutting through the lingering haze of his exhaustion. "Something real?" he repeated, his voice steady. "Alright. I'll tell you something real. I've missed you too."

The line fell quiet, their breathing the only sound moving between them. The stillness stretched—delicate, fragile—until Merritt's voice broke it.

"I should let you go," she said suddenly, her tone shifting, the fog of alcohol lifting just enough to reveal a flicker of hesitation. "I'm sure you have more important things to do. Congratulations, by the way... Mr. Prime Minister."

He could hear the smile in her voice.

"Thank you, Merritt. It would actually just be *Prime Minister*," Beau replied, teasing gently. His voice was steady, but there was a softness beneath it—something warmer, more intimate.

"Can I call you tomorrow?" he asked, the words quiet but careful, like a hand reaching through the dark. His chest tightened as he waited. This sudden thread between them was fragile, and he didn't want to pull too hard.

Would she let him in—or slip away again?

Another pause, longer this time, stretched across the line. He could almost hear her weighing the words, debating with herself. Finally, she sighed, the sound soft and gentle. "I'd like that," she said, as if admitting it to herself as much as to him.

With that, Merritt ended the call, and the line went dead.

Beau stared at the screen for a moment, her name still glowing faintly before it disappeared. Slowly, he brought his hands to his head, a jubilant smile spreading across his face. Had that really just happened? He let out a deep laugh, shaking his head in disbelief.

Rolling onto his back, he kicked at the stiff hotel sheets, his excitement bubbling over in a burst of energy he didn't know he could feel at 52-years-old. Their conversation replayed in his mind, every word, every laugh, every pause filling him with a giddy warmth he hadn't felt in longer than he could remember. His chest rose and fell in quick breaths, the thrill of it surprising even him.

Eventually, the adrenaline began to ebb, leaving behind a deep contentment. Beau adjusted the covers, pulling them snugly around him as he sank back into the pillows. His mind wandered to Merritt's voice, the way it softened when she'd said, *I'd like that.*

He smiled again, smaller this time, the kind of smile that comes from bone-deep joy. His body relaxed, his thoughts growing hazy as sleep began to pull him under.

Just before he drifted off, Beau reached for his phone, the glow of the screen casting a soft light in the dark room. The conversation still lingered in the air around him, wrapping him in it. He wanted to leave Merritt with something—words that might carry a hint of what he felt, veiled but unmistakable.

His fingers hovered over the keyboard before he began to type: *You've made tonight impossible to forget. I'll be thinking about you, Merritt. Sleep well.*

Satisfied, he pressed send, the message disappearing into the ether. Beau set the phone back on the bedside table, a faint smile still on his lips as he closed his eyes. The memory of her voice and her laugh followed him into sleep, an echo of something welcome and deeply longed for.

Chapter 21
Merritt ~ The Morning After

Merritt woke to Sophie's wet nose nuzzling her face, a persistent wake-up call against the backdrop of a throbbing headache. She groaned, cracking open one eye to find the wine glass she had carelessly left on the nightstand—an embarrassing reminder of her descent into overindulgence the night before. She couldn't recall the last time she had allowed herself to slip so far into drunkenness, to drown her thoughts and doubts in the wine. Years, at least.

Her stomach churned, forcing her upright in a panic. She stumbled toward the ensuite bathroom, her hands gripping the doorway as she collapsed in front of the toilet, retching. The tiled floor was cold against her knees, a sharp contrast to the heat rising in her face. When the nausea finally passed, she rinsed her mouth and splashed water on her face, catching a glimpse of herself in the mirror. Her reflection felt foreign—her skin pale, her hair tousled, and her expression weary.

The faint glow of morning light filtering through the curtains drew her back to the bedroom. She collapsed onto the bed, her limbs heavy, her head still spinning. Reaching for her phone, she prepared to send a quick text to Malcolm, letting him know she wouldn't be in the office. The words were already forming in her mind—"Flu, redirect calls to voicemail"—when a notification caught her eye.

A text from Beau.

Her heart jumped, her mind flashing back to the conversation they had shared in the early hours of the morning. She cringed at the memory of her brazen comments about his physique, her attraction to him spilling out in an uncharacteristically forward way. Yet amidst the embarrassment, there was a flicker of warmth, a memory of his steady, unflappable response and the undeniable sincerity of his words: *I miss you too.*

With trembling fingers, she opened his message. *You've made tonight impossible to forget. I'll be thinking about you, Merritt. Sleep well.*

A small gasp escaped her lips, followed by a squeal of delight as she hugged her knees to her chest, her cheeks flushing. Sophie tilted her head curiously, watching Merritt's reaction with amused canine intrigue. Merritt felt giddy, light, a feeling she couldn't remember the last time she'd experienced. But a sudden surge of nausea pulled her back to the present, sending her rushing to the bathroom once more.

When the sickness momentarily subsided, she leaned against the counter, breathing deeply. Her thoughts drifted back to Beau. The way he had spoken to her, the way his words lingered in her mind—it was a feeling she couldn't shake. And this time, didn't want to shake.

After sending the necessary text to Malcolm, Merritt turned on the shower, the hiss of water filling the space as steam began to rise and curl around her. She peeled off the alcohol-scented clothes she'd slept in, tossing them into the hamper with a small grimace.

Drinking too much felt indulgent. But last night had been difficult. Watching Beau on the news, his face larger than life on the screen, his eyes almost hypnotic and his voice sexy and commanding as he addressed the nation was captivating.

His words had been magnetic, but it was the tension of his ambiguous response to her text, that had lingered and bounced around her mind. The wine had been her salve, dulling the edges of her thoughts if only for a fleeting moment. Now, stepping under the too-warm stream, she let the water cascade over her, soaking her hair and soothing her aching body. She closed her eyes, trying to wash away the remnants of the previous night: the dull throb in her temples, the weight of her emotions, and the uneasy realization that her thoughts of Beau were far, far from fleeting. Whatever was unfolding, it was undeniable—she wanted to see where it would lead.

Merritt emerged from the shower, steam curling around her like a veil as she reached for a plush, forest green towel and wrapped it snugly around herself. Her warm, tawny skin glistened faintly from the heat, the room still steeped in the comforting scent of vanilla from her body wash. She moved to the counter, where the mirror was fogged in a soft haze, her reflection blurred and indistinct. Damp tendrils of hair clung to her shoulders as she leaned against the edge, letting the moment steady her before the day pressed in.

She padded back to the bedroom, her steps slow, almost hesitant, as she retrieved her phone from where she had left it. She needed to read Beau's text again, her damp fingers smudging the screen as she unlocked it.

Beau's text was waiting, his words simple but undeniable: *You've made tonight impossible to forget. I'll be thinking about you, Merritt. Sleep well.*

A breath hitched in her throat. She reread it, her heart both quickening and softening at the thought of him laying in bed somewhere, in a distant city, typing out those words. There was something about his openness, his willingness to say what he felt, that both thrilled and unnerved her.

She perched on the edge of her bed, Sophie curling up beside her, the husky's head resting on her lap. Merritt stroked Sophie's fur absently, her thoughts circling. Should she respond? What would she say? Her instinct was to push the moment aside, to let it sit unanswered, but even the idea of leaving him hanging felt wrong. Beau deserved more than silence, and she was excited to fill it.

Her thumbs hovered over the keyboard. *Good morning.* No, too formal. Last night was... lovely. Too coy, too silly. She deleted and rewrote, over and over, trying to balance her excitement and come off as somehow... cool?

Finally, she settled on something that felt honest, even

if it revealed more than she'd intended: *Last night wasn't just unforgettable for you. I don't know where this is going, Beau, but I can't stop wanting to find out—with you.*

She hesitated for just a second before hitting send, the message disappearing as her heart thudded in her chest. Sophie shifted beside her, offering a reassuring nuzzle that made Merritt smile despite herself. "Don't look at me like that," Merritt said with a weak laugh, scratching behind Sophie's ears. "I'm allowed to want something good, aren't I?"

Sophie wagged her tail, a response that Merritt took as approval. She exhaled deeply and stood, determination settling in her shoulders. She was grateful for the day off she had made for herself. It would give her time to relish in her growing feelings and her delight that Beau felt the same.

In this exact moment, she wanted more than anything to reach out to Avery. She had become so used to sharing everything that happened in life with her friend. She decided to send a quick text.

I have so much to tell you. She began. *Av, I'm not really sure what happened, but please text me back. I've had major developments...and they're all about Beau!*

Merritt hit send, pausing to see if Avery might respond. The text remained there with delivered nestled beneath her words. It was the same with all of the texts she had sent over the last few weeks.

Merritt sighed with resignation before steeling herself against the lingering nausea and then making her way downstairs. Sophie padded at her heels, her tail wagging expectantly. Merritt opened the back door, the sharp bite of lingering winter air rushing in as Sophie bounded outside, her paws leaving faint impressions in the frost. Merritt leaned against the doorframe, inhaling the crisp air, willing it to clear her head.

Sophie trotted back inside, her coat dusted with snowflakes, the coffee machine sputtered to life under Merritt's touch. The warm, earthy aroma began to fill the kitchen. The quiet hum of the morning was broken by the unmistakable chime of a FaceTime call, her phone buzzing insistently on the counter.

Glancing at the screen, she froze. It was Beau. Her heart gave an involuntary flutter, a rush of warmth spreading through her chest even as her stomach twisted itself, seeming to do backflips inside her body. She clutched the phone to her chest, smiling despite herself, but her mind raced with worry. Her hair was still damp, her face bare of makeup, and the exhaustion from last night's adventure in a wine bottle lingered in the shadows under her eyes. She hesitated for a moment, smoothing her plain sweater over her shoulders as if that might make her look more presentable, before finally answering and praying she didn't look as terrible as she felt.

"Well, good morning," he said, his boyish grin lighting up the screen. It was a smile Merritt had come to anticipate, one that tugged at something deep inside her. She couldn't help but notice the soft creases at the corners of his eyes and the tousled hair that made him look more approachable than the polished politician she had watched on the news.

Behind him, the view from the bus window blurred with the movement of snow-covered prairies speeding past, the early light casting golden streaks across the frost-covered landscape. Merritt glanced at the clock, realizing how early it must be where he is. "You've already hit the road?"

"Too early," Beau confirmed, shifting slightly in his seat to angle the camera, giving Merritt a glimpse of the snow-dusted landscape rushing past the bus windows. "First stop's a community breakfast. Figured I'd check in before the day gets chaotic." His tone was casual, but there was an undeniable warmth in his gaze that sent a pleasant heat blooming trough her. He hesitated briefly, his smile softening. "And... I wanted to talk to you," he admitted, his voice quieter now, laced with unmistakable sincerity.

She tucked a stray strand of damp hair behind her ear, her gaze lingering on the screen, captivated by the easy strength in Beau's features. Her mind flickered back to the cottage—the way his touch had felt, the heat of his body against hers—and a flush crept up her neck, spreading to her cheeks. "Well, I appreciate the check-in," she said lightly, lifting her coffee mug to take a sip in an attempt to compose herself. "You're making me feel like a total slacker over here. I've called in sick."

Beau's lips curved into a knowing smile, his voice low and smooth. "Not lazy—recovering. If I'm working hard here, it's just trying to keep up with you."

Merritt laughed softly, shaking her head. "Let's just say the wine I had last night might not agree with you. Watching your campaign coverage turned out to be... more captivating than I expected." Her cheeks warmed as the words left her mouth, but she didn't try to take them back. What was the point in pretending?

"Oh? Captivating, eh?" Beau's teasing smile widened, but there was a glimmer of something deeper in his eyes—an acknowledgment of the connection between them that neither of them could ignore. "I'll take that as a compliment."

"You should," she replied, her voice steadier now, though her heart still fluttered in her chest. She swallowed, bracing herself as she steered the conversation toward a subject that felt heavier—one she wasn't sure she was ready to broach. "When you texted me back," she began carefully, her fingers tightening slightly around her coffee mug, "I wasn't sure what it meant." Her gaze dropped for a moment before lifting to meet his. "I didn't want to push, so I poured myself another glass of wine... and then another." She let out a soft laugh, the sound tinged with self-consciousness, trying to ease the vulnerability of her confession.

Beau leaned his head back, letting out a heavy sigh. "That stupid text," he said, his voice low and filled with self-reproach. "You don't know how many messages I wrote and deleted before I sent it. It was me that didn't want to push too hard. I didn't want to scare you off." His laugh was soft, tinged with both humor and vulnerability, as he ran a hand through his hair. "Guess we were both overthinking it?"

Merritt said nothing for a moment, letting the silence settle between them as she stared at Beau's face on the screen. She nodded slowly, offering a small smile—shy and uncertain, but enough, she hoped, to show how much his words meant to her. "I guess I thought I'd just made a mess of this," she admitted finally, her voice soft with vulnerability. She took a long sip of her vanilla latte, using the motion to shield her face for just a moment longer.

"I get the feeling, Merritt, that everything with you is going to be messy," Beau said, his smile soft and genuine. "And I can't wait for it."

His words, so simple yet brimming with the promise of a future, sent Merritt's heart thudding in her chest. She looked away for a moment, her breath catching as she processed what he had just said. Without trusting herself to respond, she took another long sip of her coffee, letting its warmth steady her against the rush of emotions his words stirred.

"How are you feeling?" Beau asked after a long pause.

"Better now," Merritt admitted before she could stop herself. She shook her head, laughing nervously. "God, that was corny."

"I liked it," Beau replied without hesitation. "You don't need to overthink everything, Merritt. Just be yourself.".

The sincerity in his voice made her pause. She met his eyes on the screen, and for a moment, the world seemed to still, leaving only the charged space between them. Before she could respond, a voice called Beau's name from somewhere off-camera, breaking the moment.

Beau glanced to the side, a flicker of regret flashing across his face. "I'm sorry, Merritt. I have to go," he said, nodding toward someone offscreen. His gaze lingered on her for a beat longer.

Merritt nodded. "Go charm the rest of the country, Beau. Against those blue eyes, No one stands a chance."

"I'll try my best," he said with a wink, his smile turning playful. "But with these eyes? I think you already said it— I've got an unfair advantage." His tone was light, but there was a softness behind the words, a sincerity that lingered. "Talk soon?"

"Talk soon," Merritt agreed with a smile.

As the call ended, she stared at the now-blank screen, her chest tightening as a determined calm settled over her. Sophie nudged her leg, her warm eyes steady and expectant. Merritt smiled faintly, setting her phone down on the counter before sinking to the floor to scratch behind Sophie's ears.

"I think I'm done running from this, girl," she murmured, her fingers threading through Sophie's soft fur. The words felt solid, and real, pulling her out of the haze of hesitation she had been lost in for so long. Sophie wagged her tail, her approval immediate and unreserved.

Chapter 22
Beau ~ The Lines Crossed

As Beau ended his call with Merritt, the warmth of her voice still lingering in his thoughts, he turned in his seat to face Delphine. She had been calling his name, her tone carrying a sharp edge of curiosity that instantly set him on edge. He wasn't sure how much of his conversation with Merritt she had overheard, but from the look on her face, it was enough.

"Who was that?" Delphine asked, her voice laced with something bordering on venom. Her piercing gaze, the one that had always been able to cut through his defenses, fixed on him. After 30 years of marriage, she didn't need much to piece things together. "Who is she?" she asked again, this time more pointedly, her golden eyes, almost the same shade as her hair, glistening with unshed tears.

Beau hesitated, caught in the pull of his past with Delphine. Merritt's face lingered in his mind with all her warmth and guarded vulnerability. Yet, sitting across from him now was Delphine—the mother of his children, the woman who had been at his side through decades of triumphs and trials. Her presence was a tether, not to passion, but to the familiar, to history, and the idea of family.

"I was catching up with someone," he said finally, his tone deliberately even, though his chest tightened as he spoke. He didn't need to say more; Delphine knew how to read between the lines. Her lips parted as though to respond, but she hesitated, her expression faltering.

She looked down at her hands, wringing them together in her lap. "I thought maybe this trip would help," she admitted, her voice barely above a whisper. "That it might remind us of what we used to have. Of what we could have again."

Beau let out a slow breath, leaning back in his seat. He wanted to feel the pull of her words, the promise of the family they had built, the life they had shared. But all he felt was something close to resignation, like watching a door close he didn't have the will to hold open.

"I don't know, Delphine," he said honestly, his voice edged with weariness. "I don't know if we can go back."

Her head snapped up, her eyes glistening as she met his gaze. "Don't you think we owe it to the kids? To us? To 30 years? To at least try?"

Beau swallowed hard. He thought of their children—the laughter, the chaos, the moments of connection that had always felt like the best parts of his life. And yet, the tug he felt now wasn't love for Delphine. It wasn't even toward the family they had been.

The pull toward Merritt was undeniable, a force he felt deep in himself, drawing him closer to her even now. But the memory of her pulling away was just as fresh, lingering like a shadow. Right now, he felt like she was all in, like the connection between them was something solid that they could build on. But he'd thought that before, and it hadn't held. In their brief time together, he had already learned how much her absence could hurt, the ache it left behind when she retreated, leaving him unsure if he could risk feeling it again.

"I don't have all the answers," he said finally. "But I know that whatever we do, it has to be for the right reasons—not because we're afraid of what's next, or because you are afraid to be alone." His words held a hint of accusation.

Delphine's lips pressed into a thin line as she nodded, though there was no defeat in her posture. Her shoulders squared, her gaze hardening as she turned to stare out the bus window, her reflection a sharp silhouette against the passing scenery. "It doesn't matter what you think right now, Beau," she said, her voice laced with a calculated edge. "You'll remember, eventually, what we had. What we were."

She turned back to face him, leaning in slightly, her eyes narrowing as they locked onto his. "You're a man, Beau. And you don't forget the way I can make you feel," she said, her voice softening into a provocative purr. "You think you're over it, but we both know how quickly that will change."

Beau stiffened, his jaw tightening as her words hit their mark—not with the pull of longing she seemed to expect, but with irritation and a simmering discomfort. He leaned back in his seat, putting distance between them as he fought to keep the frustration off his face.

"Delphine," he began, "what we had isn't something I can just forget. But I also can't pretend that what's left is enough. Not for me. Not right now."

Her smile didn't falter, but there was something steely in it now, a refusal to concede. She sat back with deliberate grace, crossing her legs as she studied him with an air of confidence. "We'll see," she said simply, her tone dismissive as though she were still laying a claim he couldn't escape.

Beau exhaled, running a hand through his hair as he turned his gaze to the window and the passing scenery. His thoughts churned—a tangled web of guilt, obligation, and persistent pull of Merritt's voice in his mind. As the bus continued on, its vibrations thrumming in his chest, he leaned his head back and closed his eyes. He felt Delphine's presence, her determination a sharp counterpoint to his uncertainty, as the road stretched endlessly ahead.

* * * * *

The bus rumbled to a halt in front of a modest roadside motel, a stark contrast to the formal accommodations Beau had stayed in the night before. This small mountain town, nestled on the border of Aurivale and Cascadia—Norland's western provinces—felt a world away from the pressures of Arbourleigh. Sylvie, Quinn, and the rest of Beau's now expanded security detail began unpacking with efficiency, stationing themselves nearby to maintain a watchful presence. Tonight, Beau's team were the motel's only guests.

Once settled, the group made their way to the town's community breakfast, where Beau's natural charisma came to life. He smiled easily and worked the crowd with his signature unhurried charm, shaking hands and listening intently to the concerns of locals. It was the kind of interaction he relished—an opportunity to connect directly with the people of Norland.

Before long, Beau was escorted to a makeshift stage to address the crowd, the crisp mountain air swirling around him. His speech was billed as the main event of the day, but for Beau, it was never just about the words—it was about forging a deeper connection with the people he was honoured to serve.

"Good morning, and thank you for welcoming me to your beautiful town," Beau began. His gloved hands rested lightly on the edges of the podium draped in the vibrant orange of his party, a bold beacon against the snowy backdrop. Sylvie and Quinn stood like sentinels on either side of him, their sharp gazes scanning the gathered crowd. The audience, bundled in coats and scarves, leaned in closer.

"It's places like this—small but vibrant, filled with hardworking, resilient people—that remind me why I chose public service. Every handshake, every conversation here today has reaffirmed what I already know: the people of Norland deserve a government that works for them, not for the privileged few." Beau straightened, his gloved hand lifting briefly to gesture toward the crowd, a small but deliberate movement that emphasized his words.

"For far too long," he continued, his tone sharpening with conviction and sincerity, "corporations in our country have reaped the benefits of our labour, our resources, and our communities without giving back their fair share. It's time to turn the page on this narrative. Under our proposed reforms, no company—no matter how powerful —will escape their responsibility to pay taxes that reflect the wealth they've generated on Norlandic soil. This isn't just about fairness; it's about ensuring we have the resources to fund healthcare, education, and infrastructure for every citizen, in every corner of our great nation."

Beau paused as a wave of applause rippled through the crowd, their cheers growing in strength as he let the words settle. His gaze swept across the faces before him, his blue eyes warm yet steadfast, connecting with individuals as if each was the sole recipient of his attention.

"I've spoken with workers who've endured years of stagnant wages while CEOs reward themselves for record profits," he said, his voice carrying both steel and empathy. "That is not the Norland we believe in. A living wage is not a luxury—it's a basic right. My government will pass legislation guaranteeing that every worker can meet their needs and build a future without working three jobs or falling behind."

He paused again, letting the truth of his words resonate, then took a step back from the podium, his hands clasped lightly in front of him. The crowd edged closer, their faces lit with hope and resolve. Beau's gaze lingered on them for a beat longer before he leaned forward once more.

"And let me say this: the sharing economy has had its moment of unchecked growth. It has thrived on the backs of workers, exploiting their labour under the guise of flexibility. That ends here. We will ensure gig workers are protected by labour laws, paid a fair wage, and given the same rights as any other employee. In Norland, work will always be valued, and workers will always be respected." A cheer erupted, loud and sustained, as Beau allowed a faint smile to grace his features. He cast his eyes out toward the horizon briefly, the sharp blue of his gaze almost mirroring the winter sky above, before turning back to the crowd with renewed focus.

"Together," he said, his voice firm and filled with optimism, "we can build a Norland where opportunity is abundant, and prosperity is shared—not hoarded by the elite. Let's make this vision a reality, one step, one vote, one reform at a time. Thank you."

The crowd roared its approval, the sound reverberating through the snow-dusted streets of the mountain town. Beau stepped back from the podium, taking a final, sweeping look at the sea of faces before him. Behind him, Sylvie and Quinn stood vigilant, their steady presence a reminder of the moment's significance and the lingering shadow of Greyson's attack that had brought Beau here. Yet, the glimmer of pride on their faces spoke volumes, quietly affirming their support for the man they were sworn to protect. As Beau descended the stage to mingle with the crowd, the hopeful energy in the air felt almost tangible—a powerful testament to the vision he had boldly shared.

When Beau returned to the modest motel in the early afternoon, a wave of exhaustion settled over him. The energy he poured into these rallies, combined with the relentless whirlwind of travel and campaigning, had taken its toll. All he wanted was a hot shower and a few hours of quiet before the next wave of preparation and planning began.

As Sylvie and Quinn swept his motel room prior to him entering, Delphine appeared from her room – conveniently the one next to his own. With her presence, Beau felt the promise of an early night and recharge before the next leg of the journey to Port Rainier evaporate.

"It's all clear," Quinn reported gruffly, her eyes tracking Delphine's movements as she sauntered over to Beau.

"I have a surprise for you," Delphine purred, intercepting Beau's movements toward his room. Her voice dripped with the practiced charm that had once captivated him, her expression painted with a flirtatious, cloying grin.

"What is it?" he asked, irritation seeping into his tone as the idea of another FaceTime with Merritt crossed his mind. Frustration tightened in his chest as he felt himself yanked back into Delphine's calculated attempts to draw him back in.

She opened the door to her room. As the door swung inward, he was greeted by a chorus of cheerful voices. His three children stood inside, their excitement palpable, while Delphine's parents, Philippe and Charlotte, lingered nearby, smiling warmly as they watched the reunion unfold.

"Daddy!" Juliette exclaimed, her small frame darting toward him with unrestrained joy. She reached him first, throwing herself into his arms. Beau knelt to catch her, holding her tightly before rising to embrace his sons in turn, pulling them close and ruffling their hair in the way he knew they probably didn't love, but would accept after their long absence.

"I'm so happy to see you guys," he said, his voice thick with emotion. The unexpected sight of his children, their bright faces filled with love and excitement, was enough to overwhelm him.

Turning to Philippe and Charlotte, Beau offered a heartfelt nod. "Merci," he said, his gratitude plain in both his voice and his expression. Throughout his marriage to Delphine, her parents had been a steadfast presence, stepping in to help whenever needed. Even after his split from Delphine, their warm relationship endured, a rare constant in the shifting sands of his personal life.

The afternoon unfolded in a warm blur of family time. Philippe and Charlotte, ever considerate, retreated to their own room, leaving Beau, Delphine, and the children to themselves. The laughter of his kids filled the modest motel room, momentarily lifting the weight of his campaign and the gravity of his ambitions. They played card games on the threadbare carpet, their voices animated as they shared stories, each child eager to update their father on the moments he had missed since hitting the road. It felt like a window into a simpler life—the kind Beau had always dreamed of giving his children, full of ease, connection, and togetherness.

Delphine stayed close to him throughout, leaning into him whenever she could, her touch deliberate. At first, Beau ignored her gestures, focusing solely on his children. But as the hours wore on and he became immersed in their laughter, their stories, and the simple joy of being surrounded by family, his resolve wavered.

There was something achingly comforting in the familiarity of it all—a glimpse of the life his children had once known and a part of him desperately wanted to restore. He couldn't love Delphine again—he knew that with unshakable certainty—but the pull of giving his kids their family back tugged at him harder than anything else. Even the thought of Merritt, whose words and presence had lingered at the edge of his mind, seemed to fade beneath this consuming familiarity. If sacrificing his own desires could give his children that sense of wholeness, he wasn't sure he had the strength to resist.

As the afternoon softened into dusk and gave way to evening, Delphine rose gracefully from her perch at the foot of her motel bed. Clasping her hands together with a practiced air, she addressed their children. "Okay," she began, her tone light and sweet, "maybe you could all head next door for a bit and give your dad and me some time to talk?" She smiled warmly at Beau, who remained seated on the sagging motel loveseat, his expression neutral.

"Can we watch TV?" Juliette asked, her excitement lighting up her face.

"Yes, of course, my angel," Delphine replied, her voice dripping with affection as she reached into her pocket and handed Bastien the spare key to Beau's room – a key Beau didn't realize she possessed.

Beau rose, his movements deliberate as he embraced each of his children in turn. "I'll come over in a bit," he said.

Then, turning to Bastien, he added, "Could you call down and check if they have any cots? It looks like you and Émile might be in for an uncomfortable night." He chuckled as Bastien nodded. "Don't worry, the beds aren't any better," he promised.

Once they'd filed out, he stood in the doorway, watching as they crossed into his room. He waited until the door closed behind them and the faint sound of the deadbolt clicking into place reached his ears, reassuring him that they were safe.

When Beau turned back, Delphine had already settled herself on the couch. She sat with her legs tucked neatly beneath her, exuding an air of casual intimacy. Two small bottles of vodka, liberated from the motel's modest attempt at a minibar, sat on the rickety coffee table in front of her. She picked one up, twisting off the cap with ease as she held it up in a toast.

"Come, my love," she said, gesturing to the empty space beside her. Her smile was inviting, her tone carrying the unmistakable edge of expectation. "Join me."

Beau hesitated briefly but lowered himself onto the couch beside her. Delphine handed him the second bottle of vodka, cracking it open with a deft twist of her wrist before passing it to him. "Cheers to our babies," she said, clinking her bottle against his. The motion brought her closer, her free hand landing on his thigh—high and unmistakably intimate. "They're the best things we've ever done," she proclaimed, her voice carrying a note of wistful pride as her hand began to trace slow, lazy lengths up and down.

Beau glanced down at her hand, his jaw tightening as he resisted the instinct to push her away. Instead, he raised the bottle to his lips and took a long gulp, the sharp burn of vodka anchoring him. Despite everything else, the truth of her words struck a chord. They had created three remarkable humans together—something he could never deny, no matter how far apart they had drifted. He nodded slowly, his gaze distant as he focused on the thought of family rather than the hand creeping along his thigh.

"What are you thinking?" Delphine asked, her voice soft with suggestion. She tipped back her bottle of vodka, finishing it in one long, unbroken swig before setting the empty bottle on the coffee table. Turning toward Beau, she kept her hand firmly on his thigh while the other slid behind him, her fingers weaving gently through the short hairs at the nape of his neck.

Beau followed suit, draining the last of his vodka in a single gulp, letting the warmth spread through his chest and limbs. "I don't think you really want to know," he replied, his tone low.

Delphine's lips curved into a knowing smile, her voice dipping into a sultry register. "After all these years, my love, you are no mystery to me. I know exactly what you're thinking." Her hand left his thigh, moving with deliberate precision to undo the buttons of his crisp white shirt. Her fingers grazed his skin as she slid her hand inside, stroking him lightly. She shifted closer, lifting herself and draping her legs over his, settling into his lap with practiced ease. Her golden hair tumbled over one shoulder as she unbuttoned his shirt completely and pushed it open, her touch as familiar as it was intimate.

Without thinking, Beau's body responded, His hands moved instinctively to the backs of her thighs, sliding upward to caress the familiar curve of her hips under her skirt, his fingers pressing into the soft, supple flesh he knew so well. His fingers explored the contours of her body, reacquainting themselves with a form he had once known better than his own.

Delphine sighed softly, her breath warm against his skin as she leaned down and pressed her lips to his.

Beau didn't resist. He accepted the kiss, warm and inviting, a touch he had once cherished and now found himself relishing it once more.

Their lips met again with an intensity that quickly deepened, the kiss turning almost rough as Delphine's urgency seemed to grow. She pulled away, her breath hot against his skin as she began tracing a trail of soft, lingering kisses down his neck, across his collarbone, and lower onto his chest. Her fingers worked deftly as her mouth moved over him, unbuckling his belt and slipping open the button of his pants with ease.

She shifted, slipping gracefully from his lap to kneel before him, her movements deliberate and charged with intent. Her hands glided over the taut planes of his body, her fingers toying with the waistband of his pants, teasing at the edge of what she was about to offer. Just as she began to ease them lower, Beau's hands caught her forearms, halting her with a firm yet trembling grip.

"Let's slow down," Beau panted, his voice uneven as he struggled to steady his breath. His eyes searched hers, his expression a raw mix of conflicted desire and restraint.

Delphine's face faltered, a flicker of sadness crossing her features at his refusal. But she quickly collected herself, rising to her feet and smoothing down her skirt as Beau buttoned his pants, willing his breathing to return to normal. Turning to him, she softened her tone. "I know I hurt you," she said gently. "I'm sorry for that, my love." She leaned in, her face close to his, and attempted to kiss him.

The gesture only sharpened the memory of the pain she had inflicted on him and their family. Beau turned his head away, the rejection firm but calm.

Delphine pulled back, her expression hardening into one of indignation. "We could be so much stronger than we were," she said sharply. Then, with a bitter tone, she added, "And you can't pretend these last five years weren't your fault too."

Beau froze, her words landing like a physical blow. "five years?" he asked, his voice tentative, barely above a whisper. For Beau, Delphine's affair had been enough to end their marriage. He never dwelt on it. Instead, he buried himself in his children and his career. Was Delphine now saying the affair had been going on for five years? Had he been that blind? Could she really be that cruel?

Delphine, completely missing the pained confusion behind his reaction, barreled forward. "Everything was about you," she protested. "You ignored me, Beau."

"Five years?" Beau repeated, his voice now firmer, the shock giving way to anger. He rose abruptly from the couch, striding away from her as he began buttoning his shirt, tucking it back into his pants with clipped, precise movements.

Beau could see Delphine's mind racing behind her eyes as she caught up with what he was saying. Realizing her mistake, her tone shifted instantly to one of pleading. "My love," she began, her voice trembling, "I was just so lost."

Beau turned to face her, his hand rising to his forehead as if to steady his spinning thoughts. "What are you saying to me right now?" he demanded. "This was going on that long?" His voice cracked slightly as his mind raced, filling with scenes of their life together. The smiles that had never reached her eyes. The growing distance he had chalked up to the natural ebb of familiarity. The unexplained absences he had ignored.

A memory surfaced with painful clarity: Delphine, years ago, animatedly describing a sweet sixteen party she was planning for the youngest daughter of a billionaire client whose name she couldn't divulge. It was during his early days as Minister of Finance. Was that when this had all begun?

Delphine stammered, realizing the full weight of her words, and the truth began to spill from her in halting fragments. She confessed how the affair had begun in earnest almost immediately. The proposal, she admitted with a trembling voice, had come months before Beau had even begun to suspect her betrayal. Every detail unraveled the picture of the marriage Beau thought he had. Even the moments he had believed were real were painted in the shadows of her infidelity.

Delphine stepped toward him again, her hand outstretched, Beau gently pushed her back—not with anger, but with a quiet, final resolve. "I can't," he said simply, his voice heavy with truth. He turned away from her, a feeling of deep regret over the intimacy they had shared settling in him.

"I'm going next door," he said, his back to her as he moved toward the door.

Delphine made to follow him, but Beau turned sharply, his gaze hard. "You stay here," he said.

Without waiting for her response, Beau opened the door and stepped into the cold mountain air, its sharp bite cutting through him with a ferocity that matched the turmoil within. The chill wrapped around him, almost welcome in its harshness, a distraction from the storm raging in his chest. The door slammed shut behind him with a decisive finality. Swiping at the tears gathering in his eyes, he drew a deep, steadying breath, willing himself back into composure. With measured steps, he made his way toward the motel room where his children waited, their presence the only refuge he could trust in this moment.

At this late hour, Juliette and Émile had already drifted off. Juliette lay sprawled in the middle of the queen-sized bed, her small form tucked under a thick blanket, while

Émile rested peacefully on one of the two cots set up for the boys. Bastien, was perched on the small, threadbare couch, the television glowing softly in the dim room. The volume was low, just enough to hear, but it didn't disturb the stillness. He looked up at his dad as he entered the room.

Beau nodded, sinking down beside his son, his heartbreak a heavy weight he struggled to swallow. As he glanced at the screen, he realized Bastien was watching campaign highlights. The familiar footage played on one of the many 24-hour news channels— clips of Beau shaking hands, giving speeches, and meeting the people he hoped to serve. The pride in Bastien's expression, even in the quiet of the moment, was unmistakable, and it made Beau's chest tighten.

Beau leaned back into the couch, his shoulder brushing against Bastien's as the glow of the screen cast fleeting shadows across the room. The pride in his son's voice, though quiet, was unmistakable.

"I'm proud of you, Dad," Bastien said softly, his eyes fixed on the screen. "This whole thing—it's a lot, but it's like... you're actually making a difference."

The words settled between them, carrying a weight Beau hadn't realized he needed to hear.

"I hope so," Beau replied, his voice laced with humility. "And I appreciate you saying that." He nodded to his son, and they fell into a companionable silence, Bastien continuing to watch the news coverage while Beau's thoughts turned inward.

When he had first entered politics, he worked to ensure every single step he took had been a family decision. They had discussed the sacrifices they would all need to make, the shifts in their lives, and the direction he was heading. Even the remote possibility of taking on the leadership of the country had been put on the table, though back then, it had seemed distant and unlikely. Back then, they had faced these choices together, strong, united and as a family.

But when the actual decision came—when Greyson asked him to take over leadership of the Progressive Alliance just before a national election—Beau had made the choice alone. He hadn't sat his children down, hadn't given them the space to share their thoughts, even though he knew what it would mean for him and for them. He understood the weight it would add to their lives, thrusting them even deeper into the public eye than Delphine's affair already had.

He knew, too, that not even Eleanor's PR prowess could shield them entirely from the scrutiny that came with holding the country's top office.

Reflecting on this, a pit of guilt knotted in his stomach as he turned to look at Bastien.

"I know you didn't choose this," Beau began, his voice hushed but steady with purpose. He reached for the remote on the coffee table and clicked the TV off, plunging the room into a reflective stillness. "I should have talked to you all about it," he said, his words measured, carrying the weight of his regret. "I'm sorry, Bas."

For a moment, Bastien didn't respond. He pressed his lips together, his gaze fixed on the blank television screen. Finally, he spoke, "It's okay, Dad. We know why you're doing it." He paused, his voice resolute as he added, "You've taught us to stand for something, and you're standing for what you believe in. I think it's cool."

The words landed with great force, reverberating through Beau like the echo of something greater. His son's maturity, his ability to see past the surface and understand the deeper reasons behind Beau's choices, struck him anew. Beau swallowed hard, pride mingling with a bittersweet ache as he realized just how much Bastien had grown—how much he had shouldered in the wake of their family's upheavals.

He could think of nothing to say to his son and only nodded.

"Does all the pressure... the campaign... and everything, make you think about getting back together with Mom?" Bastien asked, his voice halting, the hesitation betraying his discomfort even as he forced the words out.

Beau worked to keep his expression calm, his nod slow and measured as he absorbed the weight of the question. He didn't want to shut his son down, didn't want to send the message that some thoughts were too messy or unwelcome to share. "Do you think about us getting back together?" he asked, his voice soft and hesitant.

Bastien was quiet for a long moment, his eyes fixed on the floor as if searching for an answer there. "I know that's what Mom wants," he said at last, his tone deliberate, each word carefully chosen. The statement hung in the air, stark and undeniable.

Beau sat with the words, letting them settle as his mind wandered to what it might mean for his children to see their family whole again. The thought tugged at him, bittersweet and heavy, a distant dream that now felt suffocating. He could picture the easy smiles of holidays past, the unbroken rhythms of shared routines—but beneath the surface, he couldn't ignore the cracks that had long been there, fractures that had widened into deep crevices and craters, carved by betrayal and lies too vast to mend.

Bastien's voice broke the silence, firmer now, pulling Beau from his thoughts. "But I don't think you should," he said, his gaze lifting to meet his father's. "You deserve more than going back to something that hurt you... and us. Just because it's easier doesn't mean it's right."

The raw honesty of his son's words sliced through the stillness. Beau's chest tightened, a mix of pride and heartbreak swelling within him as he realized how deeply his son understood not just the situation, but the man sitting beside him.

"I don't think I can do it," Beau confessed, his voice heavy with emotion. "And I am so sorry you all got hurt in this. None of this was what I wanted, and I know it's not what your mom wanted either." He rested his head in his hands as he spoke, his fingers pressing against his temple.

The room fell into a stillness once more, the kind that felt almost alive with words that didn't need to be said. Then, quietly but firmly, Bastien reached out and placed his hand on his father's shoulder. "It's okay, Dad," he said, his voice steady, carrying more reassurance than Beau felt he deserved.

Beau turned toward his son, his throat tightening, and pulled him into a firm, protective hug. The gesture said what words couldn't.

Beau pulled away, glancing at his watch. "We better get to bed," he said, his voice softer now. "We've got an early start tomorrow. You take the bed—if Juels left you any room. I'll take the other cot."

"You sure?" Bastien asked, a small smile tugging at his lips. "I wouldn't want you to break your old-man back on that thing."

The joke hung in the air for a moment, a welcome touch of levity piercing through the weight of the night. Beau chuckled, ruffling his son's hair with affection. "I'll take my chances," he said, grateful for the reprieve from the heaviness that had filled the room, this night and so much of their lives over the last year.

Beau watched as Bastien climbed into bed next to Juliette, carefully wrestling the blankets from her without waking her. "Goodnight, Dad," Bastien said softly. "Love you."

Beau couldn't help but smile, the words filling the room with a warmth that lingered. "Love you too," he replied. Turning away, he sank onto the lumpy and uncomfortable cot, his hands instinctively reaching for his phone.

Chapter 23
André ~ The Pressure Builds

André adjusted his seat in the unremarkable sedan parked half a block from Merritt's townhouse. The winter air fogged the windshield slightly, and he rubbed it clean with his sleeve, ensuring his view remained clear. Six weeks. That's how long it had been since he'd seen Beau Laurent and Merritt Clarke, and yet here he was, still tasked with keeping tabs on her. He didn't mind the work—it was clean, quiet, and well-paid. The orders had been clear: keep checking in. And now, with the latest developments, his instructions had become more specific, returning to constant surveillance.

A leak from someone in Beau's life—someone, easily pressured—had brought Merritt back into focus. She wasn't just Beau's ex anymore; she was a potential vulnerability, someone whose proximity to him could still be exploited. André didn't know the full scope of the plan; he never did. That wasn't how this worked. But the whispers were enough: Beau's enemies wanted to know if Merritt suspected anything, if she had any inkling of the threads being pulled in the background, and where she was at all times, of course.

Through the windshield, he took in Merritt's home, she had not left for work at her usual time. Instead, she was still inside. He could see through the large bay window that she was perched on her couch, a paperback in her hands.

She didn't look like someone who knew anything—no furtive glances, no nervous energy. She seemed as normal as anyone else on the street. But that was the problem, wasn't it? André knew from experience that the quiet ones often surprised you. She could be sitting on something valuable and not even realize it.

André exhaled, his breath clouding in the cold car. He had no intention of engaging her, not unless it became necessary. For now, he would follow orders, stay in the shadows, and monitor her movements. He couldn't help but wonder: did she have any idea of the storm gathering around her?

Chapter 24
Merritt ~ The Surrender

Merritt ended the call with Beau. Her heart was still racing —not just from the effortless flow of their conversation or the undeniable pull of attraction. It was the interruption that lingered in her mind, the unmistakable voice calling out to him in the background, cutting their connection short and forcing Beau's abrupt goodbye.

Merritt froze as the realization dawned. She knew that voice. She'd heard it countless times in taped depositions and brief, scandal-laden tabloid news clips, layered with charm and controversy. Delphine Moreau.

The pieces slid into place with startling clarity. Delphine, the elegant, magnetic figure at the centre of one of the most salacious cases Merritt had handled in years—the very same Delphine who had been married to Beau. She leaned against the counter, her breath catching as the implications settled over her.

Had they reconciled? Was Delphine simply visiting? Or was she still entangled in Beau's life in ways Merritt didn't want to imagine, but was right now imagining? Rationally, she reminded herself that Beau had every right to move on, or move back, in this case. After all, their connection had been brief, and she had severed it abruptly, cloaking her retreat in the guise of professionalism while hiding her true motive: self-protection.

Merritt had never revealed to Beau that she had been married, nor the truth about the abrupt ending to her marriage, a love affair that had consumed her completely but left her grasping at fragments when it was torn away without an ending at all. Beau hadn't pressed her for answers, his practiced grace offering her the space to open up on her own terms.

Beau, too, had shared only the broadest strokes about the end of his marriage, leaving Merritt to piece together the intimate details she already knew from the divorce proceedings of her own client—documents filled with private revelations she had studied carefully. They painted a picture of betrayal so deep and cutting that Merritt had felt heartbroken for Beau even as their paths trailed off in separateness over the long weeks.

Now, knowing Delphine was still present in his life, and reflecting on the recent reconciliation between her own client and his estranged wife, that heartbreak twisted into something sharper—a tangled mix of uncertainty and jealousy settled uncomfortably in her stomach along with linger nausea.

Merritt spent the rest of the day adrift, her thoughts circling back to Beau with maddening regularity. The call that had ended too soon, Delphine's unmistakable voice in the background—it all clung to her, weaving doubt and unease into her thoughts. She told herself not to overthink it, to focus on the quiet of her day, but even as she sipped yet another cup of coffee and took the opportunity of a sick day to flip absentmindedly through a novel, her mind kept pulling her back to him.

Merritt had watched Beau's speech live on the news that afternoon, perched on the edge of her couch with Sophie at her side, her heart skipping as his face filled the screen. He was captivating as always, his words stirring and commanding, but she couldn't help searching the broadcast for signs of Delphine—wondering if she lingered somewhere just out of frame. It wasn't logical, and she hated the spiral of uncertainty it sent her into, but the feeling was impossible to ignore.

After the speech ended, Merritt texted him, her fingers moving quickly over the keyboard before she could second-guess herself. She thought back to Beau's words about not holding back, about doing what felt right, and let those words guide her as she hit send.

You were magnetic out there today, Beau. Those eyes could win voters on their own—but I'm glad they're focused on bigger things. I'm proud of you.

As the message fluttered off into the void of cyberspace, Merritt felt nothing but uncertainty. She wondered if the flirtatious edge of her words would be lost on him now, especially if he was truly entangled once again in the long history he shared with Delphine. The thought settled uneasily in her chest, her growing conviction about their renewed closeness twisting itself into something sharp and stabbing into her guts.

Merritt's day dragged on. Again and again, she reached for her phone, hoping against hope to see a notification, a reply that would soothe the restless ache inside her. But each time, her recent message stared back at her, unchanging, its words taunting her with the small, damning 'delivered' nestled beneath.

As the minutes stretched into hours, even the pull of the novel she'd been reading couldn't hold Merritt's attention. Her body still felt sluggish, weighed down by the lingering effects of her hangover—an affliction that, in her twenties, would have faded by midmorning, but now, in her forties, had settled in to knock her flat for what felt like would be the rest of her life. Productivity felt out of reach, taking with it the welcome distraction of work. With no reprieve revealing itself, the ache of Beau's silence gnawed at her.

Sighing, she clicked over to the years-long text thread with Avery, scrolling through the exchange that, until recently, had been a lifeline of wit and reassurance. There was nothing new there – still no word from Avery.

The hours ticked by.

As the day stretched into evening and finally gave way to night, Merritt found herself binging a television series set against the backdrop of lush forests and breathtaking landscapes. The fictional small town was nestled near a stunning river in the heart of Cascadia, but to Merritt, the wild beauty on the screen was unmistakable—it was the same rugged terrain where she had grown up. The familiar sights stirred memories of her childhood, and the nostalgia wrapped around her like a fuzzy blanket. For a little while, as the hours slipped by, the show and her own recollections worked together to distract her restless mind.

As the first season of the show came to an end, Merritt was relieved to find it was finally an acceptable hour to call it a night. She let Sophie out into the yard for one last lap, watching as the dog completed her evening business. When Sophie returned, shaking off the cool night air, they climbed the stairs together.

Merritt slipped into bed, letting the layers of deep green linen envelop her. She lay on her back, willing her mind to quiet, but as soon as she closed her eyes, Beau's face appeared, vivid and unrelenting. His warm blue eyes, the curve of his boyish smile, the way he looked at her as if she were the only thing in his world—it all came rushing back. She flung her eyes open, her chest rising and falling with heavy breaths, trying to dispel the memory.

Turning onto her side, she shut her eyes again, but there he was, just as clear—this time smiling at her, a ghost of the passion they had shared lingering on her skin as she forced her eyes open. She groaned in frustration, rolling to her other side, only to find no escape there either. Every time she closed her eyes, she could see him, hear his voice, feel the warmth of him as if he were right there with her. His scent lingered in her imagination, intoxicating and inescapable. She let out a heavy sigh, realizing that no amount of shifting or deep breathing was going to free her from his presence in her mind.

"I can't take this," Merritt growled, her linen sheet balled tightly in her fists as she stared up at the ceiling, her frustration bubbling over. She flung her quilt aside and sat up abruptly, pausing to rest her head in her hands, her palms pressing against her temples, willing her thoughts to stop spinning. After a moment, she pushed herself to her feet.

Moving with purpose, she changed into her running gear. Sophie padded excitedly at her heels, her tail wagging in anticipation, fully aware of what this change in attire meant. Running had always been Merritt's refuge, her way of quieting the noise in her mind, and tonight, she desperately needed it to work.

They stepped out onto the empty sidewalk, their breaths rising in visible clouds of warmth against the cold. The streetlights cast soft pools of light on their path, the stillness of the night giving way to early morning hours wrapping around them. Merritt's pace quickened as Sophie trotted happily at her side, her paws clicking rhythmically against the pavement.

But as their route began to take shape, Merritt's stomach twisted. They were retracing the same path she'd walked with Beau weeks ago on New Year's Day. The memory of that day flooded back, unbidden, bringing with it the ache she'd been trying to run from.

"Fuck!" she shouted, the word slicing through the quiet as it burst from her lips—sharp, furious, and loud enough to cut over the Taylor Swift song pulsing in her earbuds. She yanked one out in frustration, her chest heaving as she came to a stop. Even her run—one of the few sacred things she still had—was betraying her.

As Merritt struggled to catch her breath, her indecision cracked. She couldn't take it anymore. A quick glance at her watch told her it would be deep into the evening where Beau was—late, but not unforgivably so. Her fingers hovered over his name, heart pounding, and before she could talk herself out of it, she tapped call. No more overthinking. No more silence. Ripping off the bandage—hearing him say there was no space left for her—seemed less cruel than the limbo she'd been stuck in all day.

The line rang, each ring stretching her nerves tighter.

A flicker of relief began to creep in as she convinced herself he wouldn't answer. Maybe she didn't want to know after all. But then, unbidden, an image flashed in her mind—Delphine's golden hair cascading over Beau's chest, her head nestled against him in the intimacy of their afterglow as their breaths evened out, their faces tilted toward one another. The thought twisted in her chest, and she silently willed Beau to pick up, if only to put her out of her misery.

Just as she was about to hang up, the line clicked over.

"Merritt?" Beau whispered, his voice thick with sleep.

"I..." she began, shifting her weight from foot to foot, suddenly at a loss for words. The resolve that had driven her to make the call dissolved.

She heard movement on the other end—a rustle of fabric, the soft creak of a door, and then the whistle of wind as Beau stepped outside. "Merritt, what is it?" His tone seemed to hold a faint edge of exasperation, and it pierced through her, leaving her feeling foolish.

"I'm sorry," she blurted out, her words tumbling awkwardly. "I just... I needed to ask you something," she stammered, the urgency of the moment faltering under her insecurities and fear.

Beau sighed, the sound quiet but unmistakable. Merritt had spent the entire day imagining herself standing in the shadow of Delphine's perfection, picturing Beau gratefully pulling his ex-wife into his arms, relishing her beauty and familiarity. The sigh hit her like a confirmation of all her fears—frustration, annoyance, the desire to humour her for the sake of closure. Tears welled in her eyes, unbidden, and she couldn't stop them from spilling over. Sophie looked up at her, concern in her posture.

"What is it?" Beau's voice came again, soft with concern. "Are you okay? What's happened?"

The gentleness in his tone cut through her spiraling thoughts, but it only made the ache in her chest deepen. Merritt wiped at her cheeks, struggling and failing to pull herself together. The words she had wanted to say now felt impossibly far away.

"I need to know," Merritt sniffed, her voice trembling, too unmoored in her thoughts to care how she sounded. The tears were audible now, accompanied by ragged sniffles she couldn't hold back. She sank to the pavement, Sophie pressing close to her side as her words dissolved into uncontrollable sobs.

The line stayed silent, save for Merritt's heavy crying and Beau's measured, steady breathing. She could picture him on the other end, perhaps wearing an impatient expression, waiting for her to compose herself or say something coherent. The thought made her cheeks burn with shame. She sniffled hard, forcing herself to steady her breath.

"I'm sorry," she choked out, her voice small and uneven. "I should go." She pulled the phone away from her ear, her thumb hovering over the screen to end the call, when she faintly heard Beau's muffled voice coming through the line.

Her breath caught, hitching in her throat amidst her uneven, hiccupping sobs. She quickly brought the phone back to her ear, wiping at her wet cheeks before they could freeze against her skin. "What was that?" she asked, her voice thick as she sniffed again, trying to make sense of what she'd just heard.

"Are you ending this?" Beau asked, his voice tinged with something Merritt couldn't quite place. "Are you ending this, again?" he repeated, more firmly this time.

Merritt's hiccupping sobs stopped abruptly, replaced by a sniff as her mind reeled in confusion. How could he think that. "No," she said quickly. "Are you?" But then, as her thoughts scrambled to catch up to his words, a new wave of uncertainty washed over her. "Wait... is there a this?" she asked, her voice trembling with vulnerability.

"Isn't there?" Beau questioned.

"That's what I was calling to ask you," she confessed, the words spilling out clumsily. Everything she had been building up in her mind all day—the fears, the hopes, the insecurities—came tumbling out in a rush. She confessed her understanding that she had no right to want something with him after how abruptly she had ended things before, but admitted she couldn't help hoping there was still something between them. She voiced her fear of him rekindling things with Delphine, of being left behind and knowing that his was a life she had no place in.

The words poured out in an unbroken stream, her voice rising and falling with the weight of her emotions. When she finally stopped, realizing she had been speaking for more than ten minutes without pause, she bit her lip and waited for his response. The cool night air pressed against her skin as she shivered, her breath visible in faint clouds as she held her phone tightly to her ear.

Silence stretched, long and heavy, and Merritt began to wonder if Beau was still on the line. She was about to speak again when his voice finally broke through the weight of all she had said.

"Merritt," the way he said her name gave it a weight that sent a shiver through her. "I don't know what to say to all of that. I don't... I don't even know where to start." Another pause, filled only by the sound of the wind whistling faintly.

"I've thought about you every day since you walked out of that café," Beau said at last, his voice low, and Merritt's heart thudded hard in her chest. "I can even picture the way you looked in that skirt," he added, his tone softening into a wistfulness that sent a jolt through her.

"I hate that day," she said suddenly, the words tumbling out before she could stop herself. "What a stupid day."

Beau chuckled softly, the sound warm in the lingering cold of winter's end. "I respect you," he said after a beat. "I respected that you wanted to focus on your career. I don't hate that day. It hurt, yeah, but it told me something important about you—that you care about your work, about what you're doing. I get that, and it's sexy as hell."

His voice shifted, a raw edge creeping in as he exhaled. "But fuck, Merritt." The curse hit her like a lightning bolt, carrying a weight she hadn't anticipated, sending fizzles of electricity coursing through her as she pushed herself up from the cold pavement. "I want you," he said, the words stark and clear. "I'm scared—of you, of this, of what it could mean. But I want this. I want you."

There was a pause, thick with unspoken emotion, and Merritt, completely overwhelmed, found herself utterly unable to fill the silence.

"Delphine is here," Beau said finally, the confession breaking the silence.

"It's not what you think... and I suppose it's not what she thinks either." He inhaled deeply, the sound heavy with regret. "We kissed," he admitted. Merritt's breath hitched audibly, and he caught it. "I'm sorry. It was—" He paused, struggling for the right words. "I've been trying to keep the pieces of my family together, for the kids. I thought maybe she was the way to do that. But it's not. She's not. I'm sorry," he repeated, his voice quieter now, carrying a weight that pressed against Merritt's chest.

Merritt swallowed hard, her throat tightening, locking the words she wanted to say somewhere deep inside her. Beau's confession struck her like a blow to the chest, leaving her breathless and her feet rooted to the cold pavement under the glow of the streetlight. Sophie tugged gently at her leash, but Merritt couldn't move. She couldn't speak.

"Merritt, say something," Beau pleaded, his voice raw and desperate. "Please tell me I haven't messed this up."

Her grip on the phone tightened, his words reverberating in her mind. *This.* That small, unassuming word, carrying the weight of everything she wanted.

He'd kissed Delphine—of course he had. She was the mother of his children, and the idea of keeping his family intact was a powerful one, impossible to fault, especially when Merritt and Beau hadn't been together for over a month. But then there was *this*!

He was tangled in a life she could never fully step into, a life filled with memories and history she couldn't compete with. But still, there was *this*—a possibility, a pull that refused to let go, asking her to believe in something that had felt impossible just hours before. The weight of *this* was immense, and it left her unable to speak.

The silence stretched until Beau spoke again, his voice hesitant but resolute. "What if you came here?" he asked. "Not here—I mean, we're leaving in the morning. But what if you came to Port Rainier?"

Merritt blinked, her heart stumbling over itself. "Do you want that?" she whispered, finally finding her voice, the words trembling on the edge of her lips.

"It's scary how much I want that," Beau replied, his voice low, breathy, and laced with something that sent a shiver through her. "I want to be with you. I would come to you if I could."

Her mind flooded with reasons not to go. The messiness of it all, the practicality of a last-minute trip, the vulnerability of stepping into something so uncertain. But beneath all that noise was the undeniable truth: she wanted to see him. She wanted *this*—whatever *this* was.

"Okay," she said softly, her voice matching the yearning in his. "Okay," she repeated, firmer this time, as if anchoring herself in the decision.

A relieved sigh came through the line, and Merritt could feel the tension in her chest begin to ease. "Okay," Beau echoed, the warmth in his voice wrapping around her. "I'll see you soon. Text me your flight details."

Then, just as the call was coming to an end, she heard him whisper: "please don't change your mind."

Merritt climbed to her feet and stood there for a moment, the cool night air biting at her cheeks, her phone still clutched in her hand. She looked down at Sophie, who gazed up at her expectantly, as though sensing something important had just happened. Merritt started walking again, her steps lighter, her breath steadier. The streetlights flickered softly overhead as the world seemed to stretch open, ready for whatever might come next.

Chapter 25
Beau ~ The Lightness Returns

Beau lay restless on the lumpy motel cot, the thin blanket twisted around his legs as he shifted for what felt like the hundredth time. No matter how heavy his limbs were, sleep refused to come. Every time he rolled over, his thoughts drifted to Merritt—her laugh, her smile, the way her glasses had slipped askew when she looked up at him on New Year's Eve, and the sound of her voice on the other end of the line that morning.

Finally, with a quiet sigh, he gave up and reached for his phone on the nightstand. It was the first time he'd touched it since their FaceTime call—somehow, through the whirlwind of his morning speech, the buzz of press, his children's arrival, and Delphine's slow, deliberate campaign to reinsert herself into his life, the rest of the world had simply fallen away.

The screen lit up in his palm.

A message from Merritt.

A slow, involuntary smile tugged at his lips. The feeling that surged through his chest was light, warm, uncomplicated—so starkly different from the sense of obligation and quiet resignation he'd felt when imagining what it might mean to let Delphine back in. Merritt wasn't a concession. She never had been.

He tapped the notification, eager to read her words.

You were magnetic out there today, Beau. Those eyes could win voters on their own—but I'm glad they're focused on bigger things. She had messaged after his speech, which meant she had been watching.

He stared at her words for a moment, savouring the feeling it stirred in him—a reminder of something brighter, something even more hopeful than his campaign. He began typing a response, his thumbs moving quickly over the keyboard, but hesitated. It was late across the country, and he hoped she was fast asleep, untouched by the weight of the day he had carried.

With a sigh, Beau deleted the draft and set his phone aside. He folded his legs and laid on his side on the cot, his head resting on a pillow that smelled slightly stale, with his hand folded beneath his head. His son's words lingered in his mind, wrapping around his heart and giving him the lightness he needed. For the first time in hours, his thoughts slowed, allowing stillness to settle over him, guiding him toward the solace of sleep.

In the stillness of the night, Beau's phone vibrated next to him, the sound faint but insistent. He reached for it quickly, careful not to wake his children. Merritt's name and her photo lit up the screen, and for a moment, he simply stared at it, his chest tightening.

"Merritt?" he said, his voice low as he stretched out the kinks that had taken root deep in his neck, shoulders, and back. The cot, as it turned out, was not the best idea after all.

Groaning softly, Beau managed to push himself to his feet, though the stiffness made it feel like a Herculean task. He moved quietly, crossing the room with measured steps before slipping out the door into the crisp night air, closing it gently behind him to keep the silence of the room intact.

Outside, the security detail had been pared down for the night—two pairs of NFC agents sitting in parked cars, their presence intentionally conspicuous. Beau offered them a wave, their sharp nods the only response as they maintained their watchful stances.

Spotting a white plastic lawn chair next to a snow-dusted ashtray, Beau lowered himself into it with a sigh. The stale stench of old cigarettes rose faintly as the snow's dampness seeped into the tray, making him recoil. He angled the chair slightly away, cradling the phone against his ear.

The moment he heard her voice, soft and unsure, hope began to slide sideways.

"I'm sorry," she said, and just like that, the floor beneath him cracked.

He leaned forward, one hand gripping his phone, the other pressed to his temple. His pulse roared in his ears. She was pulling away again—he could feel it.

"Merritt..." he managed, trying to stay calm, but his voice came out tighter than he meant. "Are you ending this? Again?"

There it was—the edge she must've heard. Not anger. Fear.

Because the truth was, he didn't think he could do it again —not with her. He'd already made peace with being alone. But she'd reminded him what it felt like to want more. To hope. And that made the idea of losing her feel worse than never having had her at all.

Then came her voice—quiet but certain.

"No. Are you?" She said tentatively.

His chest eased slightly. The ache didn't vanish, but it dulled just enough to let him breathe again.

She began slowly—tentative, halting—then the words spilled out in a rush. She told him how she'd spent the day spiralling, convinced he was slipping through her fingers, that he wanted to rebuild something familiar with Delphine. Her voice wavered as she poured out every fear that had gripped her, a confession tangled with apology. She kept saying she understood his pull to Delphine—that it made sense—and how she didn't have the right to ask for anything from him. She knew that.

Beau listened, every word wrapping around him like a thread—pulling tight, tugging at the place in him that still ached from missing her. It hurt to know he'd caused her pain with his silence today. But beneath that ache was something else: the quiet, breathtaking weight of her care. The way she opened her thoughts to him, how she admitted she'd cried over the last few weeks, how much she wanted to be with him—yet still let fear convince her to run. The DuPont divorce had just been the excuse. He heard it now, clear as anything: she hadn't stopped wanting him. She'd just been scared.

And then he told her about Delphine.

Not because he wanted to. Because he had to.

There had been a kiss, and more. Nothing had happened. But the moment had pressed in too close, and he knew it mattered. He told her everything, not hiding from the weight of it.

Then—silence.

Long, drawn out.

"Merritt," he said softly, the tremor in his voice betraying more than he wanted it to. "Say something. Please. Tell me I didn't ruin this."

Still nothing.

So he said the next thing that came to him—simple, impulsive, desperate.

"What if you came here?"

A beat. He'd started this conversation sure it was an ending, and now he feared with his carelessness with his ex-wife, he'd brought about the ending himself.

"Not here—we're leaving in the morning. But Port Rainier. Just for the weekend."

He closed his eyes, heart racing. This wasn't just about seeing her. It was about knowing she wanted to stay—if only a little longer.

When she said yes, the exhale he released was almost a laugh, full of disbelief.

"I'll see you soon," he said, the warmth threading back into his voice. "Text me your flight details."

Then quieter, like a prayer he didn't want her to hear: "Please don't change your mind."

The information came through almost impossibly fast, Merritt's swiftly arranged travel plans lighting up his screen. Beau stared at the message, his heart swelling at the thought of her eagerness.

Holding his phone to his chest, as if somehow Merritt might feel the gesture, he closed his eyes and let himself savour the moment. The cold night air bit at his skin, but it was nothing compared to the warmth radiating from within.

He didn't know how, but he knew he needed to be there—to meet her at the airport, to see her step off the plane. The thought sent a spark through him, breaking through the weariness of the night and filling him with a sense of hope.

He turned and walked back into the motel room, casting his eyes around to ensure his children were still peacefully asleep. Juliette remained sprawled across the bed, one hand clutching her stuffed rabbit, while Bastien lay beside her, his arm draped protectively over his sister. He had managed to reclaim much of his share of the blankets. Émile was curled up on the cot, his soft breaths steady and rhythmic, the blanket pulled tight up to his chin. The sight eased Beau's tensions and reservations, a sense of calm settling over him as he moved to his own cot. He sank down, the faint scent of the snow-dampened air clinging to his clothing as he folded his arms across his chest and leaned back. The silence of the room enveloped him, but his thoughts lingered on Merritt, on her impending arrival. For the first time in a long while, the path ahead didn't feel quite so heavy.

Chapter 26
Merritt ~ The Choice Made

Merritt managed only a few hours of restless sleep before it was time to start her day if she wanted to make her mid-morning flight. Though she felt slightly better than she had the morning before, her body still ached, weighed down by the remnants of too little rest. And yet, something pulled her forward—something waiting at the end of the nearly five-hour flight she dreaded. She would see Beau.

The thought was enough to propel her from bed and down the stairs to the coffee machine. As she prepared her usual vanilla latte, Sophie followed close behind, her nails clicking softly across the floor. Reaching down to stroke her fur, she whispered, "I'm sorry you can't come with me."

She had texted Avery to see if she could watch Sophie—the usual arrangement back when she and Everett would escape to tropical oases, leaving their beloved husky in Avery's doting care. This time, though, she hadn't expected a response. She didn't get one.

She was too preoccupied with thoughts of Beau to dwell on Avery's continued silence. Instead, she quickly booked Sophie into a posh pet motel—one that promised private outdoor space, a personal TV, and even chauffeured transport to and from the facility. The extravagance felt like an apology, a way to soothe the guilt of leaving her behind.

She moved through her morning routine with urgency, a blend of nerves and anticipation quickening her steps. After a fast shower, she dressed in comfortable sweats for the flight, but tucked a sleek, curve-hugging dress into her carry-on to change into later. Just modest enough to pass as practical, it hinted at something more daring—a choice grounded entirely in how Beau's gaze made her feel.

Sophie's car arrived just moments before Merritt's Voyagr, the sleek vehicle pulling up to the curb. Merritt watched as Sophie hopped eagerly into the plush interior, the driver giving Merritt a friendly nod before closing the door. The sight tugged at her heart, but before she could dwell on it, her own car pulled up behind, a nondescript grey sedan.

As the driver whisked Merritt toward the airport, they made small talk, their conversation drifting in and out as she half-listened, her thoughts consumed with anticipation. Pulling up to the drop-off zone at Arbourleigh Airport, the car slowed to a stop. Merritt shifted in her seat, reaching for the door handle when the driver turned toward her, the doors still locked.

"So, what's taking you to Port Rainier?" he asked casually.

Merritt froze, her hand hovering over the handle. For a moment, the question didn't register fully. Then it did. Port Rainier. She couldn't recall mentioning her destination. Had she? Surely she must have. There was no other way he could know. Her brow furrowed as she dismissed the flicker of unease, telling herself she must have said it during their earlier chatter. Still, a prickle of discomfort worked its way up her spine as she noticed the familiarity in his eyes, though she couldn't place him.

Her pulse quickened. She suddenly needed to get out of the car more than anything.

"I..." Merritt tried the door handle, finding it locked. Her voice tightened. "I'd like to get out now."

The driver chuckled, low and condescending. "Okay, calm down," he said, his tone sharp enough to make her flinch. "I was just curious."

To Merritt, it felt like an eternity before she heard the faint click of the locks releasing. She shoved the door open, practically tumbling out onto the pavement. Her feet caught her just in time as she staggered forward, the cold air hitting her like a splash of water. She gulped it in, her breaths ragged and sharp, trying to shake the lingering tension as the car pulled away.

Shaking her head, she told herself she was overthinking it. He was just a nosy driver, nothing more. And yet, the shadow of unease clung to her as she stepped into the bustling terminal.

Ever the anxious flyer, Merritt dreaded the flight across the country. As she boarded the plane and made her way down the aisle, her fingers hovered over her phone, her nerves bubbling to the surface. *About to board. If I survive this flight, I fully expect a hero's welcome. Also, if I don't, it's been nice knowing you*, she texted, her heart fluttering as she hit send.

Beau's reply came almost instantly: *I'll be at the gate with a parade in your honour.* A moment later, a second message followed: *Okay, maybe it'll just be me, but I promise to make it memorable.*

Merritt smiled, her chest tightening in that inexplicable way Beau always seemed to draw out of her. He had the uncanny ability to find her hidden joy and pull it effortlessly to the surface.

She could practically hear his voice in the words, rich with that easy charm that had so quickly become familiar to her. That he'd responded so quickly, knowing how full his day must be, made the gesture feel even more significant. Sliding into her seat and buckling her belt, Merritt read the messages again, the tension in her shoulders easing slightly.

The flight passed quickly, thanks in no small part to the motion sickness tablet Merritt had taken to knock herself out. She slept through nearly the entire journey, waking just in time to groggily change into the dress she'd packed, the curve-hugging fabric helping her feel a little more put together. She tied her hair up in a bun, then slid back into her seat, bracing herself for descent.

As soon as the pilot announced that passengers could turn their mobile devices back on, Merritt reached for her phone, fingers fumbling slightly in her haste. She tapped her foot impatiently, waiting for a signal. At last, the network bars lit up, and a message came through almost instantly: *I'm here.*

It was followed by a poorly framed selfie of Beau standing in what looked like the arrivals area—his face partially cut off, with Sylvie and Quinn visible in the background, both of them looking unamused in a way that made her smile.

Her chest lifted as she typed back, *You did bring me a parade*, then slipped the phone into her purse and rose to collect her carry-on. Anticipation surged through her, sweeping away the last of the anxiety she'd carried all morning.

She stepped through the automatic doors and into the crowded arrivals hall, the noise and movement around her fading into a blur as her heart picked up speed. Her gaze scanned the crowd, darting past families, couples, and business travellers—until it landed on him.

Beau stood just ahead, tall and steady amid the swirl of people, his broad shoulders unmistakable. Their eyes locked, and for a heartbeat, the terminal fell away. Sylvie and Quinn flanked him like sentinels, but she barely noticed them.

All she saw was him.

She didn't think—she moved. Her steps quickened, then turned into a full stride. When they met, it was sudden, unrestrained, and inevitable. Beau wrapped his arms around her and pulled her close, holding her like he needed her. She melted into him, her face tucked into the curve of his neck. He smelled like cedar and something warm and unmistakably his—familiar in a way that made her knees go weak.

She inhaled sharply, breath hitching, as tears threatened to spill.

"Hi," she whispered against his neck, the word trembling in her mouth.

Beau pulled back just enough to take her in, his hands framing her face like he was afraid she might disappear. "Merritt," he whispered, her name slipping from his lips with a tenderness that unraveled something deep and trembling inside her. "You're here."

She nodded, unable to speak past the ache in her throat. His thumb brushed along her cheek, catching a tear as it fell. They stood like that—suspended—while the world blurred around them. The hum of the airport, the shuffle of travellers, the weight of other people's lives—all of it faded, distant and irrelevant.

"I'm here," she finally managed, the words no more than breath.

Then he kissed her.

It wasn't tentative. It wasn't hesitant. It was the kind of kiss that rewrote the days they'd lost. That said more than words ever could. She melted into it, into him, into the sheer relief of being held by someone who wanted her there. The tight knot of the past few weeks loosened all at once, breaking open beneath his touch.

A voice cut through the moment like a crack of light: "Alright, that's probably enough, you two."

Quinn. Dry, pointed—but not unkind.

They broke apart, breathless, and she turned to find a small crowd gathered—phones raised, screens glowing, strangers openly watching. Her skin prickled. It hit her all at once—who he was. Who she was kissing. He wasn't just Beau. He was the Prime Minister of Norland.

But his hand never left her back—solid, certain, and unapologetically there—as Quinn and Sylvie closed in with the smooth, efficient precision of a detail that had done this a hundred times before.

"Nice to see you again," Sylvie murmured over her shoulder, her voice low, almost fond, as they began weaving through the crowd.

Quinn flanked them on the other side, deflecting cameras with a flick of her hand and a glare sharp enough to scatter anyone in their path.

Merritt let herself be moved, let herself lean into the warmth at her side, the strength of the man beside her, the strange blur of movement and meaning.

When the Escalade door finally shut behind them with a quiet, definitive thud, it was like the world stopped again. Just them. Just silence.

And all she could hear was the sound of her heart, crashing into his.

For a moment, the world outside the Escalade ceased to exist. Inside, silence settled—soft, charged, intimate. Their gazes locked, the distance between them buzzing with unspoken words as Sylvie steered the vehicle smoothly through the streets of Port Rainier. Neither moved. Neither spoke. They just sat in it—the stillness, the closeness, the gravity of being here, together, again.

"I've got the whole weekend," Beau said at last. "It gets crazy from here," he added, a note of caution threading through the warmth. "But I wanted this weekend to be just us. The kids flew back to Arbourleigh with Delphine and her parents."

She didn't speak. She didn't need to. Her chest tightened, his words folding gently over her. Instead, she reached across the space between them and took his hand. Brought it to her lips. Pressed a kiss into his palm —a silent thank you for this moment, for his thoughtfulness, for him.

"I don't know if you'd want to," he continued, more tentative now, "but I thought we could head to Silver Reach tomorrow. I mean... if that's okay with you. I can make other plans. We've got the whole weekend." A soft laugh escaped him.

Her breath caught. Silver Reach. Home. The frozen northern city of Cascadia where everything began—where joy and grief lived side by side in memory. She nodded, perhaps a little too quickly, her hand still holding his, her eyes searching his face, hoping he could see just how much that offer meant.

"I'd love that," she whispered.

The Escalade pulled into the underground parking beneath Beau's hotel, its warm lights glowing against the cold concrete. They rode the elevator in silence, anticipation thrumming like static between them. Even Sylvie and Quinn seemed slightly ill at ease in the charged air.

When the elevator doors slid open, the security team stepped out first. A quick sweep of the suite followed—swift, professional, barely a pause.

"Um, enjoy," Quinn said at last, offering Beau a salute that somehow managed to be both awkward and fond. It was the warmest expression Merritt had ever seen on her usually stony face.

Sylvie looped an arm casually around Quinn's waist, guiding her back toward the elevator with a knowing smile. The two of them disappeared to the floor below, where the team's suites waited—leaving Beau and Merritt alone in the quiet sanctuary above the city.

She glanced over at him with a raised brow, half-smiling. He met her look with a subtle shrug. "I think they're dating," he said with a smile.

Her gaze drifted from his face to the room around them —and stopped. Her breath caught.

Floor-to-ceiling windows stretched across one wall, framing a view so stunning it felt unreal. The city glittered below, golden light spilling across the waterfront like scattered stars. Beyond, the Pacific stretched into darkness, vast and endless, moonlight dancing over its surface like silver threads. The beauty of it settled over her like a hush.

She could feel his gaze on her—steady, wordless, almost reverent. Stepping closer to the window, she let herself lean into the glass, her breath misting against the cool surface. The moonlight bathed everything in silver, casting her in its quiet glow. Outside, the city sparkled and the ocean stretched toward forever, but all she could feel was the gravity of this moment. Of him.

She didn't hear him move, but she felt him—his presence at her back, the warmth of him folding around her as his arms slid gently around her waist. She exhaled softly, tilting her head back just enough to let her hand find his cheek, her fingertips tracing the familiar line of his jaw. Solid. Real. Here.

His lips found her neck—slow, unhurried kisses that sent heat blooming beneath her skin. His breath was warm, the rhythm of it brushing over her like something sacred. Every inch of space between them disappeared.

"How would you feel about a shower?" he whispered against her skin, his voice low and rough, the question laced with tenderness and desire. His hands rested at her hips, thumbs drawing slow, lazy circles over the fabric of her dress.

"You look so beautiful," he added, the words hushed— but laced with awe, like a truth he couldn't not speak.

And in that moment, wrapped in moonlight and his touch, Merritt believed him.

She turned to face him, heart pounding. Their eyes met, and the air between them pulled tight. He didn't speak. He didn't need to. The hunger in his gaze said everything.

Slowly, she nodded, lips parting as her hands reached for the buttons of his shirt. She worked through them one by one, her fingers brushing warm skin with every undone inch. He stood perfectly still, watching her.

Without a word, he took her hand and led her into the bathroom. The lights were dim, the marble glowing with soft reflections from the city outside. He turned on the shower, and the sudden sound of rushing water seemed to deepen the quiet around them.

When he turned back, he said nothing—just reached for her.

His fingers found the zipper at her back, slow and deliberate as he eased it down. The fabric slipped from her shoulders in a whisper, then pooled at her feet. She stood still, breath caught, bare in the amber glow of the city lights, the curve of her collarbone rising and falling with every heartbeat.

His eyes darkened, swept over her like flame over silk.

He stepped in close, his hands tracing the slope of her shoulders, gliding down her arms. His touch was featherlight, reverent—like he didn't know whether to worship her or fall apart at her feet.

Her hands moved to his chest, pushing the shirt from his frame, fingers exploring the lean strength beneath. When she dragged her palms down his stomach, the muscles there tensed under her touch. His lips found hers— hungry, open, claiming. She kissed him back with everything she had, her body already trembling with the need she'd tried so hard to keep buried.

The heat between them rose as they stepped into the shower. Steam curled around their bodies, water cascading in ribbons down their skin. His hands roamed her slowly, deliberately, skimming over her ribs, her waist, her hips. When he gripped her thighs and lifted her against the cool tile, she gasped into his mouth, legs wrapping instinctively around him.

"Tell me you want this," he growled against her throat, his voice thick with hunger. "Tell me you want *me*."

Her breath caught. Fingernails dragging down his back, she gasped, "Beau, I fucking want you. Don't stop."

He didn't.

His mouth was everywhere—her neck, her collarbone, the curve of her breast. Every kiss was an ache. Every touch an unraveling. Her back arched, body bowing to him, chasing every rush of sensation he gave her. His name left her lips again and again, half-moan, half-prayer.

He moved with a slow intensity, like he had nowhere else to be, like every second inside her was sacred. Her body met his rhythm without thought, without fear—just need, sharp and rising, until it drowned everything else.

He whispered her name against her skin, over and over, like it meant something more now. Like it belonged to him.

And she let it.

The moment broke her open. She came apart in his arms, clinging to him like he was the only thing holding her to the earth. He followed with a low, broken whisper of her name, his body pressed deep into hers, trembling with the slow, consuming wave of it.

Afterward, they didn't move right away.

The water still ran, streaming over them in rivulets as he held her there, forehead resting against hers. Her breath came in soft gasps, heart thundering against her ribs. He traced small, lazy circles against her lower back, holding her to him even now, as if afraid she'd vanish if he let go.

Then, wordlessly, he turned off the water and lifted her again—strong arms steady beneath her thighs as he carried her into the bedroom. He laid her gently across the satin sheets, the cool fabric kissing her skin. Sliding in beside her, he drew her in close, wrapped around her like a shelter.

She could feel the echo of him still inside her, the ache sweet and deep. His fingers brushed slowly over her bare hip, not ready to let her go. Not yet.

"I think I love you, Mer," he whispered, his voice barely audible.

Her heart stuttered.

She turned her face toward his, searching those steady blue eyes that had undone her the moment she'd first met them. Her throat tightened, but she didn't flinch.

"I think I love you too," she said, the words breaking from her like breath held too long.

Neither of them spoke. Words would have only narrowed what was vast between them. Instead, she let herself be held, surrounded by the rhythm of his breath—calm and steady, like a tide pulling her back to something safe. Something hers. The ache she'd carried for so long quieted beneath the sound of it. In the hush of the room, with his warmth all around her and the water's memory still on her skin, time stopped asking to be measured.

She tried to stay awake. To hold on. To carve the feeling of this night into bone, into blood, into forever. Every beat of her heart whispered stay, stay, stay.

And then—softly, like testing the strength of a thread she hoped might hold—she whispered into the dark, "I *do* love you."

His response wasn't words. Not at first. It was a smile, curving against the crown of her head. Immediate. Unmistakable. The warmth of it bloomed through her chest, stealing her breath.

He didn't rush to speak. He just pulled her closer, as if to hold the truth of what she'd said between them, letting the silence stretch and settle like something sacred.

When he finally did answer, his voice came quiet and certain, wrapped in the magnitude of everything he felt.

"I *do* love you too, Merritt," he murmured.

He said it like it mattered. Like he'd meant to say it forever.

And as his words curled around her in the quiet, Merritt let her eyes drift shut, sleep finding her easily in the place she'd always been safest—his arms.

Chapter 27
Beau ~ Her

When Beau opened his eyes, the room was dim—washed in the soft, silvered light of a Port Rainier morning. Overcast. Quiet. The kind of hush that blurred time.

He reached instinctively across the bed, his hand searching for the warmth of her.

But all it met was the cool sweep of satin sheets.

His chest tightened. The room, once filled with her breath and body and laughter, felt suddenly cavernous. Empty.

Rubbing both hands over his face, he sat up, dragging sleep with him like a weight. He swung his legs over the edge of the bed and stood, pulling on a pair of boxer shorts as he crossed the suite.

"Mer?" he called out, voice low and rough from sleep. It hung in the quiet, unanswered.

The silence pressed in.

Had she left?

Again?

A familiar ache stirred low in his gut. The kind of ache you get when hope starts to retreat too fast.

He moved through the suite with purpose, heading toward the small kitchenette, chasing clarity—or at the very least, caffeine. But before he could reach the machine, the faint, unmistakable smell of burnt coffee met him halfway.

He rounded the corner and found it: a cheap drip coffee maker, nearly full, sitting like a failed offering on the counter. And beside the carafe, a single cup sat untouched —still steaming faintly. Next to it, a piece of paper, folded cleanly in half.

His breath hitched.

He stepped forward and picked up the note.

This is gross. Save yourself. Don't drink it. I'll be back with supplies.

At the bottom, in her neat, steady handwriting, were two words that hit him harder than anything else had in a long time: *Love, Merritt.*

Beau exhaled sharply, the knot in his chest loosening all at once. The fear unraveled. The heaviness lifted.

She hadn't left. She hadn't disappeared.

She'd just gone out for better coffee.

Merritt was still here.

And apparently, a coffee snob.

He leaned back against the counter, smiling to himself as the tension in his body faded. He could definitely live with that.

He took her note's advice, leaving the scorched hotel brew untouched. Instead, he stepped into the shower, letting the hot water hammer away the last threads of sleep and uncertainty. As steam filled the room and clarity settled in, he thought of the day ahead—of winding roads and the northern city that had shaped the woman who now filled his every thought.

The sound of the suite door opening pulled him back.

Moments later, a soft knock tapped against the open bathroom door.

He turned toward the sound, towelling water from his face. "Mer?"

Her voice didn't answer—her grin did, already curved and wicked as she leaned against the doorframe. One hand on her hip, the other holding out a coffee cup like a gift, the logo of some local shop scrawled in bold across it.

"You missed the show," he teased, wrapping the plush towel low around his hips.

She glanced him over shamelessly appreciative. "I don't know. Looks like I caught the encore."

He reached for the cup, amused. "What's this?"

"The best coffee in Port Rainier," she declared. "Wicked. My favourite." Her tone was light but full of pride, like she'd hunted it down just for the pleasure of watching him sip it.

He took a cautious sip—then a longer one.

"That's actually... really good," he admitted, eyes narrowing as if annoyed by how easily she'd impressed him. "Didn't realize I was dealing with a full-blown coffee elitist."

"You're welcome," she said, arms crossing loosely as she watched him. "I basically saved your life."

His mouth shifted into a slow smile. "I don't know," he said, stepping forward, water still dripping from his hair onto her shoulder as he wrapped his arms around her waist, "I think I could get used to being rescued by you."

She laughed, shoving lightly at his damp chest. "Okay, hero. Dry off. Get dressed. We've got places to be."

He smirked, lifting the cup again. "Careful," he cautioned. "You know you are speaking to your Prime Minister."

She stepped in, close enough that her breath brushed his jaw, her tone dropping low and dangerous. "And as I recall," she murmured, guiding his hands back to her waist, "the government's supposed to serve the people."

His grip tightened.

His smile changed.

"I've never been more committed to public service," he said quietly, voice thick with warmth—and something just beneath it.

* * * * *

They pulled out of the city just after ten, a small motorcade slipping through the slick streets of Port Rainier, headlights cutting clean lines through the grey morning. The city fell away behind them in stages—glass towers, coffee shops, traffic, tension—until all that remained was open road and a horizon smudged with snow.

He felt it almost immediately: the shift.

The silence. The space. The soft weightlessness of being with her, away from everything else.

With her beside him—and the bold, trembling newness of what they were becoming—the coming election, only a short while away, felt like a storm he could still keep at bay. The presence of additional security vehicles, the low murmur of radio chatter, even the quiet professionalism of Quinn and Sylvie in the front seats—none of it touched the stillness between them.

Outside, Cascadia's coastline unfurled like a dream: dense evergreens cloaked in snow, cliffs dissolving into the dark sweep of the Pacific, and the endless pale sky overhead, heavy with light. The road stretched on, wet and winding, tires humming against the pavement in a rhythm that settled deep into his chest.

Beau glanced sideways. Merritt was staring out the window, her hand resting on the edge of her seat, relaxed. Peaceful.

And then, after a long stretch of silence: "I don't know if you'd want to," she said softly, still looking at the trees. "But maybe we could stop at my mom's?"

She turned to him then—eyes steady, unsure and brave at the same time.

He reached across the leather, threading his fingers through hers. "I'd love to."

From the front, Sylvie cleared her throat. "We'll need to plan it out. It won't be subtle," she said gently. "You should give her a heads-up. It's going to be more than just the two of you showing up."

Quinn was already on her phone, muttering something about secondary routes and timing.

Merritt pulled out her phone, hesitated over the keyboard for a beat too long, then typed something quick and neutral—practical, even—hoping it didn't sound as strange as it felt to send.

They drove on.

And with the road rolling out in front of them, she began to speak again.

Softly at first, then steadier.

She told him about her parents' divorce—how it split her childhood cleanly in two: before and after. Summers with her father in Arbourleigh, where his quiet loneliness seeped into everything, a kind of sadness that lived in the corners of rooms and between silences. Her mother's swift remarriage to Talon Swiftwater had felt like a replacement, a reshuffling of a life she was no longer part of. Two sisters came from her mother's second union. Eventually, at sixteen, ache—paired with the deep, unspoken pull of her father's solitude—led her to move in with him full-time in Arbourleigh.

She told him how that early fracture had shaped her path. How becoming a divorce attorney felt like a way to give structure to the chaos she'd grown up in. A way to soften the blow for families caught in the same storm. To make it hurt a little less.

And she told him about her father's diagnosis. How the cancer came fast and ruthless. How she moved up her wedding so he could walk her down the aisle. How he died the day she returned from her honeymoon—as if he'd held on just long enough to see her begin again.

She didn't cry. But her voice trembled at the edges, like she was carefully holding the story together as she gave it to him.

He listened, silent and sure, letting the details settle between them without interruption.

But one word landed differently than the others.

Wedding.

She'd never mentioned it before. Not once. It wasn't the fact of it that got to him, but the not-knowing. The feeling that he was still learning things he hadn't thought to ask, and she didn't seem to want to share.

Still, he kept his expression calm. His hand never left hers.

This was the first time she'd really opened the door.

And he wasn't about to let it close.

* * * * *

When they arrived at the modest house where Merritt's mother lived—the home that had shaped Merritt's childhood—a small woman with glowing brown skin stepped onto the porch to greet them. Her face lit up with a warm smile, and before Beau could even process the moment, she wrapped him in an unguarded embrace.

"I'm Naya," she said, her voice rich and welcoming as she stepped back, her hands lingering lightly on his arms. The resemblance to Merritt was undeniable—the same warm, deep brown eyes, the same tawny glow to her skin—but where Merritt carried the world with caution, her mother seemed to greet it with open arms.

Naya quickly ushered them inside with an easy laugh, her joy infectious as she held the door wide for Beau, Merritt, Sylvie, and Quinn. The remaining NFC agents stayed outside, a reminder of Beau's role and the weight he carried with him, even here.

Inside, the house was cozy and lived-in, filled with the scent of cedar and freshly brewed tea. Naya led them into the living room and gestured for them to sit. Despite Beau's polite protests, she addressed him only as "Prime Minister," her tone imbued with genuine respect.

"You can call me Beau," he offered, a soft smile playing on his lips.

"Absolutely not," Naya said with cheerful defiance. Then, more firmly: "Prime Minister."

There was no tour of the house, no walk through memory. After Merritt had moved to Arbourleigh with her father, Naya had erased her daughter's presence almost immediately. Merritt's tiny back bedroom had been repurposed for one of her younger sisters so the two girls wouldn't have to share. Over tea, Naya spoke with regret about how she'd handled those years—her voice edged with remorse as she admitted she hadn't known how to hold space for Merritt then. She expressed deep gratitude for their reconciliation after her second husband passed away—a grief that had pulled them back together in a way neither had expected.

The conversation lightened from there. Naya, animated and expressive, told Beau she had voted for Greyson Hartwell in all three of his terms, her pride unmistakable. Beau smiled and thanked her, accepting her warmth with genuine appreciation.

After a while, Merritt rose and stretched slightly. "Mom, don't you have any coffee?" she asked, nodding at the neat tea set laid out before them. "Tea is just herb-flavoured water," she added with a theatrical sigh.

"Oh, that stuff's bad for you," Naya replied, waving a dismissive hand. "But if you must, there's some in the kitchen. I'll make it. Would you like a cup, Prime Minister?"

Merritt reached out and placed a gentle hand over her mother's. "I'll make it, thank you."

She turned to Beau then, a teasing smile playing on her lips. "Would you like a cup... *Prime Minister?*" she asked, her brown eyes sparkling with mischief.

Beau chuckled, warmed by her playful tone. "I would," he said, returning her smile.

As Merritt disappeared into the kitchen, Naya leaned in, her voice lowering to a quiet, conspiratorial murmur. "I believe in your policies," she began, her expression suddenly serious. Beau nodded, unsure where the conversation was headed. "But my daughter," she added, tilting her head toward the kitchen, "don't hurt her."

"I don't intend to," Beau replied lightly, though her pointed tone gave him pause.

Naya's gaze softened, but there was a flicker of steel beneath the warmth. "After Everett, I'm just glad to see her putting herself out there again—though this," she said, lifting her phone, the screen glowing in the dim light, "was a surprise."

Displayed was a headline, the image unmistakable: Beau and Merritt embracing at the airport the night before. The news had already spread.

"Everett?" Beau asked carefully, though part of his mind snagged on the thought that Merritt might not yet know about the publicity—or how she'd feel when she did.

"Her husband," Naya said, matter-of-factly, unaware that the name landed like fresh news. "He passed away... what, not quite two years ago now?"

The words struck Beau like a sudden gust of cold air. His chest tightened. His heart ached for Merritt—for the grief she must carry, even as she walked through the world with such strength.

"I didn't think she'd ever move on," Naya confessed, her voice dipping lower, her expression tender. "She's fragile, even if she doesn't show it. So, you be nice," she added, her smile warm but her tone edged with unmistakable gravity. "Prime Minister," she added with a playful smirk.

"I fully intend to be," Beau said earnestly, just as Merritt reappeared, balancing two mugs in her hands.

Beau rose to meet her, his fingers brushing against hers as he took the mug. Their eyes met, and in the meeting of their eyes, he felt an even deeper tenderness bloom within him.

"It's only instant," Merritt warned, her voice light, though there was a hint of apology in her tone. "But I need the caffeine." Her gaze flicked between her mother and Beau. "Were you two talking about me?"

Both Naya and Beau raised their shoulders in unison, wearing matching innocent smiles.

"No idea what you're talking about," Naya said with a proud smirk, as Beau sipped his coffee, steering the conversation in another direction.

As the visit drew to a close, Beau and Merritt stepped out into the deep northern night. The street was quiet, the dark vast and still. Only the faint yellow glow of the porch light lit their path. The air bit with cold as Beau offered his hand, steadying Merritt down the icy front steps and guiding her to the car. Sylvie held back slightly, giving Beau the space to open Merritt's door before slipping into her own seat beside Quinn.

* * * * *

The drive to the cabin was quiet, the road winding through dense forest beneath a sky scattered with stars. Isolation wrapped around them like a blanket, the world narrowing to the hum of the engine and the faint crunch of snow beneath the tires.

Their destination was a small, secluded A-frame cabin, its wide windows framing a sweeping view of the surrounding forest. Inside, the space was simple but warm, the air scented with cedar and dominated by a large stone fireplace. While Beau and Merritt would share the main cabin, Sylvie and Quinn had arranged for the rest of the security detail to be housed in nearby cabins, with two sets of NFC agents stationed in cars just outside.

Beau took Merritt's bag as they stepped inside, setting it gently near the door. He watched as she took in the space.

"What do you think?"

Merritt glanced around, her eyes drifting over the vaulted ceiling, the massive fireplace, the wide glass panels that opened up to the dark beauty of the forest. "It's beautiful," she breathed, shivering slightly as she stepped toward the hearth. "Let's get a fire going."

Beau leaned against the doorframe, a teasing smile on his lips. "Mer, should I really trust you with fire?"

She arched a brow, unfazed, and knelt to begin stacking the logs with practiced ease.

"So," she said after a beat, her tone light but edged with curiosity. "What did you and Mom talk about while I was in the kitchen?"

Beau didn't answer right away. Instead, he moved slowly across the cabin, hands tucked into the pockets of his jeans as Merritt stoked the fire—her motions steady, but her attention clearly split.

After a moment, she stood and crossed the room to him, slipping her arm around his waist. "Well?" she prompted, tilting her head to catch his gaze.

He turned to face her fully, his hands resting gently on her shoulders. He bent slightly, eyes searching hers, the question sitting heavier now that it was real between them.

"You didn't tell me you were married before," he said, his voice quiet, trying to stay steady.

Merritt's gaze dropped, her body tensing beneath his touch. "I was," she said at last, the words barely audible.

"I know," Beau replied gently. "And?" He remained quiet, giving her time and space.

She hesitated, her breath catching as though the air itself had turned against her. When she finally spoke, her voice was thin and frayed. "He died," she said, the words trembling on her lips. Her eyes filled, the tears spilling over in aching sobs that she couldn't hold back.

Without hesitation, Beau pulled her into his arms, holding her tightly as her grief rose between them like a tide. "I'm so sorry, Mer," he whispered, steady and soft, his hand stroking her hair, offering presence where words fell short. After a pause, he asked gently, "Why didn't you tell me?"

He meant it kindly, but couldn't quite keep the edge of hurt from his voice.

As her sobs began to settle, Merritt rested her head against his chest, her voice barely above a whisper. "I'm sorry. It's just not something I'm very good at talking about," she admitted. "I mean, I used to talk to Avery. But when's the right time to tell someone you're dating that you're a widow? 'Oh, by the way... I was married. He died. Oops, forgot to mention it.'" She gave a short, humourless laugh that caught in her throat.

Beau held her a little tighter. "You don't ever have to hide from me," he murmured. "You can tell me anything."

She wiped at her cheeks. "I wasn't looking for anything serious when I met Everett," she said slowly, as if peeling back layers she hadn't touched in a long time. "I was in law school—driven, tunnel vision. I didn't think I had room for anyone else. But then... he showed up."

A faint, wistful smile tugged at her lips. "We met on a dating app. Our first date wasn't anything special—just walking and talking for hours. But it felt like breathing. It felt like home."

Beau listened quietly, a tightness forming in his chest. He didn't want to feel jealous—it wasn't that—but there was something sacred in the way she spoke of Everett, something that made him feel like a late arrival to a story he couldn't rewrite. Still, he reminded himself: every step she'd taken had led her here, to him.

Then she told him the rest—about the argument, the way Everett had left in anger, and the accident that followed. Beau's hand tightened gently around hers.

Her voice grew smaller. "I think that's why I tried so hard not to get close to you," she admitted, her vulnerability slicing through the quiet. "Losing him... it broke something in me. I don't know if I could survive that kind of pain again."

Beau bent down, pressing a soft kiss to her hairline. "I'm not going anywhere," he said, steady and sure. He guided her to the couch, wrapping her in his arms as the last of her tears slipped free. She nestled into him, her breathing slowing until she drifted off against his shoulder.

Beau stayed still, holding her. And as the fire crackled softly nearby, he understood with aching clarity just how much strength it had taken for her to let him in.

Gently, Beau gathered Merritt into his arms, her body light against his—but the weight of her grief, her story, her past, was something he carried willingly. As he laid her down on the bed, he tucked the quilt around her with reverent care, as though he could protect her from everything that had ever caused her pain. He slipped in beside her, his arm curling around her waist, drawing her close.

Her breath was soft and steady, the rhythm of someone who had finally allowed herself to rest. Her vulnerability was not lost on him—it was a rare and sacred kind of trust. And Beau felt it all: her history, her hesitation, the bravery it took for her to let him in.

He didn't retreat from it.

He embraced it.

In the hush of the dark, as their bodies aligned and her warmth seeped into him, gratitude rose in his chest like a tide. For the first time in years, he felt the unmistakable certainty that he was exactly where he was meant to be— not just lying beside her, but holding all that she was, and everything she was still learning to let him carry.

Chapter 28
Merritt ~ The Return to Us

The morning felt lighter. So did Merritt.

She and Beau moved easily around the cabin—showering together, dressing, preparing breakfast. There was a gentle rhythm to it all, the kind that settles into the body before the mind even catches up. Their conversation drifted from topic to topic, aimless but comforting, the kind of chatter that didn't need direction. Silences stretched between them, companionable and warm, as natural as the fire Beau had kept burning since the night before. Merritt found herself soaking it in—the simple domesticity, the easy harmony, the way they seemed to fit.

Later that morning, they set off to explore the wilderness. Merritt led Beau through the breathtaking forests that had shaped her childhood, each step a return to the girl she used to be. Sylvie and Quinn came along, their presence never intrusive, and Merritt noticed the way the two women drifted easily in and out of conversation, seemingly content just to be near one another. The trail to Shane Lake in Forests for the World Park was steeped in soft laughter and shared awe. Merritt caught herself smiling often as Beau matched her pace effortlessly, his energy and curiosity slotting so easily into the landscape of her memories.

By midday, they were back in Silver Reach, standing at the foot of the stairs to a sleek Challenger jet bound for Arbourleigh. Merritt hesitated. Her pulse picked up. Flying had always unnerved her, and the thought of climbing into the narrow body of a small jet made her stomach turn.

Beau noticed. He reached for her hand. "We'll be fine, Mer," he said gently.

His voice was calm, reassuring, but her nerves still flared. She nodded anyway, swallowing the lump in her throat and letting him guide her up the steps.

Inside, she gripped his hand tightly, her knuckles whitening as the aircraft taxied for takeoff.

"I'll never understand how you do this all the time," she muttered, trying for humour, though her voice was thin with dread.

Beau gave her a smile, his hand steady on hers. "You've got me," he said.

And somehow, that helped. She didn't let go for the duration of the flight, but she breathed easier. The sound of him beside her—the calm rhythm of his breath, the stillness he carried—was enough to get her through.

When they landed in Arbourleigh and the engines finally powered down, Merritt exhaled a quiet breath of relief. They had one last evening ahead of them—one last pause before politics and duty pulled them back into the shape of their separate lives.

Even as there was nowhere else she'd rather be than with Beau, Merritt understood the complexities of their desire. Love like theirs—discovered later in life—still carried the all-consuming intensity of youthful romance, but now it had to be measured against the undeniable constraints of time and the unyielding demands of professional ambition and long-standing commitments. There was a little less future at her disposal now, and it weighed on Merritt's mind—not as a shadow, but as a sharp reminder of how precious their time together truly was. She knew their moments would be parceled out in the narrow spaces between careers, obligations, and the lives they had carefully built before finding one another.

Beau's final debate before the election loomed just ahead, set for the following evening—the very same night Merritt was slated to give the keynote at the Women in Law and Justice conference. It wasn't just another speech. For Merritt, it was one of the proudest milestones of her career—a culmination of the work she'd done to carve out space for herself and other women in a system built to keep them out. Once, she might have considered making room for love by bending, reshuffling a commitment, showing up for Beau's big moment. But that wasn't who she was. Not anymore. Her work was not something she slotted in around someone else's importance—it was her foundation. Her purpose. Her non-negotiable.

And Beau understood that. More than that—he respected it. He didn't just tolerate her ambition; he admired it. That reverence made her fall harder for him than any blue-eyed stare or broad-shouldered embrace ever could. There was something undeniably magnetic about a man who didn't need her to make herself smaller to fit into his world.

Still, knowing she was supported didn't make it easier. As they sat in the back of the Escalade—Sylvie once again at the wheel, Quinn riding shotgun—Merritt gazed out the window, the landscape of Arbourleigh blurring past. They were headed to her townhouse, but her thoughts stretched far beyond it.

She wanted him. She wanted the steadiness of his presence, the peace she hadn't realised she'd been craving. But she also wanted her life. The career she'd fought to build. The purpose that had shaped her.

The SUV slowed to a stop in front of her home, and Merritt's stomach dropped. A small group of reporters stood on the sidewalk, cameras in hand, eyes trained on the Escalade.

Her fingers instinctively tightened around Beau's.

"It's okay," he said gently, already sensing the spike in her pulse. "I've got you."

His voice was calm, steady—but Merritt's world had shifted again. And this time, the cameras were rolling.

Sylvie and Quinn stepped out of the Escalade first, moving with the precision of people trained to anticipate risk.

They created a small perimeter, allowing Beau and Merritt to make it to her townhouse without incident.

The moment the door clicked shut behind them, Merritt let out a sharp, frustrated breath. "Fuck." She gave herself a small shake, trying to dispel the adrenaline still pulsing through her system.

The Arbourleigh airport had been chaos—a blur of flashing cameras and shouted questions. She hadn't even registered the full extent of it until she saw the front pages at the newsstand: her and Beau's embrace at the Port Ranier airport, splashed across every major outlet. She found herself thinking of Avery, wondering what she'd say, wishing she'd answer her messages.

"You okay?" Beau asked, watching her carefully as she leaned down to unlace her boots.

"I mean..." she started, then trailed off. She placed her boots neatly on the rack inside her front closet—everything in its place, like always. "I don't know," she said finally.

Without missing a beat, she turned her attention to Beau's coat, hanging it up before nudging his shoes into alignment with a little too much care. Her hands moved through the familiar rituals of order: closing blinds, adjusting curtains, checking that everything was just as it should be.

Beau stepped forward and gently caught her hand. "Merritt," he said, calm but firm. One brow arched, steady and knowing. "This is going to get worse from here."

She let out a long, quiet sigh. "I know," she admitted, meeting his eyes briefly before looking away.

On the drive from the airport, she'd given in to temptation and clicked on one of the articles. Her firm's bio photo greeted her under the headline:

*From Courtrooms to Campaign Trails: Meet Beau
Laurent's Rumoured Flame.*

*Beau Laurent, Norland's newly appointed Prime Minister
following Greyson Hartwell's resignation, is no stranger to
the spotlight as he blazes across the country on the campaign
trail. But this week, it isn't his bold policies or the upcoming
election that have Norlanders buzzing—it's his personal
life.*

*Photos of Laurent embracing a woman at Port Ranier's
airport surfaced earlier this week, sparking widespread
curiosity about Merritt Clarke, the accomplished family law
attorney who has captured the Prime Minister's attention.*

*Clarke, 41, is a compassionate yet formidable figure in
Norland's legal world. Based in Arbourleigh, she has built a
reputation as a successful divorce attorney who takes on
challenging cases with both empathy and precision. Most
notably, Clarke briefly represented tech billionaire Sebastian
DuPont during his high-profile split from Genevieve
DuPont, though the couple later reconciled.*

*Her personal life, however, has been far more private—
until now. Clarke was previously married to Everett Cole, a
venture capitalist, who tragically passed away in a car
accident nearly two years ago. The pair had been together
for 13 years, their partnership described by insiders and
those close to Clarke as one of mutual ambition and respect.*

*Raised in Cascadia before relocating to Arbourleigh as a
teenager, Clarke's early life and the divorce of her parents
shaped her dedication to family law. Her commitment to her
career remains steadfast; she is scheduled to deliver the
keynote speech at the Women in Law and Justice conference,
coinciding with Laurent's final debate before the election.*

*However, the public reaction to this budding romance has
already drawn sharp commentary, including from
Laurent's ex-wife, Delphine Moreau, and the former flame*

of Clarke's high-profile client DuPont. In a statement posted to Moreau's Instagram account, the former first-lady wrote:

"Beau Laurent has always been a man of immense ambition and dedication, qualities I greatly admired during our years together. I trust he'll receive the same level of understanding and support in his new relationship—though I imagine that can be a steep learning curve for some, especially someone as career driven as Ms. Clarke."

The statement, though outwardly gracious, has been widely interpreted as a thinly veiled jab at Merritt Clarke, questioning her capacity to navigate the demands of such a high-profile partnership. Commentators have speculated whether Moreau's words reflect genuine concern or a calculated reminder of her own years spent at Laurent's side.

The timing underscores the challenges of their romance. With both deeply entrenched in demanding careers, their relationship is sure to face scrutiny—especially as Laurent begins his tenure as Prime Minister and polls suggest his victory in the election is all but certain.

For now, Clarke and Laurent remain silent about their relationship, leaving the nation to speculate about the power couple navigating love, ambition, and life under the brightest spotlight Norland has to offer.

She'd squeezed Beau's hand when she read it, stunned by how much of her life had already been laid bare. Now, standing in the supposed safety of her home, it felt anything but safe.

Seeing Everett's name there—his death reduced to a passing line in a puff piece—made something in her recoil. It wasn't just the invasion of privacy. It was the way her grief had been flattened, commodified, made fodder for speculation. The sanctity of her past, of the love she'd lost, felt cracked open.

"Merritt," Beau said softly, his voice drawing her back. "We can do this. I'm not going to wish any of it were different—this is where I need to be, and I want you here with me. But if I could shield you from all of this... the spotlight, the noise—I would."

Merritt didn't respond right away. She admired Beau—his resolve, his vision. What he carried was so much bigger than the two of them. His ideas stretched across a country, reshaping it with every decision, and she believed in that future as fiercely as he did. He bore the weight of leadership with intention, and she wanted to be there beside him as he shaped it into something better.

"It's not always going to be this intense," Sylvie offered from the other side of the room. "Eventually, they'll lose interest in your love story and move on to what you're wearing, how much you weigh, whether you broke some unwritten rule—y'know, the usual." She smiled, but the humour was threaded with truth.

"I'll get used to it," Merritt said at last, her voice lighter than expected. The thought of Beau made everything feel a little more manageable. With him, she could handle the scrutiny.

A knock at the door pulled her upright, her stomach tightening with a jolt. She peeked through the blinds before opening it, her body easing when she saw Sophie trotting up the steps at the end of her leash, led by one of the NFC agents.

"Thanks," she said quickly, her tone clipped as she reached for Sophie—who wasted no time breaking free to barrel inside. For a moment, Merritt lingered on the threshold. Across the street, beyond the small crowd of onlookers, a grey sedan idled. The driver stared, unblinking. Unashamed.

She swallowed the discomfort and stepped back inside, quietly closing the door behind her.

Sophie was already investigating the corners of the entryway, her tail wagging with wild delight as she reacquainted herself with familiar scents. Merritt knelt to greet her, burying a hand in her thick coat. The dog turned quickly to nudge Beau's hand, tail thumping against the wall like a metronome of joy, entirely unaware of the unease still clinging to the air.

That night, they stretched out on the couch with Sophie curled between them. Sylvie and Quinn had taken the evening off, leaving the two in the quiet watch of agents outside. It was the first true pocket of peace since returning to the capital.

They watched episode after episode of a '90s sitcom they both knew by heart—the kind of show that didn't demand anything from them. Their hands found each other across the back cushion, fingers lacing lightly above Sophie. The low glow of the television painted the room in soft gold, casting them in a kind of stillness that felt worlds away from the noise waiting outside. For a while, nothing else existed but this—these slow, quiet hours.

But time, as it always did, moved too quickly. And as sleep began to pull at the edges of her mind, Merritt led him up the stairs and down the hallway.

The bedroom door opened to a space she hadn't yet reshaped. It still bore Everett's imprint. As she climbed into bed, the ache of memory stirred, sharp and sudden. She watched Beau unbutton his shirt, his movements unhurried, his presence so welcome. To him, it was simply a moment between them. But for her, the room held more—it held echoes. She felt herself stretching to make space for them both.

I'm sorry, she whispered silently into the quiet of her mind.

She pictured Everett's warm smile, the one that had made her feel seen and loved. He had been her first true home. And now, here was Beau—offering something new. Not a replacement, but a continuation. Not an erasure, but an expansion.

Beau slid beneath the covers and drew close, his body pressing into hers, chasing off the chill of lingering grief. She nestled into the warmth of him, her head resting against his shoulder. Sophie circled once at their feet before settling in with a heavy sigh.

Despite the ghosts that lingered and the uncertainties still ahead, Merritt felt something deep and profound—peace. A soft kind of permission. She could carry Everett's memory without closing herself off to what was in front of her. There was room for both—for grief and for love, for who she had been and who she was becoming. For the first time in a long while, she wasn't just surviving.

Chapter 29
Beau ~ The Steadying

Beau adjusted his tie for the third time, fingers gliding over the silk with measured precision. Around him, the hum of preparation played out in familiar rhythm—staff moving briskly with purpose, Sylvie and Quinn stationed by the door, their eyes sharp. His reflection was composed, unreadable, but beneath the surface his thoughts surged, tangled with the gravity of what lay ahead. This wasn't just another campaign milestone. Tonight's debate was pivotal—a chance to crystallize his vision for Norland and to stand unflinching against the inevitable barrage from Victor Hargrave, the rat-eyed leader of the Norlandic Conservative Union.

The faint murmur of voices drifted in from the hall, a low backdrop to the stillness in the room. Beau's eyes moved to the notes scattered across the table in front of him. He didn't need them—every figure, every policy was etched into him. But going over them, again and again, had always been his armour.

As he waited backstage, his thoughts veered toward Merritt. He pulled out his phone and reread her message.

Good luck tonight, Beau. Not that you need it—I know you've got this. Just go out there and be the man who fights for what matters. I'm proud of you, and I'll be cheering you on from here. Always.

A faint smile pulled at his lips, her unwavering support woven into every word.

Thanks, Mer. Knowing you're with me means more than you know. Good luck with your speech tonight. You'll crush it. XX, he had written back, then slid the phone into his pocket.

With a steadying breath, he gathered his notes and adjusted his tie one last time as Sylvie gave a brief nod of confirmation. The low murmur of the audience seeped through the walls, growing louder as he was ushered toward the staging area. Just beyond the curtain, the stage lights blazed, casting stark outlines around the podium where Lissa Tremblay stood, preparing to introduce the candidates. A veteran anchor with decades covering Norlandic politics, she was known for her sharp questions and unshakable presence—no one would be getting an easy pass tonight, and Beau wouldn't expect one.

"First," Lissa began, her voice calm but authoritative, "welcome Jacques Desrosiers, leader of the Montclair First Coalition, or MFC. An outspoken proponent of Montclair independence and cultural preservation, Mr. Desrosiers seeks to ensure Norland's French-speaking regions are given the autonomy and recognition they deserve."

The audience broke into polite applause as Desrosiers walked onto the stage with measured strides, nodding briefly to the crowd.

"Next, representing the Green Future Party, we have Imogen Delacroix," Lissa continued. "A passionate advocate for environmental sustainability and renewable energy, Ms. Delacroix's vision centres on combating climate change and creating a greener future for Norland." Imogen stepped onto the stage, her smile warm as she waved to the audience. The applause swelled slightly, a reflection of her growing popularity among younger voters.

"And now, please welcome to the stage Victor Hargrave, leader of the Norlandic Conservative Union," Lissa announced. "A staunch advocate for fiscal responsibility and resource development, Mr. Hargrave has built his platform on reducing government spending and ensuring Norland remains competitive in a global economy." The crowd's response was louder this time, a mix of cheers and scattered boos as Hargrave strode onto the stage, a self-assured grin plastered across his face. Beau couldn't help but notice the smug confidence in his opponent's demeanour, a deliberate projection designed to dominate the room.

Finally, it was just Beau waiting in the wings. He inhaled deeply, steadying himself as the applause from Hargrave's introduction began to fade. This was it—the moment to lay his vision bare before the nation one last time before Norlanders would head to the polls.

Lissa Tremblay's voice carried through the auditorium, calm and composed. "And finally, representing the Progressive Alliance, we have Norland's newly appointed Prime Minister, Beau Laurent. Known for his commitment to workers' rights, expanded universal healthcare, and bold environmental reforms, Mr. Laurent is championing a people-centred vision for Norland. His platform includes ensuring corporations pay their fair share in taxes, introducing a living wage for all workers, and creating a future built on equity and opportunity. Tonight, Mr. Laurent takes the stage to secure his mandate from the people of Norland."

The crowd erupted into thunderous applause as Beau stepped onto the stage, his smile broad and assured. Raising a hand confidently in greeting, he scanned the audience, their energy feeding his resolve. This wasn't just about politics—it was about people, and the country he believed Norland could become.

The debate began predictably, each leader using their opening remarks to solidify their platform and take subtle, and not-so-subtle, shots at their opponents. Jacques Desrosiers leaned heavily on his calls for Montclair's independence, painting it as a solution to the cultural and economic disparities he claimed Norland had ignored for too long. Imogen Delacroix, in her calm yet passionate tone, emphasized the urgent need for environmental action, positioning herself as the only leader willing to tackle climate change with the seriousness it required.

Victor Hargrave was, as expected, combative and unrelenting. His focus on economic growth and reducing government spending was wrapped in sharp rhetoric aimed directly at Beau. Hargrave wasted no time questioning Beau's plans to introduce a living wage and increase taxes on corporations, calling them reckless and out of touch with Norland's economic realities.

Beau, for his part, remained calm under fire. He used Hargrave's attacks as opportunities to highlight the moral foundation of his platform. He spoke directly to Norlanders about the importance of fairness—how asking corporations to contribute their fair share was essential for funding universal healthcare, ensuring every worker earned a living wage, and building a more sustainable economy.

As the debate progressed, tensions rose. Exchanges between Hargrave and Beau grew sharper, particularly on the economy, while Imogen held her ground as a steady voice for environmental reform. Jacques found moments to inject his arguments for regional autonomy but was largely sidelined as the debate turned into a duel between Beau and Hargrave.

The debate moved into its second half, with Lissa shifting focus to the influence of powerful corporations and their leaders on the election. Lissa Tremblay turned to Hargrave, her tone measured as she began to press him.

"Mr. Hargrave, critics have accused you of being little more than a puppet for tech billionaire Sebastian DuPont, whose financial contributions and vocal support for your campaign have raised concerns about undue corporate influence in this race. How do you respond to those allegations?"

Hargrave's smile faltered for a moment before he leaned into the podium, his tone dripping with sarcasm. "Well, I suppose if anyone's an expert on Sebastian DuPont, it would be the Prime Minister. After all, he's the man who stole your wife, isn't he, Beau?"

The room buzzed with a mix of sharp intakes of breath and scattered murmurs as Hargrave straightened his posture, a smug smile creeping back onto his face.

Beau's expression stayed composed, but his gaze sharpened. He took a steady step forward, his voice clear and resolute. "This debate is about Norland's future—not cheap personal attacks. Norlanders are tired of leaders caught up in division and petty distractions.

They want someone who will rise above the noise and answer to them—not to billionaires or their bottom lines."

He paused, letting the silence draw out as his eyes swept across the room.

"That's why I'll make sure corporations like Mr. DuPont's pay their fair share—so we can build a country where every worker earns a living wage, and every person has the chance to thrive. Fairness isn't a buzzword. It's a promise. And I intend to keep it."

The audience erupted into applause, Lissa raising her hand to regain order as Beau stepped back, his steady gaze never leaving Hargrave.

As the debate drew to a close, Lissa turned to the candidates for their final remarks. The room settled into a tense silence; the weight of the moment palpable as each leader delivered their closing arguments.

When it was Beau's turn, he stepped forward, his voice steady but filled with intensity. "Tonight, we've heard a lot of words, a lot of plans, and more than a few attacks. But what this comes down to isn't about who can land the sharpest jab or spin the cleverest line—it's about you. The people of Norland."

He paused, his gaze sweeping the audience and the cameras that broadcast to millions. "I believe in a Norland where every worker earns a living wage, where corporations contribute their fair share to ensure our schools, our hospitals, and our communities are strong. I believe in a Norland that leads the fight against climate change, that doesn't just talk about equity but delivers it to every citizen, no matter where they come from or how much they have."

Beau's voice grew stronger, carrying the weight of his convictions. "This election isn't about me. It's about us— what we value, what we're willing to fight for, and the kind of future we want to build together. I'm asking for your trust, not because it's my turn, but because I will always put you first. Let's choose hope. Let's choose fairness. Let's choose progress."

The room erupted into applause, a crescendo of cheers that underscored the gravity of his words. As Beau stepped back, he met Lissa's nod of acknowledgment, the debate winding to a close. The spotlight dimmed, but the questions, the stakes, and the vision for Norland burned brighter than ever in Beau's mind.

Backstage, Beau was met with a flurry of activity. Sylvie was already there, Quinn by her side, their expressions revealing a rare twin flicker of pride as Sylvie handed him a water bottle. "You nailed it," she said, her words as measured as always but carrying a weight of sincerity.

Inside the dressing room, his campaign team erupted into cheers as he entered, their faces lit with excitement and relief. "That was masterful," one aide said, holding up a phone displaying the early social media reactions pouring in. "Hargrave's jab didn't even land. You turned it into a total win."

Beau smiled, allowing himself a moment to exhale. The tension that had gripped him all evening began to release as he accepted the congratulations, his mind already turning toward the next steps.

As the team celebrated around him, Beau's phone buzzed in his pocket. He pulled it out and read Merritt's name on the screen.

You were incredible tonight. Watching you fight so passionately for fairness and equality—it's impossible not to believe in you, in everything you stand for. Honestly, it's kind of unfair how sexy that is. I'm so proud of you, Beau.

He tucked the phone back into his pocket, her encouragement carrying him forward.

Sylvie tapped his shoulder, her voice gently breaking through his thoughts. "Car's ready, sir."

Though he'd asked her more than once not to, she'd taken to using the formal address since his appointment—a quiet nod to the weight of his new role, and perhaps her own way of showing respect.

The celebration quieted as he grabbed his coat and followed Sylvie toward the back entrance, Quinn trailing behind them. The crisp night air met him as he stepped outside, the dark streets of Arbourleigh lit by the glow of streetlights. The Escalade waited at the curb, engine humming faintly, Quinn—uncharacteristically—sliding into the driver's seat. He climbed into the back, the door clicking shut as the city began to blur past the windows.

Inside, the atmosphere was quiet. Reflective. He rested his head against the back of the seat, the night playing over in his mind. The debate had gone well—better than he'd let himself imagine. But now, with the adrenaline fading, a loneliness crept in. The kids were with Delphine tonight. When he got home, he'd be alone.

And he didn't want to be alone.

Can you come over? he typed quickly, sending the message to Merritt before doubt could slow him. *I could send Sylvie to pick you up,* he added.

Her reply came almost instantly.

Is it a sleepover?

The playful tone matched his own, a spark of warmth in the hush of the night.

I'm not sure how much sleeping there will be, he replied, adding a winking emoji. *I'm hoping for next to none, if I'm being honest.*

Can Sophie come too? I'll call a Voyagr. You don't need to send Sylvie! she responded.

It's Sophie I'm most looking forward to seeing, he joked, just as the Escalade turned into the underground garage.

As he climbed the stairs from the garage, Sylvie and Quinn at his side, he broke the silence. "Merritt's coming over," he said casually.

Sylvie's lips twitched, a smile threatening to break through.

"Is it safe for her?" Quinn asked, her voice tightening. "Shouldn't she have security now that the two of you kissing in an airport is literally everywhere?"

He stopped mid-step.

He hadn't thought about it. Not once. Delphine and the kids had always had their own security detail. Even after the divorce, an NFC agent remained with his ex-wife at all times.

And now that the question had been asked, it bloomed inside him like cold water pouring through warm certainty. The campaign had drawn attention. Since their reunion at Port Rainier, so had Merritt. And he'd invited her into his orbit without a second thought.

As he waited for her to arrive, a faint unease settled in— tight and unwelcome—coiling around the edges of his anticipation.

Chapter 30
André ~ The Trap Set

Plans had changed, just as André always knew they would.

He had tracked the woman to the Women in Law and Justice Conference at the gleaming new Eleanor Hartwell Conference Centre. The venue buzzed with energy, a sea of sharp suits and polished ambition, and André stood out like a wolf among sheep. When curious glances came his way, he deflected with feigned allyship, his polite smile masking the cold calculation beneath.

As the evening wore on, André's attention drifted between the stage and the updates from the final leadership debate he was following on his phone. Each notification only confirmed what he already suspected: Victor Hargrave, his employer's candidate, was losing ground. The debate wasn't shifting the tide; if anything, it was cementing the momentum for the opposing camp. The future his employer had invested in was slipping away, and André knew what that meant. Escalation was inevitable.

The woman concluded her speech to warm applause, her voice resonating with conviction that grated against André's nerves. As the crowd thinned and the event wound down, he shadowed her discreetly. When she hailed a taxi and disappeared into the night, André followed at a distance, his pulse steady. She returned to her townhouse, its warm light spilling into the quiet street.

Then, just half an hour later, she stepped outside again, calling for a Voyagr. A flicker of surprise passed through André, replaced quickly by a sharper focus. Luck, or something darker, was on his side tonight. He was ready.

Chapter 31
Beau ~ The Rising Pressure

When the doorbell rang, it felt like it had taken a lifetime for Merritt to arrive.

Beau moved before thinking. Fear gripped his chest, sharp and choking, a single thought pulsing beneath his ribs: *Please let her be okay.*

He ignored Quinn's barked protest—"It's not protocol!"— and reached the door in a handful of urgent strides. The moment he pulled it open, his heart surged.

She was there. She was fine.

Merritt stood on the threshold, cheeks flushed from the cold, an overnight bag slung over one shoulder, Sophie at her side. She smiled—and everything in him exhaled.

Then it all fractured.

Sophie pulled forward with a joyful bark, tugging hard on the leash. Merritt stumbled, thrown off balance, tumbling awkwardly into the entryway as the bag slipped from her shoulder.

And then—

"Beau!" Quinn's voice cut through the moment like a blade, sharp and laced with alarm. *"Down!"*

She'd seen the threat first. But too late.

The driver of the Voyagr—just a blur a second ago—was suddenly there, stepping forward. His arm raised. A glint of metal caught the evening light.

The shot cracked through the night—quieter than he would have expected, given the devastation it unleashed.

Pain exploded in Beau's chest.

He staggered back, gasping, a sudden wetness spreading

across the starched white dress shirt he hadn't bothered to change out of. His legs buckled. The floor rushed up toward him.

More gunfire.

"Down!" Quinn screamed again, throwing herself in front of the shooter. She took a bullet—he heard it. The raw grunt that followed. But she kept moving, body slamming into the attacker, dragging him down in a violent blur of limbs and fury.

Sylvie was already there, weapon drawn. Her expression was cold steel as she fired once—clean, decisive.

Across the lawn, more NFC agents moved forward. Shouts. Footsteps. The aftermath of chaos.

And through it all—Merritt.

She dropped to her knees beside him, breath ragged. Her white sweater was already off, her hands pressing it hard against his chest. He could feel the warmth of her palms through the growing wetness. Her face swam in his vision, blurred by pain, by panic, by something far more terrifying than either.

"No," she whispered, over and over, her voice cracking like glass. "No. No—no—*no.*"

He couldn't tell if she was talking to him, to herself, or to something higher than either of them.

The lights above dimmed. Sound narrowed. The world began to tilt.

But her voice—her voice was the last thing that reached him, fierce and desperate.

He wanted to tell her he was sorry. That he was okay. That he loved her.

"I'm not going anywhere," he managed as everything went quiet.

Chapter 32
Merritt ~ The Shattering

"No," Merritt said firmly, her voice trembling but resolute. The word came again, sharper this time, cutting cleanly through the chaos. "No," she said louder.

The NFC agent hovering over her hesitated, his hand twitching like he might move her by force. "Ma'am," he said, tone clipped but controlled, "you need to step aside so we can—"

"No!" she snapped, pressing harder against Beau's chest. Her makeshift bandage—her sweater—was soaked through with blood. She didn't care. She was half-naked, her chest covered only by a sheer bra, knees burning against the cold floor, but she didn't move. Couldn't move. She wouldn't.

Around her, the world blurred into noise—Sylvie barking orders, Quinn's laboured breaths as she was helped upright and escorted toward a waiting car, the rising wail of sirens in the distance. But Merritt heard none of it.

All she saw was his face—pale, slack, eyes barely open.

"No," she said again, her voice stronger now, even as tears spilled down her cheeks. "I'm staying right here. I'm not letting him go."

And she didn't.

She stayed rooted in place until the paramedics arrived. A young woman knelt beside her, gently touching her elbow.

"We've got it from here," the medic said, calm and steady, already reaching for Beau.

Merritt's hands lingered one second longer before she pulled them away. She watched helplessly as they moved quickly, efficiently—lifting him onto the stretcher, carrying him out the door and into the waiting ambulance.

Merritt collapsed forward. Her blood-soaked sweater

clutched to her bare skin, her breaths sharp and ragged as the immensity of what had just happened crashed over her. Through her sobs, she clung to Beau's last words—*I'm not going anywhere*—though now they felt like smoke in her hands.

Sophie pressed close, the husky's tongue licking her tear-streaked cheeks, keeping her from slipping completely into the chaos.

Boots pounded across the foyer, and suddenly she was surrounded. NFC agents. Guns drawn. Faces taut.

"She's okay," Sylvie said firmly, stepping between her and the advancing wall of gear. She crouched beside her. "They need to take you in."

"No," Merritt whispered, voice cracking. "I didn't do anything."

"I know," Sylvie said gently. "But it's procedure. I promise I'll stay with you."

She helped her to her feet. Merritt barely registered how stiff her jeans had become, soaked through with Beau's blood. She clutched her sweater against her chest until Sylvie gently pried it away and sealed it in an evidence bag.

"Sophie," she murmured, glancing back at the house.

"I've got her," Sylvie assured her. "She'll be safe."

Inside the cruiser, Merritt folded into herself. The cold didn't register. Neither did the hum of the engine or the quiet voices up front. Only the silence. Only the fear.

At the NFC field office, she moved like a ghost through sterile halls and into an interrogation room. Lights buzzed overhead. Agents cycled through with calm, clinical questions.

She tried to answer. She remembered the driver—too chatty, too familiar. He'd insisted on walking her to the door. She should have stopped him. She didn't.

They mentioned the shooter—André Buchner. Shot by Sylvie. Quinn, too, hit in the shoulder. Both in surgery. But no one said Beau's name.

That silence was deafening.

Then came a shift in tone: questions about Sebastian DuPont. She muttered something about attorney-client privilege, but her mind was already moving.

She remembered the shell corporations. The server warehouse in Cascadia. The offshore ownership of Voyagr. Hargrave dodging Tremblay's questions about DuPont at the debate.

Pieces clicked.

And still—no news of Beau.

Sylvie returned with a blanket and draped it around Merritt's shoulders. "Come on," she said quietly, guiding her to the bathroom.

Inside, she helped her peel off her blood-soaked jeans and underwear, working with brisk, practiced care. Each item sealed in a plastic bag. Then: "This was all I could grab from lost and found."

Merritt blinked at the bundle—faded blue sweatpants and a giant hoodie with a stretched-out Wu-Tang Clan logo. She pulled it over her head. The sleeves swallowed her hands. The absurdity of it nearly broke her. If she laughed, she wouldn't stop.

Her reflection in the mirror was unrecognizable, and she was almost grateful she couldn't see it clearly without her glasses. She imagined herself pale. Empty. Terrified.

"How is he?" she managed to ask turning away from herself and back to Sylvie. "Is he..."

Sylvie's voice trembled. "He's alive."

The breath left Merritt's lungs. She collapsed into Sylvie's arms, sobbing with relief.

They drove to the hospital in silence.

But the silence screamed.

Merritt sat curled in the front seat, arms wrapped tightly around her chest, the fabric of the hoodie clinging like armour. Her mind circled back to Everett—to the moment the call came. The disbelief. The desperate drive to the hospital. The sick, hollow silence of identifying a damaged body. How she had begged the universe to give her more time. How she'd lost him anyway.

She couldn't lose Beau. Not now. Not him.

At the hospital, Sylvie guided her through layers of security. No one questioned her presence. The waiting room was still, the lights harsh. She sat, waiting. Watching.

More people arrived. Aides. Staff. Then the children—red-eyed and shaken. Bastien, Émile, Juliette huddled together. No Delphine.

Merritt's thoughts spiralled—back to DuPont, the warehouse, the connection she couldn't unsee.

"This is Merritt," Sylvie said gently, nudging the children forward.

Merritt stood, adjusting the hoodie's sleeves. "It's lovely to meet you," she said softly, though she had already kind of met Juliette briefly.

The children nodded politely, their grief too big for introductions.

Time dragged forward in long, indistinguishable stretches. The soft rustle of clothing, the occasional buzz of a phone, the squeak of rubber soles against linoleum —everything felt muffled, like sound underwater. Merritt stared at the door, willing someone to walk through it with answers.

And then, finally, a doctor appeared.

"He's stable," she said. "In the ICU. Conscious."

Merritt stood before she knew she had moved. "Can we see him?"

A beat. Then a nod. "Follow me."

The ICU was silent save for the hum of machines. Beau lay still in the bed, pale and barely recognizable beneath the tangle of wires and monitors.

Juliette crept to his side. "Daddy," she whispered.

Bastien and Émile followed. Bastien reached for Beau's hand. "We're here," he said.

Beau's eyes fluttered. His lips moved, barely. No sound.

Merritt stayed in the doorway. Couldn't move. Couldn't breathe.

He was alive. But he looked like he might not be for long.

She'd come so close to losing love again.

Eventually, the nurse approached, her voice soft as she asked the children to head home and get some rest. Bastien was the last to let go, his hand slipping reluctantly from his father's.

Merritt didn't move.

The nurse turned to her. "You should get some rest too."

"I'm staying," she said quietly, but with a certainty that left no room for argument.

There was a pause. Then the nurse gave a small nod and slipped out, closing the door behind her.

Merritt lowered herself into the chair beside the bed. Her body ached with exhaustion, but she stayed upright, eyes fixed on Beau.

She wasn't going anywhere. Not when he was still fighting. Not when he'd almost slipped away. Not when she'd already lived through this kind of loss once.

If she had to lose someone again, she was damn well going to be there when it happened—and face it head-on.

Chapter 33
Beau ~ The Aftermath

Beau's eyes fluttered open to a room washed in sterile white. The brightness hit him like a blade, and he winced, retreating into the safety of darkness. Behind closed lids, colour bloomed and fractured—vivid, senseless shapes spinning through the fog in his mind.

He fought his way back.

When his eyes opened again, slower this time, the light still hurt, but he endured it—long enough to see her.

She stood across the room in clothes that looked borrowed from another life—baggy, mismatched sweats in wild colours, the emblem on her oversized hoodie unmistakable: Wu-Tang Clan.

A flicker of recognition broke through the haze. It didn't make sense, not yet. But it was her. Merritt.

Then the image dissolved, swallowed by the dark as his eyes slipped closed once more.

When his eyes opened again, she was still there. The harsh light seemed to spotlight the maroon flakes snaking up her neck, smudged over the collar of her hoodie, and smeared onto her cheek. His chest tightened, and his breathing hitched as panic clawed its way up from the depths of his exhaustion. Was that blood? Was she hurt?

His eyes closed involuntarily, his body felt like cement, but when he opened his eyes again, her presence remained—haunting, steady. Her hair was tied in a messy knot atop her head, her face washed out, the dark smudges under her eyes telling of a night full of tears and devoid of rest. His gaze lingered on the maroon streaks again, now realizing with mounting horror that it was blood.

Guilt clamped down on his chest, sharp and unrelenting. His thoughts were slow, muddled by pain and exhaustion, but one burned through with terrifying clarity: he hadn't listened to Quinn. He hadn't considered the risk to Merritt. His gaze caught on the blood streaked across her neck and cheek, and panic surged. Was she hurt? Had she been caught in the crossfire because of him? The thought twisted inside him, sick and spiralling. She looked so fragile—disheveled, blood-smeared, drowning in clothes that dwarfed her frame—it seemed impossible she wasn't injured. The chaos he'd failed to prevent stood before him now, too real to escape, too heavy to bear.

Beau blinked up at her, vision swimming. "Merritt?" he rasped, his voice barely there. "Why are you dressed like that? Where are your glasses?" His brow furrowed as he tried to make sense of the hoodie and streaks of maroon. "Are you hurt? Is that... is that jam?" His head lolled slightly as he tried to sit up, only for pain to clamp down hard across his chest, stealing his breath. He winced, collapsing back into the pillows. "Did we have pancakes?" he muttered, dazed.

His words trailed off, the absurd image of breakfast lingering for a beat before the haze began to clear. Something pulled at him—an itch at the back of his mind that refused to quiet. "Wait..." he murmured, blinking slowly. "Was this... my fault?" The question slipped out before he could stop it, cracking through the silence with a raw edge of fear. He shifted again, trying to rise, but pain surged up like a wave, fierce and immediate. His chest clenched, his limbs heavy and slow, his breathing jagged.

His eyes found hers—blood on her cheek, hair a tangled knot, hoodie far too big—and the confusion in him deepened. He didn't understand. He just knew she shouldn't look like that.

Merritt crossed the room in a few quiet steps, a smile finding its way through the worry on her face as she perched gently on the edge of the bed beside him.

"No," she whispered, brushing the hair from his brow. Her touch was careful, calming. She leaned in, pressing a tender kiss to his forehead before pulling back, her eyes steady on his.

"None of this was your fault."

"Beau, I'm okay," she reassured him, her hand moving absently to stroke the greying strands at his temples. "It's you," she said, her voice thick with emotion as she lifted one of his hands to her lips, pressing a featherlight kiss to the back of it. His eyes flickered down to his hand, taking in the IV needle taped to the pale skin.

Beau managed to lift his head, the effort monumental, every muscle straining against exhaustion. His eyes darted around the room, taking in the sterile machinery, its cold hum a sharp contrast to the warmth Merritt brought simply by being there. The exertion left him reeling, and his head fell back onto the pillow, heavy and final, as if even gravity conspired against him. But Merritt's hand clung to his.

"You were trying to leave me," Merritt whispered, her voice trembling, just audible over the soft beeping of the monitors.

With what little strength he had, Beau shifted, pain blooming through his chest as he pulled her closer. Her face hovered above his, blurred at the edges, but close enough.

"No," he rasped, his grip tightening weakly around her fingers. "I'm not going anywhere."

Then everything faded again.

Chapter 34
Merritt ~ The Waiting

In the days following the attempt on Beau's life, Merritt was kept at a distance. "It's for everyone's safety," Sylvie had said, and that was that. The justification may have been reasonable, but the enforced separation gnawed at her. She wanted to be near him—not waiting in silence, not reduced to second-hand updates.

To the outside world, Merritt Clarke had become a headline. Her relationship with Beau—once quiet, private—was now the subject of speculation, analysis, and tabloid frenzy. News outlets dissected her past, her career, her fashion, her every move. Photos of her leaving the NFC field office in a borrowed hoodie had gone viral.

And Avery still hadn't called.

Merritt was certain her friend had seen the coverage—of Beau's shooting, of their relationship, of Merritt smeared with his blood—but the silence remained unbroken, and increasingly impossible to understand.

At Beau's insistence, a private security firm now shadowed Merritt's every step. Two hulking bodyguards flanked her like shadows: waiting outside her office, trailing her on shortened runs with Sophie, idling in an unmarked car outside her house through the night. Their presence, while meant to reassure, only added to her sense of confinement. Her world had shrunk to three places: home, work, and the narrow sidewalks she was allowed to jog.

Messages from Beau arrived in short, infrequent bursts—whenever he had the strength. Each one was a tether, a flicker of light in the long stretches of waiting. Merritt reread them constantly, clinging to his affection in the quiet hours between updates from Sylvie. Beau was stable. Quinn was recovering, though the bullet had done significant damage. Merritt took in each report with a kind of reverent hunger, needing more than words could give her.

She tried to lose herself in work, but her firm had quietly

begun scaling back her caseload. Clients grew scarce. Colleagues offered tight smiles and careful glances. Merritt knew what they were thinking—*Is she a liability now?*

Evenings were the hardest. She curled up on the couch with Sophie, the husky pressed close, her warmth a balm as the news cycled endlessly. Footage of Beau's home flooded the screen—crime scene tape flickering in the breeze, NFC agents standing guard, the soft wash of sunrise caught on the driveway where everything had gone still.

Tonight, Lissa Tremblay's face filled Merritt's television screen, her tone steady and authoritative as she addressed the latest developments.

"Breaking developments tonight," the anchor began, "as new evidence links tech magnate Sebastian DuPont to last week's assassination attempt on Prime Minister Beau Laurent."

Merritt's breath caught, her hand freezing in Sophie's fur.

Tremblay continued, her voice measured. "According to newly obtained financial records and leaked internal communications, DuPont—founder of several major tech ventures—is confirmed to be the largest private donor to Victor Hargrave's Norlandic Conservative Union. Analysts believe the shooting may have been a last-ditch effort to destabilize the election, now just two days away, after earlier attempts to damage the Progressive Alliance platform failed."

Footage cut to the perimeter of Beau's home, police tape snapping in the breeze, NFC agents stationed at the perimeter. The house looked like a crime scene from a film. But Merritt had been there. She could still smell the blood.

"The shooter, André Buchner, remains in hospital following his arrest," Tremblay reported. "Sources confirm he will be charged under federal anti-terrorism laws. NFC officer Quinn McAllister, injured in the line of duty, remains in stable condition but. Her future with the agency is uncertain."

A photograph of DuPont flashed on screen—charismatic, polished, smiling behind a podium at a tech conference.

"DuPont's financial empire is now under federal investigation. Investigators have traced funds from a shell company linked to DuPont to the alleged shooter just days before the attack. Authorities have also confirmed that Buchner was the Voyagr driver who dropped Merritt Clarke—identified as a close associate of the Prime Minister—at his residence on the night of the shooting."

Merritt stared at the screen, her own name sounding foreign in Tremblay's voice.

"The Voyagr platform, though legally separated from DuPont's known holdings, is now believed to be indirectly owned through a cascade of offshore corporations. Investigators have seized servers from a Cascadia warehouse recently transferred to DuPont's wife, Genevieve. Sources confirm those servers contained location data and access logs with high-level permissions— raising significant concerns over potential misuse of user information, including sensitive addresses by Voyagr."

The screen shifted to footage of Delphine Moreau entering a press event, her smile tight and camera-ready.

"Former spouse of the Prime Minister, Delphine Moreau, is not believed to have been involved. While her affair with DuPont during her marriage to Laurent drew intense media scrutiny, new communications suggest the relationship may have been orchestrated to spark scandal within the Progressive Alliance. The affair ended abruptly after Laurent—then Minister of Finance—weathered the political fallout."

A brief photo montage played: Delphine with DuPont,

Delphine alone. Then Hargrave.

"Victor Hargrave has denied knowledge of DuPont's actions. However, leaked documents show DuPont not only financed Hargrave's campaign through various intermediaries, but also provided advanced voter analytics tools and supported coordinated efforts to discredit Progressive leadership. One of those efforts now appears to include the stabbing of former Prime Minister Greyson Hartwell—an incident previously believed to be isolated."

Merritt sat frozen, her mouth dry.

"DuPont has not issued a public statement. His legal team maintains his innocence."

Then, another photo of Merritt appeared on screen, the image taken the night of the shooting. She was wrapped in a grey blanket, the Wu-Tang hoodie barely visible underneath. Blood stained her cheek.

"Merritt Clarke, a prominent divorce attorney and personal partner of the Prime Minister, has declined public comment. She is not considered a suspect in the investigation."

Sophie shifted beside her, sensing the tension.

Lissa Tremblay's face returned to the screen. "Prime Minister Laurent remains in recovery. He is expected to make his first public appearance tomorrow as the country prepares for one of the most consequential elections in Norland's history."

The broadcast faded to commercial.

Merritt stared at the empty screen, the silence in the room suddenly too loud.

her hand flew to her mouth as the depth of the conspiracy sank in. She'd known the financial disclosures would cause ripples—but not this. Not a plot so sweeping and cold-blooded it made her stomach churn. Quietly leaking DuPont's offshore holdings and corporate ties had meant crossing an unthinkable line. She'd broken attorney-client privilege—something she had sworn never to do. But watching it unfold now, seeing how deeply it cut into Beau's life, into his recovery, she felt no regret. Only weight. The weight of knowing she'd helped unmask something uglier than she could have imagined.

She reached for her phone, her fingers trembling as she typed a message to Beau: *I just saw the broadcast. I can't believe how far they went. None of this changes what you've built. You're stronger than all of it—and I'm here for you. Always.*

His reply came quickly: *I know. They've thrown everything at me, but they can't take what matters. I'm still here. You're still here. My kids are safe. That's enough.*

I love you! Merritt texted.

I love you too, Mer. More than I can put into words, he wrote. Then, after a pause: *I'm speaking from here tomorrow. I'd love for you to be here. With me.*

From Sylvie, Merritt had learned that Beau had been moved back to his residence, where a private hospital room had been set up. The arrangement gave him greater privacy and security as he recovered—shielded from cameras and curious eyes.

Absolutely, she replied. Then, after a beat: *If they'll let me.*

His response came instantly, laced with familiar wit: *Mer, how many times do I have to remind you? I am the Prime Minister.*

A winking emoji followed, then a single crimson heart.

Merritt sat on the edge of the couch, Sophie's head heavy on her knee, her fingers absently stroking soft fur. Beau's words glowed on her phone, the crimson heart lingering like a promise. Her thumb brushed the screen, a small smile pulling at her lips.

The chaos of the past few days had nearly pulled her under—but Beau's message, and the way she felt about him, cut through it. Even now, wounded and vulnerable, he was steady. A reminder of the strength they shared. Of everything they'd both fought for.

She thought of the choice she'd made—the leak that had toppled DuPont's empire. It had been privileged information, given in trust during DuPont's divorce. And yet, when weighed against the consequences of staying silent, the decision had been painfully clear.

With Sylvie's help, it had been done carefully, discreetly. No one would trace it back to her. The sanctity of privilege still mattered—but so did justice. And tonight, watching the fallout unfold, Merritt felt no regret. That betrayal had been necessary. And if one day she had to answer for it, she would stand by it.

She rose, tucking her phone into her pocket, her resolve sharpening. Tomorrow, she would see him. Tomorrow, she would be at his side—not as a bystander, but as someone who had risked everything for him.

As Sophie padded after her up the stairs, Merritt let herself exhale—a long breath that finally eased the tightness in her chest.

Chapter 35
Beau ~ The Address

Beau's recovery felt excruciatingly slow. He pushed himself hard, demanding progress faster than his doctors thought wise. Returning home had been a hard-won victory—one he clung to with ferocity. It wasn't just about escaping the indignities of hospital life. It was about reclaiming control. Being home was its own kind of declaration: *Despite everything, I'm still standing.*

He loved this house—the life he'd built inside it—and he refused to let anyone take that from him. Not even as the blood stains lingered on the foyer floor.

His visitors were few, his days tightly controlled. His children came daily—their presence a needed reprieve—while aides and NFC agents moved through the halls, keeping him updated on the ever-widening conspiracy.

What stunned him most was how far back the threads reached—back to the calculated seduction of Delphine following his appointment as Minister of Finance. The realisation that his life had been entwined in this web for so long reopened wounds he'd thought had scarred over. He was deeply grateful to Eleanor Hartwell, whose brilliance had shielded him and his children from the worst of it, even if her deft manoeuvring hadn't been enough to spare Greyson.

The thought of Greyson ached. His friend had been another casualty of the same ruthless scheme—a leader undone by the very forces that had tried to dismantle Beau. Yet despite it all, Greyson still came to visit during Beau's recovery, a show of loyalty and a reminder of their shared purpose: the Progressive Alliance, and the future they both believed Norland deserved.

"You've got to fight through this," Greyson had said, his voice heavy. "The party needs you. The people need you. And Merritt..." He'd grinned, the corner of his mouth lifting in a rare tease, referencing the now-famous photos from Port Rainier.

Beau hadn't needed the prompt. The stakes of his recovery were not lost on him. The choices ahead were enormous, but for him, there was no hesitation. He would run. And if Norland gave him that chance, he would fight with everything he had to bring his vision of a fairer, stronger country to life.

In the hours leading up to his live, televised address— delivered not from a grand podium, but from his own home—Beau was surrounded by a small army of aides and speechwriters. Their voices filled the room with careful conviction, stitching together words of resilience and resolve, threading a fragile hope through the storm of violence and betrayal. Beau listened closely, weighing every phrase. He didn't want vengeance in his voice—he wanted vision. Something that would outlast fear.

When the final draft was printed and stacked neatly on a side table, the nurses stepped in to help him dress. They moved around him with efficiency, adjusting his collar, straightening his jacket, fastening cufflinks with steady hands. Each gesture reminded him that his strength was still returning, inch by inch. But he was here. He was standing.

The door opened, and Sylvie stepped in—then moved aside to let Merritt enter behind her.

Beau turned toward the sound, and the smile that spread across his face was instant, unguarded. Their eyes met, and for one suspended second, the noise of strategy, scandal, and high political stakes faded. All he saw was her.

"Can I touch you?" Merritt asked softly, stopping just a few steps from him. Her voice trembled with hesitation, her posture cautious—like one wrong move might end him. There was warmth in her gaze, but also a flicker of fear, as if she couldn't quite believe he was truly standing there.

"I'd really like to hug you," she added, her words barely above a whisper.

Beau's smile deepened. "I think I can manage that," he said, his voice edged with the same ache and awe that filled her own.

He took a careful step forward, moving with intention. His arms came around her slowly, gently—avoiding the dressing at his chest, mindful of every healing nerve. But the second she was in his arms, something in him gave way. He drew her closer, his breath catching as he buried his face in the curve of her shoulder. The familiar scent of vanilla wrapped around him like a lifeline.

Neither of them moved.

"You saved my life," he whispered into her skin, the words raw. And before he let her go, he pressed a soft, aching kiss just above her collarbone, as if to mark the place where gratitude met love.

A producer's voice cut through their stillness, brisk and insistent, pulling Beau out of the moment. He was guided away for final adjustments, surrounded by a flurry of movement. Aides and nurses moved with precision—adjusting his collar, straightening his jacket, checking the lighting—every detail calibrated to project strength, steadiness, and hope.

He took his seat beneath the harsh glare of studio lights, the hum of the cameras rising like static in the air. His chest ached beneath his bandages, each breath a reminder of how close he'd come to losing everything. But he held himself still, composed. Ready.

The countdown began, the producer's voice in his ear, marking the final seconds.

Beau's eyes shifted across the room—to her. Merritt stood near the edge of the set, half in shadow, her arms crossed tightly over the soft fabric of her sweater. Her gaze never wavered. In the steady warmth of her eyes, he found what he needed.

When the cue came, Beau turned to face the camera. He drew a deep breath, held it for half a second, and spoke—not just to the nation that waited with bated breath, but to the woman whose unexpected presence had changed everything.

"Good evening," Beau began.

"Tonight, I want to speak to the challenges we face as a nation—the uncertainty, the fear, and the forces that try to divide and tear us down. These past weeks have been a stark reminder of how far some will go to protect their power, their privilege and to silence the voices calling for change. But let me tell you this: no matter how calculated their efforts; they will never overcome the strength of hope and resilience that binds us together.

"In recent days, the truth about the attacks on my life and the efforts to undermine this government have come to light. These were not random acts. They were calculated attempts to silence the voices that demand equality and fight for equity—voices that represent every person in Norland who has ever believed in building a fairer, brighter future. These efforts were designed to protect the wealth and influence of the powerful few, keeping opportunities out of reach for far too many. But they have failed. They failed because the spirit of this nation, the belief that fairness and justice must extend to everyone, cannot and will not be defeated.

"My purpose has always been clear: to work toward a Norland where every person has a real opportunity to succeed, regardless of where they come from or the barriers they face. A Norland where the child of a single parent in the heart of Rider's Rest has the same access to education and opportunity as the child of a CEO here in Arbourleigh. A Norland where workers are valued for their labour, where a living wage is not a privilege but a right. A Norland where fairness is not just an aspiration but a reality we build together.

"This vision has not changed. If anything, the challenges of these past weeks have made it even stronger. The attacks against me, against this government, against what we stand for, have reminded me of one simple truth: those who cheat, who harm, who deceive, do so because they fear what we can achieve. They fear a world where their power is no longer unchecked. They fear progress. And they should.

"To those who have fought so hard to keep Norland divided, who have sought to protect their wealth and influence at the expense of others, let me say this: you have not won. You will not win. This country belongs to its people—not to the few, not to the privileged, but to all of us. And together, we will rebuild what you tried to break.

"I know many of you are tired—tired of the weight of inequality, the frustration of working harder only to fall further behind, and the anger of watching those at the top grow richer while others struggle just to get by. But I also know this: you are stronger than those challenges. We are stronger together. And together, we can build a future that is truly for everyone—a future where no one is left behind, no matter their ethnicity, sexual orientation, gender identity, or any other part of who they are. This is the Norland we deserve, and this is the Norland we will create.

"This is our moment to rise above. Our moment to show that good, no matter how fiercely it is challenged, will always prevail. So tomorrow, when you cast your vote, I ask you to remember this: we are not just voting for policies or platforms. We are voting for the kind of Norland we want to leave behind for those who come after us—a Norland built on fairness, kindness, and the belief that every person matters.

"Thank you, and I promise you this: together, we will move forward, stronger than ever."

As the broadcast ended, the room erupted into applause, the sound filling the space with a mix of relief and admiration. Beau shifted in his chair, bracing his hands on the armrests as he pushed himself to his feet. The effort was slow, his body still protesting every movement, but determination flickered in his eyes.

The nurses moved toward him immediately, concern etched into their faces, but Beau waved them off with a grumble. "I'm fine," he said, his voice weary, brushing away their hovering hands.

His gaze locked onto Merritt, standing quietly in the corner, her arms folded across her chest. Without hesitation, he made his way toward her. She straightened as he approached, her expression softening, and by the time he reached her, the noise of the room seemed to fade.

As Merritt wrapped her arms around him, Beau winced slightly, a sharp breath escaping through his teeth.

"Fuck," she blurted, immediately stepping back, her eyes wide with panic. "I'm so sorry!" Her hand flew to her mouth, guilt written all over her face.

"Oh no," Beau said, his voice laced with dry humor. "It's just that I got shot a couple of days ago, so, you know, I'm a bit fragile. No big deal." He laughed softly as he stepped forward, closing the space she had created between them.

This time, he gently encircled her in his arms, his movements slow but sure. "See?" he murmured, his chin finding the perfect spot on the top of her shoulder. "Still standing. Still fine. Still not going anywhere."

"You were amazing," Merritt said softly into his ear, their embrace unbroken. Then, a teasing smile played on her lips. "I think I might actually vote for you."

Beau laughed as he held her a little closer. "Your vote is the one that matters the most," he whispered. After a moment, he pulled back just enough to meet her gaze.

"Will you stay tonight?" he asked, his voice quieter now, almost tentative. "I know our last sleepover didn't exactly go as planned..." A faint smile pulled at his lips, but he felt a vulnerability in the way he searched her face, as though her answer mattered more than he could say.

Merritt smiled, her hand rising instinctively to touch his face. Her fingers grazed his cheek, the touch electric amidst the tumult of what they had endured. "I'd like that," she said simply, her words laced with beginnings, second chances and continuations. To Beau, it felt like more than an answer—it was an offering of trust, a surrender to the connection between them. Despite everything that had come before, she was giving herself permission to step forward, to lean into whatever came on the edge of after.

Beau exhaled, the tension in his body dissolving. "Good," he said, that single word carrying everything they had spent their time together building and then diving into. His arms tightened around her again.

They stood like that for a long moment, suspended in the warmth of each other's presence.

"I don't know what tomorrow will bring," Beau said quietly, his voice tight with worry. "It feels like everything is on the line—more than just policy or progress. Politics doesn't feel like governance anymore. It's become a battlefield for morality." He paused, shaking his head. "We're re-litigating fights we had laid to rest decades ago, and instead of building on that, we're waging war on equality, fairness, and basic human dignity."

His hands slipped from Merritt's waist as he began to pace, his steps slow but purposeful—the measured movement of a man still healing, but unwilling to remain still. "This isn't politics," he said, glancing at her. "It's cruelty, dressed up as conviction. It's about silencing anyone who doesn't fit into the narrow worldview of the loudest and the cruelest. And that's what we're up against."

Merritt stepped in and placed her hands gently on his

shoulders. "We can't control tomorrow," she said, her voice calm and certain. "You've done everything you can —and for what it's worth, I believe in you."

She kissed his cheek, slow and warm, then pulled back just enough to meet his eyes. "But no more speeches tonight, Prime Minister. Tonight is just us. We'll worry about tomorrow, tomorrow."

With a smile, Merritt slipped her hand into his and led him out of the room, now vacant and cluttered with dormant camera equipment. The hallway beyond was softly lit, calm and still, and the worry over tomorrow seemed to ease with every step.

"Merritt," Beau said, gently pulling her to a stop. She turned to face him.

"Where exactly are you taking me?" he asked, a playful smile on his lips. "You've never even made it up here, despite my best efforts to change that."

Her grin deepened. "Not yet. But I'm a quick study," she said, gesturing down the hallway with a casual flick of her hand. "I figured one of these doors must lead to a bedroom. I guess I was just hoping to get lucky?"

Beau laughed, the sound easy and unguarded. "If getting lucky is the goal, let me at least improve your odds by pointing you in the right direction."

He took the lead, guiding her gently down the hall. When they reached his room, he pushed open the door to reveal a space bathed in the amber light of dusk. Long shadows stretched across the floor, softening the sharp edges of the day and casting everything in a warm, glow.

At the foot of the bed, Beau paused, catching his breath. He turned to face her, his hand still wrapped in hers, and with a faint, steady smile, guided her down to the corner of the bed.

Beau tightened his grip on Merritt's hand, steadying himself as he wavered slightly—then dropped to one knee. His heart thundered in his chest, every beat a blend of nerves and absolute certainty. This wasn't the grand moment he'd imagined when he bought the ring just a week ago. But as his movements faltered, the pain of healing still present in every motion, it felt right. Honest. A mirror of their love—imperfect, unvarnished, and all the more beautiful for it.

From where he knelt, he looked up at her, gaze unwavering despite the tremble in his limbs and the pain in his chest. Slowly, he reached into the inner pocket of his navy jacket. His fingers brushed the silk lining before closing around the velvet box. Deep emerald green, it caught the room's soft light as he drew it out and cradled it in his hand.

"I didn't plan it like this," Beau said gently, opening the box to reveal a princess-cut green diamond encircled by a halo of white. "I saw this ring while we were driving through the mountains. And I thought of you."

Merritt didn't speak. Her eyes held his.

"I told myself I'd wait for the perfect moment," he continued, voice steady but wavering as if holding back tears. "That I'd find some quiet, perfect setting to ask you this. But the truth is, there are no perfect moments. There's only this one—and somehow, ours have always been perfect in their imperfection."

He paused, emotion rising like a tide. "I know it's soon," he admitted softly, his voice barely above a whisper. "But I also know what I feel. And I know it's real."

He took a breath. "You've made me braver than I ever thought I could be. You reminded me that there's still something worth fighting for—not in politics, not in noise, but here. With you."

His voice cracked, and he blinked against the tears blurring his vision, cheeks flushing with raw vulnerability.

"What I'm trying to say," he said, his words catching in his throat, "is that I love you. Somehow, even more in this second chance than I ever thought possible. And if you'll let me, I want to spend the rest of my life proving that—proving that even in our mess, even in everything we've come through, we can build something extraordinary."

He reached for the ring, the green diamond flashing like hope in his palm. "Merritt Clarke, will you marry me?"

Chapter 36
Merritt ~ Diving into After

For a moment, Merritt didn't move. Her mind spun, her heart pounding—but her answer was already written in every beat. Of course it was *yes*. How could it be anything else? And yet, as her eyes held Beau's, time seemed to suspend itself. She felt it then—the past she'd once been afraid to leave making room, at last, for something new.

The ache of losing Everett hadn't vanished; it never would. But somehow, in this moment, there was space for both grief and hope. Space for more love. For Beau.

"Mer?" Beau's voice was soft, laced with emotion, his eyes shimmering with tears.

She blinked, her breath hitching as her lips parted, searching for words that didn't quite come. "I just..." she faltered. "Can we stay like this a second longer?" Her voice was faint but steady, trusting the stillness to say what she couldn't. She needed to hold onto this—this fragile, perfect second—before time dared to move again.

Beau nodded, and the tears slipped free, silent streaks down his face. Merritt reached out, brushing them away with the tips of her fingers. Then, leaning in, she kissed him—slow and deep—letting everything she felt pass between them in that one, unguarded moment.

Her lips brushed his ear as she whispered, "Of course I'll marry you."

Carefully, Beau slid the ring onto her finger, his hand trembling slightly. As he rose unsteadily to his feet, Merritt was there—arms wrapped around him, centering him with a touch that felt as essential as air.

She kissed him again, soft and searching, her lips trailing along the line of his jaw to the curve of his neck. Her hands moved with purpose, slipping his suit jacket from his shoulders and letting it fall to the floor. One by one, her fingers found the buttons of his crisp white dress shirt, undoing them slowly. With each inch of fabric pulled away, the bandages over his chest came into view—stark against his skin, a sobering reminder of how close they'd come to losing everything.

Her hand came to rest over his heart, her touch featherlight, afraid to press too hard. Beneath her palm, she felt the steady rhythm—fragile, resilient, and wholly his. "Beau," she whispered, his name breaking in her throat like a prayer.

He brought his hands to her face, cupping it with infinite care, his thumbs brushing away a tear she hadn't realized had fallen. "I'm here," he said, the tenderness in his voice wrapping around her like warmth on a cold night. "And I'm not going anywhere."

She kissed him again, deeper this time. Her hands moved to his waist, their motions deliberate and gentle, as if nothing beyond this moment mattered. The world outside the room faded, eclipsed by their shadows melting together in the warm light of dusk.

Guiding him carefully to the bed, she followed, helping him ease down with care. He winced, a pained breath catching in his throat as the movement stirred the pain in his chest, but he didn't let go of her hand. She climbed in beside him, curling her body around his with tenderness, every motion shaped by the awareness of his healing.

A soft shuffle of paws echoed in the quiet, and then Sophie leapt onto the bed. She circled once, then settled at their feet with a heavy sigh.

Merritt smiled faintly, brushing her hand along Beau's side. He let out a long breath, his body slowly relaxing into hers, one hand resting over hers where it lay gently over his bandaged chest.

She held him that way, feeling the slow rise and fall of his breath beneath her palm. Her face tucked into the curve of his neck, where the gentle thud of his pulse reassured her—he was here. He was safe.

With her arms around him and Sophie curled at their feet, Merritt let her eyes fall closed. Night had fully settled in, but in the darkness, she clung to the certainty of this moment—of them.

Whatever tomorrow held, it could wait.

For now, she had him.

Chapter 37
Beau ~ The Future They Chose

When Beau's alarm chimed, he awoke to the warmth of Merritt's arm still wrapped securely around him, her body pressed against his. For a moment, he allowed himself to stay there, breathing her in, the ache in his chest pulling at him as he shifted to face her. He rolled carefully onto his side, their foreheads brushing as his lips found hers. She stirred under his kiss, her eyes fluttering open to meet his. A faint smile spread across her face.

As the kiss ended, he pulled back slightly, watching her as sleep slowly released its hold. She stretched languidly, her body arching toward him before she pressed her lips to his once more, brief but tender. She lay back again, her dark hair fanning out across the pillow, her arms reaching above her head in a gesture of contentment.

He stayed, watching her until the persistent ache in his chest became too much to ignore. He swung his legs over the edge of the bed and rose, padding barefoot to the ensuite. The door remained open as he fumbled for his pain medication, swallowing the pills with a handful of water scooped from the faucet. He could see Merritt's gaze on him, reflected in the mirror above the basin.

"What do you see?" he asked her, their eyes meeting in the mirror.

She sat up, pulling Beau's sheets around her. "The future," she said. "Mine, and the nations." Her steps were soft as she crossed the bedroom, the sheet trailing behind her. She came to stand behind him, her hand brushing his shoulder before her lips followed, pressing a kiss there, tender and deep. Then she turned his face to hers, her eyes holding his as her lips found his mouth.

Merritt turned, letting the sheet slip from her fingers as she stepped into Beau's shower. She turned the water on, the gentle hiss filling the room as steam began to rise. Beau leaned back against the counter, his gaze following her until the glass fogged over, her figure dissolving into a shadow moving behind the blurred pane. He watched as she tilted her head back under the stream, washing her hair, her silhouette serene in the hot cascade of water.

When she emerged, her damp hair clung to her shoulders, droplets tracing rivulets down her skin. She reached for Beau's towel, wrapping it snugly around herself, the fabric seeming to embrace her as much as he longed to. He couldn't supress the small, sideways grin that played at his lips. He couldn't help but admire her, every part of her—not just the parts she shared with him, but all of her. Her focus, her dedication, her unapologetic independence. Merritt was hers first, and that, he realized, was what made her presence in his life even more extraordinary.

She passed him on her way back to the bedroom. He followed, lingering by the doorway as she dressed in yesterday's clothes, tying her wet hair into a loose braid. The simple ritual of her morning felt as intentional as the woman herself. When she glanced at her watch, her pace quickened slightly.

"I'm going to be late," Merritt said, her voice matter-of-fact as her fingers moved quickly over her phone, texting her private security team to let them know she was ready. A knock sounded at the front door—an unwelcome reminder of the day waiting beyond it, and all that hung in the balance.

Beau crossed the room and came to stand in front of her, his hands resting gently at her waist. He leaned in to kiss her, his lips brushing hers in a moment that lingered just long enough. "I'll see you tonight?" he asked softly, one brow lifted.

"Of course," Merritt said, smiling.

Sophie stirred from her spot on the bed, brushing against Merritt's leg. Merritt reached down to scratch behind her ears, then straightened as the knock came again, firmer this time.

"Leave her here," Beau said. "Consider her my insurance policy—you'll have to come back for her."

Merritt's hand lingered on Sophie's head as she glanced back at him, a playful glint in her eyes. "As long as you want me, I'll always come back. But yeah, I'm always coming back for this girl."

Beau's smile deepened. "I'll hold you to that."

She leaned in, pressing a soft kiss to his mouth. "You've got this," she murmured. "So don't waste the day being nervous. Go win a country."

As the front door closed behind her, Beau moved to the window that overlooked the driveway. He watched as she glanced back over her shoulder, raising a hand in a small wave before slipping into the waiting car. He lifted his own in return, holding it aloft until the vehicle disappeared from sight.

Only then did he turn back into the house—Sophie already trailing his movements like a loyal shadow.

The morning unraveled in a blur of routine and hovering hands. The nurses overseeing his recovery fluttered about as he ate his breakfast—fresh fruit and what they optimistically called "nutritious" oats. Beau had other names for the lukewarm mush, none polite. Sophie rested nearby with her chin on his foot, casting him sympathetic glances, as if she, too, found the meal an affront.

After breakfast, the nurses descended again, guiding him through a shower with the same brisk efficiency they applied to changing a dressing. Their hands were gentle but insistent, their fussing barely concealed beneath a veneer of professionalism. He bore it all with restrained grumbling, though his pride prickled at needing help for something so personal.

"Prime Minister or not," one of them teased as she adjusted his bandage, "you can't add a husky and a girlfriend to your recovery and pretend that doesn't count as added strain."

Beau smirked. "Sophie's doing all the heavy lifting."

By late morning, they escorted him to his main-floor office—a journey he insisted he could manage solo, only to be shadowed the entire way. Once settled into the leather chair behind his desk, Sophie flopped beside him with a sigh.

From there, Beau's focus shifted to the people who had made this moment possible. He spent the morning making calls to longtime supporters, his voice warm with gratitude. Between texts to volunteers and short check-ins with key aides, he found himself buoyed by both the memory of the night before and the promise of the day ahead.

A few pre-arranged interviews with national media channels filled the midday hours, conducted from the controlled quiet of his home office. His tone was steady, hopeful, and his words carefully measured. There was nothing left to campaign for, nothing left to prove. Only the waiting remained. In mere hours, Norlanders would choose their next Prime Minister.

With the polls open, he was carefully escorted to visit two nearby polling stations under tight security. Each visit was brief but meaningful—a show of trust in the democratic process, a signal that he was still standing. He smiled for the cameras, exchanged pleasantries, and posed for a handful of photos that would be shared online by his team. Back in the car, he recorded short videos encouraging citizens to vote. "Today is your chance," he said, voice warm, "to shape the future we'll share."

By evening, Beau returned home, the energy of the day giving way to simmering anticipation. His campaign team had gathered in the living room, their voices weaving through the space as early results began to roll in. Beau settled onto the large sectional, his body grateful for the reprieve. Sophie trotted over and curled up at his feet with a soft sigh. He scanned the room, catching snippets of conversation, bursts of laughter, and the undercurrent of cautious hope that threaded through it all.

Shortly after dusk, Merritt arrived. From his seat, Beau watched as Sylvie opened the door, taking the overnight bag from her hands. Merritt stepped inside, scanning the crowded room until her eyes found his. Sophie, already sprawled at Beau's feet, perked up at the sound of the door and bounded over to greet her, tail wagging like a banner of celebration. Merritt dropped to her knees to greet the husky, scratching behind her ears before rising and weaving through the crowd.

When she reached him, the aide seated at Beau's side shifted, making room. Merritt settled in beside him, curling her legs beneath her. "This is it," she said with a mix of excitement and reassurance in her voice. She leaned in, pressing a kiss to his cheek before draping an arm around his shoulders. Her presence, like always, settled something inside him.

Beau glanced at her, his chest tightening—not with pain, but with something deeper, more enduring. Gratitude, and the overwhelming sense that whatever happened tonight, he already had what mattered most.

The room quieted as the first results began to appear on the screen. The broadcasters spoke with deliberate calm, their voices tinged with the anticipation that gripped everyone watching. Beau's team leaned forward collectively; their murmurs soft but charged as they analyzed the early numbers. It was still too soon to draw conclusions, but the map began to light up with the first ridings reporting, small flickers of orange, blue, and green punctuating the vast grey of the nation.

Beau sat back, his gaze on the television, though the words

and numbers felt distant, like a tide rushing in just out of reach. His advisors spoke in bursts—celebrations, cautions—but it all blurred together. Then he felt it—Merritt's hand on his shoulder, a subtle squeeze that pulled him back into the room. Not with force, but with presence. He turned toward her, catching the certainty in her eyes—calm, but bright with conviction. She didn't speak. She didn't have to. He was quickly learning how much could be said in her stillness, how deeply she could reassure him with nothing more than a look. With her, silence never felt empty. It felt full. Solid. Like faith.

The results began to roll in faster as the eastern provinces reported. One riding flipped in his party's favour, then another, the coloured orange markers slowly spreading across the map. Cheers broke out among the team as a bellwether riding—a traditionally conservative stronghold—turned orange. It was a small victory but significant, and Beau allowed himself a flicker of hope.

As the hours passed, the map continued to fill, riding after riding reporting with dizzying speed. The broadcasters shifted their tone, their commentary more animated as trends began to emerge. The votes weren't just promising—they were historic. In provinces like Montclair and Cascadia, where his party had fought tooth and nail, the results were resounding. In Aurivale, where his platform had faced deep skepticism, they were holding their ground. The numbers were undeniable: Beau's party was surging.

The room erupted as a major milestone was declared. "Progressive Alliance poised to form the next government," Lissa Tremblay announced, her voice slicing through the tension like a thunderclap. Beau's breath caught in his chest, the importance of the moment pressing down and lifting him all at once. Around him, his team broke into applause and jubilant embraces, the room alive with an energy that felt almost electric.

Merritt turned to him, her smile radiant, her eyes shimmering with pride. "You did it," she whispered, her voice barely audible above the celebration. She cupped his face with both hands, guiding his gaze to hers before kissing him deeply, a gesture filled with certainty and unrestrained joy. The moment was theirs, but a campaign volunteer caught it on her phone, the image immortalizing in love and triumph.

Beau sank into the moment with Merritt, his eyes never leaving hers as his hands cradled her face in return. The sounds of the room faded into the background, the world narrowing to just the two of them. Then, from the television, the words broke through like a lightning strike: "Beau Laurent, Norland's next Prime Minister."

The room erupted into cheers and applause. Merritt threw her arms around Beau's neck, her laughter mingling with the joyous cries of his team. Sophie barked excitedly, weaving through the crowd with her tail wagging furiously, as if she, too, understood the magnitude of the moment.

Beau's ears buzzed, the noise of the room blurring at the edges, as Merritt slipped her arm under his to help him rise to his feet. His body protested, the ache in his chest sharp and insistent, but he pushed through it, driven by the sheer weight of the moment.

"Prime Minister," Merritt addressed him with pride.

He grinned, his hands finding her waist and pulling her close. "You can still call me Beau," he teased, his voice rough with emotion as he kissed her deeply. The world seemed to disappear again.

Despite the pain lancing through his chest, Beau spun her gently, dipping her in his arms as her laughter spilled out like music. He kissed her again, this time slower, savouring the moment as the room roared around them. For the first time in a long time, Beau allowed himself to believe in the promise of what was to come.

* * * * *

The evening wore on with celebration despite the late hour. There were toasts and laughter, champagne and tearful hugs. They toasted the future a dozen times over, to Beau, to progress—then again to Beau.

Eventually, the crowd thinned.

In the early hours of morning, coats were shrugged on, goodbyes were said, and one by one, the house emptied out. What remained was stillness.

Even Sophie was done, her head resting on her paws as she lay curled up at the far end of the couch, too tired to lift it when Merritt walked by.

Merritt turned off the last lamp, leaving the living room cast in soft shadows and the glow of the moonlight. She turned toward Beau, expecting him to suggest they head to bed.

But he didn't move.

He stayed where he was—reclined on the deep sectional, shirt untucked, tie long gone, his chest rising and falling slowly beneath the edge of a blanket draped over him. The exhaustion in his face was unmistakable, but so was the glint in his eyes.

When she walked closer, he reached out and caught her hand. His grip was gentle but sure. "Don't go just yet," he said.

She arched an eyebrow. "I thought you weren't allowed any strenuous activity?" she teased, the intention in his expression leaving little room for doubt.

He tugged her down onto the couch beside him,

wincing slightly as he shifted to make space for her along his side.

"I'll risk it," he muttered, slipping a finger beneath her chin to tilt her face toward his. "I've been waiting all damn night to celebrate properly with you."

His hand slid around her waist, drawing her gently over his lap. She straddled him without hesitation, her knees sinking into the cushions on either side of his thighs, their bodies already falling into rhythm.

"Beau," she whispered, fingertips brushing his cheek without pulling away, "you're still healing—"

"I know," he said softly, pressing his lips to her jaw, his breath warm against her skin. "I'm healing, not dead. And you—" his voice dipped, rough with want—"you look so incredible right now."

The words pulled a small sound from her—half laugh, half exhale—as she leaned in to his lips.

He kissed her deeper, tasting the night on her skin, the tension they hadn't yet shaken, and something else too— something that felt like coming back to life.

His hands slid beneath her sweater, fingertips tracing the warm length of her spine. She felt so good—soft, real, right here. She arched slightly as he explored, and the small, breathy sound she made nearly undid him.

Her fingers moved to his shirt, slow and sure, and he stilled at the feel of her undoing each button. She peeled the fabric apart with care, eyes flicking to the edge of the bandage across his ribs.

When her hand brushed it, pain flared sharp and quick— but it was eclipsed by the heat of her touch, by the way she looked at him like she still wanted him, especially now.

He hissed through his teeth.

She pulled back instinctively, but he caught her wrist and held it there—right over his heart. "I'm good," he said. "Don't stop."

He needed her too badly to pretend otherwise. The ache in his chest was nothing compared to this—the ache to feel her move against him, around him, to lose himself in the heat of her skin and the sound of her breath and the way she always gave herself to him like there was no one else in the world.

He pulled her back to him, and this time, when their bodies met, there was no space left between them. Heat surged as clothes were shed in slow, aching increments— her sweater lifted, his shirt peeled open, the brush of skin on skin enough to make his breath stutter in his throat.

They kissed like they were starving. Not frantic—just hungry in that deep, serene way that burned from the inside out.

When she sank onto him, it stole the air from his lungs. His hands gripped her hips, holding her steady as his eyes swept over her, hunger and awe tangled in every breath.

"Merritt," he whispered, voice frayed, reverent. His fingers flexed against her skin, trying to hold on and let go all at once.

She moved over him slowly, beautifully, and it was everything—heat and tension and surrender wrapped into a rhythm that was theirs alone. He couldn't look away. Couldn't stop touching her. The curve of her waist beneath his hands. The way she gasped when he angled his hips. The rise and fall of her body against his, over and over, until time bent around them.

He was losing track of everything but her—her body, her breath, the way she said his name like it meant salvation.

He buried his face in her neck, murmuring into her skin, not even sure what he was saying. Just the truth, over and over. That he needed her. That he never wanted to be without her. That this, *this*, was the thing that had kept him going.

When release came, it wasn't a crash—it was a slow, relentless wave. A tightening. A shattering. A falling apart inside the safety of her hands.

They stayed like that, suspended in the after, bodies slick and tangled, hearts still racing. She curled into him, one hand on his chest, her thumb absently stroking the edge bandage he barely felt anymore.

He reached for the blanket and pulled it over them both, tucking it behind her shoulder—the gesture tender, possessive, permanent.

Outside, the city stretched toward morning.

Inside, there was only heat. Only skin. Only her.

"I think," he said, brushing his lips against her bare shoulder, "that might be my favourite win of the night."

They stayed like that, their bodies still joined, the warmth between them sinking deep. Eventually, they drifted into sleep—Merritt's head tucked under his chin, his hand still resting at the small of her back. Sophie lay curled at the edge of the sectional, her soft breathing the only sound in the otherwise silent house.

* * * * *

The morning crept in slowly, the sky outside shifting from deep navy to pale grey. Merritt stirred first, her cheek pressed against Beau's chest, the weight of sleep still thick in her limbs. The couch was warm. Familiar. So was the steady rise and fall of his breathing next to her.

She stirred, awareness slowly returning—the couch, the weight of a blanket, the solid warmth of Beau next to her—just as the front door opened.

There was the unmistakable jingle of keys, the creak of hinges, and then the low murmur of Sylvie's voice greeting someone. A moment later, light footsteps approached across the hardwood.

Beau blinked awake just in time to see two unfamiliar nurses—cheerful, efficient, and clearly unprepared to find the Prime Minister wrapped in nothing but a throw blanket, his entirely unclothed fiancé nestled at his side.

Merritt made a noise—half gasp, half groan—and ducked her head beneath the blanket without ceremony, her hair disappearing in a rush against his ribs. He could feel her body curl tighter, both mortified and laughing under her breath.

Beau let out a slow exhale, more amused than anything, and reached for the edge of the blanket, shifting it a little higher over Merritt.

Sylvie stepped into the room behind the nurses, coffee in hand. She paused just long enough for one brow to lift—barely perceptible—before smoothing her expression into something cool and impeccably professional.

She gave Beau a once-over, noted Merritt's distinct lack of visibility, and took a sip. "You do realize you're scheduled to give a national address in less than two hours?" she said, a dry laugh slipping past her lips before she turned and ushered the nurses toward the kitchen.

"At this rate," Merritt mumbled from beneath the blanket, "every member of your staff is going to see me naked."

Beau smiled, pulled the blanket down just enough to press a kiss to the top of her head. "Worth it," he said, voice warm with amusement.

* * * * *

Later, Beau and Merritt were whisked to Civic Plaza at Dominion House to deliver Beau's victory speech. Merritt walked beside him, her hand clasped firmly in his as they ascended the steps together. The crowd gathered below was ecstatic, their cheers swelling like a wave, filling the crisp morning air with an energy that felt almost electric.

It wasn't just the political victory they were celebrating—it was the story of Beau and Merritt, a love affair that had captivated the nation as much as the election itself overnight. Many in the crowd held up the morning's newspapers, the front page dominated by the now-iconic photograph of Merritt cradling Beau's face, her lips pressed to his in an unmistakable kiss. The pale-green diamond of her engagement ring sparkled prominently in the image, a symbol of the personal triumph intertwined with the political one.

Victory and Vows: Beau Laurent's Win Sealed with Love, the headlines proclaimed. The photograph had become more than just a moment captured—it was a symbol of hope and unity, resonating with a nation hungry for both. Beau felt the warmth of the crowd's support washing over him, their cheers buoying him as he prepared to speak. As he stood before the gathered crowd, Merritt at his side, he couldn't help but feel the depth of the moment—both for the country he now led and for the life they were building together.

"Good morning, Norland," Beau began, his voice rich with emotion.

"Today, we do more than turn a page—we illuminate it. Last night, you chose to shed light in the places that have long been overshadowed by darkness. You chose compassion over cruelty, progress over stagnation, and hope over despair. You chose to believe in the strength of unity and the power of what we can accomplish when we stand together.

"This victory is not mine—it is ours. It belongs to every volunteer who spent their evenings knocking on doors, to every family who sat together at their kitchen tables debating the kind of nation we want to become, one we can be proud to call home. It belongs to every person who cast their vote believing in a fairer, brighter future for every Norlander. It belongs to those who dared to hope, even when hope felt impossible.

"Our campaign was never about me—it was about you. It was about seeing the overlooked, hearing the unheard, and giving voice to those who felt silenced. We promised equality, fairness, and the unshakable belief that no one should be left behind. Today, I renew that promise. This moment marks not the end of a campaign, but the beginning of a responsibility—a responsibility to lead with humility, compassion, and service.

"I stand here today because of the people who lifted me when I felt the weight of the world on my shoulders. To my colleagues, my friends, and the many hands who made this campaign possible—thank you. To my children—you are my light and my reason. You remind me every day of the kind of Norland I want to leave behind to you and your generation who make up our future. To Merritt— your faith in me has been my anchor and my guide. You have taught me that love is not just a gift but a responsibility, one I will carry with me always. And to Greyson Hartwell—your leadership and dedication to this nation leave behind a legacy of integrity that I will strive to honour as I move forward.

"As we step into this new chapter, let us remember: Norland's progress is never the work of one person but the collective will of a people who refuse to give up. The road ahead will not be easy—change never is. But I believe in this country. I believe in its people. And I believe in the extraordinary things we can build together.

"So, today, Norland, we begin again. With light to guide us. With hope to unite us. And with a promise to create something remarkable, together. Let's get to work."

As the cheers of the crowd swelled, Beau stepped back from the podium and into Merritt's waiting arms, his words lingering in the air as the crowd continued to cheer. For a moment, he allowed himself to pause, to breathe, to absorb the faces of those who had gathered. Merritt's hand rested lightly on his back as they ended their embrace.

He stepped back, his hand finding hers as he lifted it to his lips and kissed it gently. Their fingers intertwined, they stood together at the edge of the stage, their united front a silent symbol of gratitude and resolve. Merritt squeezed his hand softly, her touch saying everything she didn't need to put into words: *I'm here. I'm with you.*

The crowd's cheers grew louder, a wave of sound that seemed to echo the energy of the season and the moment. The early March air carried the first stirrings of spring, the faint scent of renewal mingling with the hope and anticipation of a nation poised on the brink of change. For Beau, the moment transcended the noise. The world narrowed to the warmth of Merritt's hand in his, the promise in her eyes, and the vision of the future they would build—not just for themselves but for the country they both believed in.

As they turned to leave the stage, Merritt's hand never left Beau's, her grip as steady as his resolve. Beau glanced at her, a smile at the corners of his lips, then looked ahead, his chest filling with something deeper than pride. It was hope.

Together, they stepped forward, into the unknown, into possibility, and into a future they would shape—side by side.

Epilogue
Avery ~ The Breaking and the Becoming

Rewatching the election coverage, I sat curled on Luca's couch, the television casting a warm, flickering glow across the dimly lit living room. The glass of red wine in my hand trembled slightly, though I wasn't cold. Beau's face filled the screen—those bright blue eyes of his alive with fire and conviction as he delivered his victory speech. I could feel the crowd's energy even from here, the way their cheers surged and swelled like waves. But it wasn't Beau I was focused on. It was Merritt.

She stood just behind him, steady and sure, her dark eyes shining with pride. When he stepped back and into her arms, my stomach twisted. The camera caught every detail—how she wrapped him up so fiercely, protectively, and the way her whole face softened, broke open with a smile so full of love it nearly knocked the air from my lungs. That used to be familiar.

Not Beau, not the love—but the way Merritt stood, so rooted, so sure of herself. The way she looked at him with such open pride. I used to see that side of her. I used to hear her thoughts before she even said them.

We used to share everything. But somewhere along the way—quietly, gradually—I stopped replying. I stopped calling. I let the silence grow. And now, watching her from this distance, I couldn't shake the feeling that I'd disappeared from her life without her even noticing.

"You're crying again," Luca said from the kitchen, his voice slicing through the stillness, edged with something cold. I looked up to see him leaning against the counter, watching me too closely.

"Honestly, Avery, you're too emotional for your own good. It's just a speech. We didn't even vote for that loser."

I touched my cheek, surprised to feel it wet. "I'm

fine," I whispered.

But I wasn't. Not really. I didn't know what this ache was exactly—guilt, maybe. Or just grief. Not because Merritt was happy, but because I felt so far from her happiness. The distance hadn't been intentional. It had just... happened. Life moved, and I'd focused on my relationship with Luca. That was what you were supposed to do, wasn't it? Prioritize your partner. Merritt would understand that. Wouldn't she?

"You know," Luca started, his voice taking on that tone he always used when he wanted me to think he was just offering a thought—not steering one, "Merritt has always had a knack for making everything about her. It's not a criticism. Just an observation."

I didn't say anything, but my jaw tensed.

"She thrives on being the centre of attention," he went on, swirling the bourbon in his glass like he was telling me the weather. "Maybe she didn't notice you pulling away. Or maybe she did—and just saw it as inevitable. People like her? They adapt fast. Especially when someone like Beau Laurent is around. Why would she look back?"

My grip on the wineglass tightened, fingers straining white. I wanted to argue, to tell him he was wrong. That Merritt had called, texted, reached out again and again. That she had always cared. But his words were already working their way under my skin, planting seeds I didn't want to water. What if she really had let go of me?

"She's happy," I said finally, barely able to get it out.

Luca crossed the room slowly, deliberately, and placed a hand on my shoulder. To someone else, it might've looked like comfort. But I felt the weight of it—subtle, heavy, meant to hold me in place.

"There it is," he murmured. "You're starting to see it. People drift apart, Avery. It's natural. It's inevitable. She has her life. And you have yours."

His thumb brushed along my collarbone, a touch that made my whole body tense.

"You have me," he said, voice like a promise and a prison all at once. "Isn't that enough?"

You've reached The End
But...
The Stories Never Stop

Welcome to Norland: a fictional country full of complicated politics, quiet scandals, emotional slow burns, and men who say emotionally competent things that make us fall a little bit in love with them with every single sentences they speak. (Looking directly at you, Beau.)

The Norland Series is a collection of interconnected novels set against the backdrop of this messy, wildly beautiful country — where grief and hope, public lives and private hearts, are always tangled together. Not every story will centre Merritt and Beau, but don't worry: they'll always be nearby, occasionally walking into scenes just to remind you why we're all unwell over Beau's bone structure, blue eyes, and emotional intelligence.

If you love romance with depth, politics with consequences, and characters who are trying really hard not to spiral publicly (but sometimes do anyway), you're in the right place.

For updates, new releases, and more Norland stories, visit BrittWolfe.com. Or don't — but just know we'll be over here swooning without you.

See you in the next slow burn.

About The Author
Britt Wolfe

Britt Wolfe is a Canadian author who writes emotionally charged, character-driven love stories full of grief, tenderness, and people trying very hard not to cry in public (but often failing). When she's not buried inside the world of Norland—where power moves quietly and men like Beau exist to make us all swoon—she's usually writing something else entirely, drinking coffee she forgot she made, or pestering her husband Sean with unsolicited plot readings at highly inconvenient hours.

Britt lives in Calgary with her wildly patient, smoking hot, husband, their incredible husky Sophie, and their occasionally possessed cat Lena—all of whom have earned co-author credits at this point.

You can find her online at BrittWolfe.com, where she's probably already lost inside her next fictional universe.

 brittwolfe.author@gmail.com

 BrittWolfeAuthor

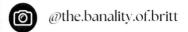 @the.banality.of.britt

 BrittWolfe.com

Manufactured by Amazon.ca
Acheson, AB

16918435R00223